Saturday Writers 2017

Carol,
My dear friend, confident and
staunch supporter,
May you be blessed with Gd's
glory in all you do .

Saturday Writers

Diane How

Seven Deadly Sins
Seven Heavenly Virtues

Anthology #11

Saturday Writers 2017

ISBN-13: 978-1986984966

Cover design by Cyn Watson
Cover illustration by Cyn Watson

First Edition: December 2017
10 9 8 7 6 5 4 3 2 1

Saturday Writers

Seven Deadly Sins
Seven Heavenly Virtues

Anthology #11

Edited by
Bradley D. Watson

Saturday Writers 2017

Editor's Note

Books like this are always a collaboration of many talented people. The anthology you hold in your hand is no exception. A lot of hard work went into it, but it was a labor of love for all those involved.

Saturday Writers has been in existence since 2002, recently obtaining non-profit status, and takes its motto, "Writers encouraging writers," seriously. The group consists of people from all walks of life and all genres of writing. Participants range in age from their 20s to their 80s. Writing experience includes teachers, well-published authors, and those brand new to the field. Poetry, memoir, essay, screenplay, copywriting, and conventional stories are all represented.

Our annual anthologies are a direct result of our desire to encourage our writers. A contest theme is chosen each year, and the authors submit their works based on monthly prompts. The judges then choose the best offerings and we include them in our publication.

The 2017 theme was "The Seven Deadly Sins and Seven Heavenly Virtues." Each monthly prompt allowed our writers to shine as they wrote memorable stories, poems, and works, many of which are included in this volume.

As a bonus, we have also included the winners of the first annual Poet Laureate's contest, hosted by our Poet Laureate, Robert Sebacher.

We hope the writings you hold bring you joy, and perhaps encourage the writer within you.

The editor wishes to thank all the members and officers/chairs who spent time helping to prepare this latest collection of winners—Rose Callahan, Nicki Jacobsmeyer, Jeanne Felfe, Susan Gore Zahra, Tom Klein, Tammy Lough—as well as all those who submitted works for these contests or helped find judges. To Rose, Susan, and Tammy, thanks for rising to the challenge of helping with proofreading. This anthology would not be in our hands without their help. You have my undying gratitude.

A special thanks to Cyn Watson for conceiving and creating the amazing cover that graces these pages.

-Bradley D. Watson, Editor

* * *

Table of Contents

From Lust to Chastity

The Valentine's Day Surprise
Tammy Lough

"Happy birthday, babe," Danny said, sitting with Claire at the red, high-top table inside Crossroads Sports Bar. Smiling, he pulled a thin, rectangular box from his jacket pocket and slid it across the table.

Claire diverted her attention from the baseball game playing on six ginormous screens. Wrapped in glossy white paper with a tiny bow, the shape of the box was an immediate disappointment. She removed the red bow, which Danny snatched off the table and pressed to her forehead. She smiled and unwrapped the gift, setting the lid to the side. Yes, the 24-karat rose-gold bangle looked amazing, but they both knew it wasn't what she wanted.

"It's beautiful, you know," she said, lifting the bracelet from its cotton bed. "Danny?" She met his admiral-blue eyes. "Be straight with me. Am I wasting my time? Because, if I am—"

"C'mon Claire," he interrupted, splaying his arms wide. "You know I love you." He leaned in close. "Don't I tell you all the time how much you mean to me?"

After tipping his beer for a long swig, he shook his head. "I'm just not ready for the marriage thing," He signaled for another bottle.

"The marriage thing?" Claire threw him a glowering stare. "Seriously, Danny, you sound like a twelve-year-old. You're a grown man, and grown men make commitments."

"I don't know what's wrong with me, babe. But, I do love you." He cupped his hand over hers. "Please, give me more time?"

"More time?" Claire inhaled a deep breath and released it slowly. "We've been together for five years. You're running low on time, and I'm running out of patience."

Claire handed him the bangle and lifted her wrist. He clasped the bracelet closed, then kissed her hand.

"It is gorgeous, you know. It's not that—"

"I know." Danny nodded in agreement.

#

"Pick up, pick up the phone," Claire said into her cell phone, continuing to pace the length of her bedroom. Two rings down and going on a third, her anticipation built. She would share her over-the-top news in mere seconds. "C'mon, answer your phone," she whispered. Finally, her mother's singsong voice sounded in her ear.

"Hello?"

"Mom!"

"Claire, is that you? Are you all right, dear?"

The words flew from Clair's lips like confetti from an air compressor. "Danny might, no, not might, Danny's going to propose. He's going to propose on Valentine's Day!"

"Slow down, honey. Danny is what?"

"He's going to propose, and I know it for a fact. I'm going to get a ring. An engagement ring with a big, sparkling diamond." She danced her hand in the air and wriggled her fingers. "Oh, heavens, my nails are a mess. I need to get them done this afternoon."

"Why do you think Danny is going to propose, dear? Did he tell you?"

"Well, no, he didn't *tell* me, but Kara Donaldson, you remember Kara? She led that Bible study we went to last summer. Anyway, she told me while delivering mail at Randy's Jewelry Emporium this morning, she saw Danny standing at the counter holding a burgundy ring box and making a purchase. What fits nice and neat inside of a ring box? A ring. Not just any ring, either. Danny bought me an engagement ring."

"It certainly sounds that way, dear. I am—"

"We've been together five whole years," Claire interrupted. "And, it's Valentine's Day. The timing is perfect, and it's going to happen."

"Really? Oh, my goodness," her mother said. "Well, I guess it *is* about time."

"Yes," Claire said, chuckling. "It is."

"I'm excited for you, darling. Will you keep me posted?"

"I'll let you know what's going on, and it *is* going to happen. I'll call you right after Danny proposes. Well, not *right* after."

"Stop right there," her mom said with a chuckle. "That's a road I'm not traveling with you or your sister. Good luck, honey."

"Thanks, Mom. I love you."

"Good-bye, darling. I love you, too."

#

Claire admired her glossy "Red-Hot-Red" manicured nails as she drove home from Polish Me Pretty Salon on Pig-Tail Alley. A perfect match for the red, low-cut sweetheart neckline and high hemline cocktail dress she bought to wear for her evening with Danny. He'd be lusting for her long before the main course arrived. Claire giggled, then looked around at nearby cars to see if anyone watched. *Mental note to self, scuff up the bottoms of my new, strappy red stiletto's or risk a face-plant at the restaurant.*

Placing her palms on top of the steering wheel, she fanned her fingers, envisioning her sparkling diamond ring. She wondered what style Danny chose to symbolize their eternal love. They never really talked about it. To be honest, if he proposed with a beer tab, she'd think it was the most beautiful token of love she'd ever seen. She hoped the diamond was at least one carat. Her Danny was a proud man, and one way to show off to his buddies would be the size of her diamond. Especially Angelo and Tony. He'd never let one of those guys show him up, not in a million years.

After returning home, she melted into her favorite cushy chair, wrapped herself in an afghan to remove the February chill, and picked up her journal from the end table. Instead of listing her daily gratitude's, she found herself drawing rings of every size and shape. She wanted Danny to propose so badly, it physically hurt. Her past dreams of falling in love never included the absence of, and therefore the unfulfilled desire for, a lifelong commitment. A couple declared their love and progressed to the next step. Danny should have proposed long before five years. Her mind ran through reel after reel of scenarios he might use to ask for her hand. If Danny didn't propose this evening, she'd need to cut her losses and move forward.

She slid a yoga DVD into the player and followed the yogini's stretching moves to release the tension throughout her body. Occasionally, she stopped to admire her nails and imagine the diamond that would grace her finger. She removed the DVD and prepared for Danny's arrival.

#

Claire answered Danny's signature six knocks at the door: two loud, two soft, and two loud. She never had to wonder who it was when her sweetheart came calling.

"Wow," Danny said, his eyes wide as he took in Claire's ensemble for the evening. He smiled and opened his arms wide for a hug. "Come here." He shut the door with a kick from his foot. "You look amazing, and I mean a-MAZING!!"

"Thank you," she said, tugging his tie. "You look a-MAZING yourself."

"I can't wait to show you off, sweetheart." He twirled her in a circle. "Do you have any idea how bad I want you right now?"

Claire winked, then turned to pick up her purse from the entry table. "About as bad as I want you. That's why we're going out that door. One more minute alone and we'll lose our dinner reservation and be forced to call for a pizza,"

"I opt for you, and pizza," he said with a deep growl.

"Tomorrow night," she said. "But this is Valentine's Day. Let's go celebrate."

"After you, my love," said Danny with a sweep of his arm. "And Claire?"

She turned. "Yeah?"

"I love you more than anything in this world." He took her key and locked the door behind him. "I just want you to know that."

She put her hands on his shoulders and tiptoed for a kiss. "And, I love you infinity."

#

Claire fidgeted all through dinner. The anticipation of his proposal caused her to talk faster and at least one octave higher than normal. She hoped he got down on one knee. *I wonder what he'll say.*

The word "disappointed" was too mild to describe the hurt Claire felt when they finished their chateaubriand with still no proposal. This evening, when she opened the door to let him into her apartment, he was complimentary, affectionate, and loving. He left no doubt as to his appreciation of her shapely figure, either. He even reminded her of his love. So why no proposal? He also left no doubt during dinner when she followed his gaze lingering on the view the cut of her dress afforded. She had leaned in and whispered, "My lustful Neanderthal," when his desire to take her was indisputably displayed by his inability to control what she teased as his "Roman hands and Russian fingers."

Then, she remembered a movie where an engagement ring peeked from within a strawberry sorbet. *Danny's sharp. He's going to do something unique.* The waiter interrupted her thoughts when he presented their final dish. But, no amount of swirling her dessert spoon in the decadent chocolate mousse revealed a ring. She felt her teeth clench and tried to relax her jaw.

#

Thirty minutes later, she tucked her hands into the slanted pockets of her wool dress coat as she and Danny walked toward the door to her apartment. Tears stung Claire's eyes. He hadn't given her so much as a rose, much less an engagement ring. Her chest felt heavy, and for the first time she knew what it meant to feel her heart break in two. Then, Danny nudged her to change direction and led her to the nearby apartment complex's courtyard.

"I have a surprise for you," he said, wiping bits of fallen foliage from a wrought-iron bench. He motioned for her to sit.

Claire knew without a doubt that the moment, *the moment*, was mere seconds away. She expected a ring at Christmas, felt sure on New Year's Eve, and then on her birthday. The culmination of their five-year relationship came down to this one special moment.

Danny moved closer but remained standing. He reached into his right coat pocket in what seemed slower-than-slow motion and brought forth a burgundy ring box.

Claire took an inward breath.

He faced the box toward her and watched her expression as he opened the lid.

She saw the sparkling of diamonds and gasped. She looked up at Danny, then back to the pair of diamond stud earrings.

"Are you surprised?" Danny asked before sneaking his hand toward the red velvet ring box in his left coat pocket.

He bent to his knee and smiled at the woman he would love to infinity.

Accidental Chastity
Susan Gore Zahra

It wasn't that lust never entered my adolescent mind. Every lustful thought was lassoed and hogtied in ropes woven from cords of puritanical, paranoid misinformation. I locked them in a mental vault where I kept ideas that made no sense but sounded important enough to be kept safe until a time when I could finally parse them out.

My mother's attempts at explaining where babies came from amounted to the statement, "God creates a miracle," followed by a deluge of tears. My father managed to find something to clean or repair whenever conversation moved toward babies or any other female topic. His instructions for driving a car with manual transmission included a lengthy dissertation on the anatomy of the internal combustion engine, how cogs on gears engaged and disengaged, and when to use which gears. When he finished, I had to ask if this had anything to do with the mystery pedal between the brake and the gas. I shudder to think what necessary piece of information he might have left out of the birds-and-bees instruction.

Grandma Verna took my education upon herself when I was ready to start seventh grade. She sat across from me at her kitchen table, looking anywhere except at me.

"You are getting to the age where boys might try something."

"Like what?"

Grandma looked at the ceiling, then down the hall. She glanced at me, tapping the upper sleeve of her dress.

"Like touching your shoulder."

"Oh. Why?"

"Just don't let them."

Every boy in grade school had touched my shoulder when we were outside playing tag during recess. In junior high, there was no recess or playing tag. However, there were 1500 kids crammed into the hallways between classes. There were boys ranging from cherub-cheeked seventh-graders to peach-fuzzed ninth-graders sporting letter sweaters with "66" announcing their graduation year. There were girls hunched over notebooks that camouflaged their presence or lack of training bras alongside young women wearing their boyfriends' letter sweaters. All sorts of anonymous hands touched my shoulders. Some of those hands probably belonged to boys. None of those shoulder taps had any effect that I could see.

Then, there was Keith. Keith was my age and lived down the hill, around the corner. My sister, Betsi, was a year younger than we were. His sister, Cathy, was a year younger than Betsi. At home, away from eighth and ninth graders who were starting to wear makeup and after shave, we were still kids who hollered, "Can you come play?" from our front porch or their backyard. We still played tag. Keith still touched my shoulder when he was "it." So did Betsi and Cathy. I suffered the humiliation of being the eternal "it" because I was so slow and awkward. I gladly would have avoided letting Keith or either of our sisters touch my shoulder, but I just couldn't run any faster.

Seventh grade was a year filled with mysteries, such as why a used car salesman by night was allowed to teach science by day. He had only two lesson plans: dictate the objectives and concepts from the teacher's edition while we wrote them in our notebooks; and teach us the rules to whatever sport was in season. If the boys were going to become real men, they were going to have to play some sport, and if the girls were going to catch a husband, we were going to have to be able to discuss sports intelligently with the boys.

I loved science. I wanted to be a scientist when I grew up. Sitting through the last hour of the day with Mr. Used-Car-Salesman explaining the different strategies for determining whether to punt or pass was agony.

Keith had the world's best science teacher. Every day I bolted out of that miserable excuse for a science class to meet Keith. He described his class in vivid detail as we walked home together.

On a rainy day, my mom and Grandma Verna drove up. Keith and I crammed into the back seat of our Volkswagen Beetle with Betsi and my two-year-old sister, and continued discussing his teacher's dissection of an earthworm.

"Did you know earthworms are bisexual?"

"No! What's bisexual?" I knew that sexual had something to do with being a boy or a girl. I had never heard a prefix attached to the word before.

"That means they can be both mothers and fathers."

"Wow!"

We moved on to discuss earthworms' ganglia and their ability to survive being cut into several pieces. Mom dropped Keith off at his house, and my sisters and me off at our house. She took Grandma the rest of the way up the hill to her house. It seemed like at least an hour before she got back home from driving only the length of our houses and the space between.

"Don't ever talk to Keith about sex again!" Mom screamed. Then she started crying.

"When did I talk to Keith about sex?"

"In the car!"

"We were talking about earthworms."

"Bisexual earthworms. Don't talk to Keith about earthworms again."

"Mom, that wasn't sex. That was science."

"Then don't talk to Keith about science again!"

No more playing tag with Keith. No more talking about science with Keith. What else was left to do with Keith? My future seemed to be doomed to sitting in silence and ignorance.

One day, Mr. Used-Car-Salesman pointed out a girl who had what appeared to be a hickey on her neck. He deviated from his sports agenda to explain the science of venereal diseases because our parents were all either too scared or too stupid to know anything about sex, and it was obviously time for some of us to know how to avoid VD. He explained the disease process in terms of breaking out in huge, oozing sores, followed by going crazy and then dying. This happened when girls didn't behave themselves with boys and mucous membranes came into contact.

The girl with the hickey was in tears. The rest of us were sinking low in our seats, trying not to make eye contact with anyone else, except for the boy across the aisle from me. He was sitting tall and smirking. He raised his hand as straight as the torch on the Statue of Liberty.

"What are mucous membranes?"

Mr. Used-Car-Salesmen stared him down.

"Those are the linings of your nose and mouth."

Suddenly, everything was clear. Germs behaved differently in boys and girls. If a girl sneezed on me, I would catch a cold. If a boy sneezed on me, I would break out in huge, oozing sores. Then I would go crazy and die. No wonder Grandma Verna told me not to let a boy touch me on the shoulder—he would be close enough to sneeze on me. The thing with Keith in the car had nothing to do with earthworms or science. If he had sneezed, I would have broken out in nasty sores, gone crazy, and died. So would my sisters, and maybe even Mom and Grandma. Our whole family could have been wiped out.

There were a few logical flaws that I failed to see as I slid farther underneath my desk, trying to stay shielded from any male sneezing.

A couple of years later, Betsi had picked up enough information from the junior high restroom stalls to try to correct my thinking. Her version, which turned out to be reasonably accurate, sounded more absurd than my germ theory. Why else would there be so many TV ads for Clorox, Lysol, and cold remedies? The odor of Vicks VapoRub probably repelled boy germs the way garlic repelled vampires.

I was not a fun date in high school. One poor young man tried a second date before labeling me a "door handle hugger." He said he preferred going out with girls who would at least let go of the door handle by the second date. When seatbelts became standard equipment, I kept mine on at all times, even while parked.

But there was one rather exceptional fellow. Mike listened to the classical music station instead of the rock station. He was handsome, quiet, and polite. Most attractive of all, he played oboe in band and orchestra. I played bassoon. We could spend hours and hours making music together and commiserating about our love-hate relationship with double reeds.

Spring brought contest season, and the invitation to spend more time together in the intimate setting of a woodwind quintet. We shared a seat in the school van coming back from contest our sophomore year. In the afterglow of a performance good enough to promise keeping our quintet together for the rest of our high school years, we could relax.

I felt his hand wrap around mine. I was so terrified that I wanted to jump out the window and run. Not only were we risking death, we could be expelled for breaking the school's no fraternizing rule.

Mike's touch felt warm, his grip firm enough that I knew it was intentional, yet light enough that I could pull away if I wanted to. I wanted to hold his hand forever. Warnings from Grandma Verna and Mr. Used-Car-Salesman drifted away, carrying my fear of catching some horrible disease with them. Chastity became less an accident and more a choice to wait for the love that lives and grows for a lifetime.

First love faded, replaced by a full spectrum of relationships, from infatuation to the life-long love of my husband. We met in much the same way in which I met my first love. Ray and I both played bassoon in college band and orchestra. We shared a love of classical music and a love-hate relationship with our double reeds. Ray also played saxophone and enjoyed jazz as well as classical music. He introduced a both/and acceptance of life into my either/or world. Our desire for each other could coexist with the chastity that enabled us to forsake all others.

Ray and I decided to give our children more accurate information about sex than our families had given us. Our efforts were supported by the school offering age- and gender-appropriate classes taught by the school nurse for the fourth, fifth, and sixth graders.

Our daughter bounded through the door the day of her first class, asking to have a private conversation about the most wonderful, exciting things she had ever heard. Kathy showed me the materials the nurse passed out and asked questions.

Although I provided factual and appropriate information, I was trembling inside. I realized my daughter was shifting gears from childhood into womanhood. I wondered if my mother's tears had been more from the sense of something precious slipping away than from ignorance when she equated every birth with the parting of the Red Sea.

Kathy ended our conversation with a hug and thanks for being so easy to talk to. She said some of her friends couldn't talk to their mothers about anything like that. I hoped for their sake that Mr. Used-Car-Salesman was retired.

The Race
Jeanne Felfe

With trained precision, I bend and extend my left leg behind me, my right knee underneath me, lining up fingertips on the gritty yellow starting tape, something I've done thousands of times—perhaps thousands each year since the first over twelve years ago—but this is the one that counts. It's what I've worked toward to the exclusion of all else—dolls, boys, even family. Nothing compared...nothing came close.

Ten seconds drag out in slow speed, sweat already sliding down my brow. I glance left, then right, into eyes like mine, emblazoned with the lust for Gold.

The roar of the crowd fades as my breath settles and pulls from deep within my core, muscles tense in anticipation of the starter's shot that will change everything. Forever.

Instinct kicks in at the blast. My arms and legs pump, seemingly of their own accord. I am never so free, so...me, than in this zone. Feet churn the rubber track, propelling me ever closer to the finish. My breath comes in hot bursts.

A rustle of movement bleeds into my peripheral vision as she pulls ahead. Anyone but her, I think. But she surges two strides ahead of me. Fire bursts from my lungs. I dig deeper. I close the gap to one step.

An instant later, her ankle twists—she goes down, her quest for Gold over in a flash of red and bone white. Her anguished scream permeates the air and I leap over legs strewn in my path.

Four steps past her, my way to the ribbon clear, I pull up and spin on the ball of my left foot, careful to stay in my lane. Other runners whizz by as I jog to her and extend my hand.

She stares at me for a second from a face twisted and tortured before grabbing it.

I pull her upright and slide her arm over my shoulder, around my neck. We hobble to the finish line, last, but across.

The medics relieve me and haul her away on a stretcher.

I sink to my knees, the realization of what I've done draining the last of my fury. Tears, restrained and unfallen, burn the backs of my eyes.

* * *

At the bottom of the athlete ramp, I slam open the door to the locker room and am assaulted by the stench of unfulfilled triumphs. She is on an ambulance gurney just inside, her ankle wrapped in ice, her face shrouded in pain and defeat. The EMT sticks a foot out to stop the door so he can wheel her out.

Holding up one hand, she chokes, "Wait."

Her sullen eyes find mine, her fire having died on the track, along with her dreams. "Why?" she asks, her voice hoarse and coated in anguish. "You don't even like me."

I hesitate. She's right…I don't, but didn't realize she knew. I see myself through her eyes. Driven. Focused. Lonely?

The words of my long dead father echo in my head as I respond. "Sometimes the only thing to do is the right thing. My dad always said I would know what that meant when it happened."

"But you gave up certain Gold…for me."

A lopsided grin creases my face. "You know, I don't actually *dislike* you. It's just that you were the only one who could've beaten me. I didn't want to win like that."

She nods in understanding. "Yeah, I wouldn't want to win that way either." She pauses and draws a long, slow breath. "But I don't think I would have stopped for you."

"I would have said the same, yesterday."

I walk out of the locker room, head high. At twenty, there will be at least one more Olympics for me. But there might never be another chance to feel this good.

The Ring
R.G. Weismiller

Today starts like every Saturday for me. Hoisting my clothing on my shoulder, I swagger out of the dry cleaners. I know I deserve the best of everything—suits, cars, and women. The clothes are mere tools for climbing the corporate ladder. Because I look so good in them, females can't keep their hands off of me. My success allowed me to purchase an Audi convertible, further enticing members of the opposite sex. My eyes focus on its sleekness, letting me ignore other patrons as they plod from their dreadful minivans and unexciting sedans.

As the trunk lid pops open, the purring of an engine passes me, nurturing everyone's envy but mine. A blue Corvette screeches into a parking space near the business. A man, who I nicknamed Todd, pops from the vehicle with a bundle of clothes. Although introductions have never occurred, I know we are brothers of a mutual admiration society—single, handsome, and successful.

Sliding into my car, I notice a small box wrapped with a beautiful white ribbon in the passenger seat. A note leans against the package. The meticulous handwritten words read:

> **This was for my beloved who is no more.**
> **May you find someone who is worthy of it.**

Wondering where the package came from, I spring out of my car, scrutinizing the surroundings. Light traffic flows on the street. A few pedestrians stroll about. No cars are speeding away and no one is running. Someone must have placed it through the opened window while I picked up my clothes.

In my car, I slip the ribbon off without breaking it and open the package, finding a ring sitting in a black velvet lined box.

Sparkling small diamonds encircle a large, brilliant emerald cut diamond. A rainbow of colors dance as I turn the ring in the sunlight, mesmerizing me. Not being proficient about gems, I surmise the size of the center stone to be about two carats.

However, such a ring means commitment. The note hints at some fairy tale version of love. None of my flings have ever lasted more than a few months. Eventually boredom creeps into the affair. When the conversations stall and become tedious, so does the bedroom. It's time to move on. I know there are women who anticipate the opportunity to be with me.

I have no problems finding a replacement. My friends' wives always want to introduce me to someone. Single women at work beat down my office door to introduce themselves. Even my mother seems to always find someone for me, following with hints how wonderful grandchildren would be in her life.

Meagan—an extremely attractive svelte brunette with the looks of a goddess—is my current flame. However, our relationship is fading. Lately her demands of my time are growing on my nerves. She says when we are together, I'm preoccupied.

She is right. I'm obsessing about a voluptuous blonde named Christie instead of her. Those thoughts evolve into desires, fantasizing about her shapely legs and curvaceous body. For the past month, she has come to my place whenever her time permits. Her wedding ring has been absent. For two hours, the passion is next to heaven. I've never met anyone like her.

Looking at the ring, I'm reminded of my career. There could be advantages to abdicating the single life. At a recent social gathering, a vice president approached me about becoming a director. The conversation centered on my performance. He smiled when he alluded to how being married would be beneficial in securing the position. At the party the wives, with their elegance, grace the men they stand next to. I must choose such a woman for this ring. One who will help advance my career, and more importantly be a trophy wife.

Although stunningly beautiful, Meagan has not fit into those social gatherings, claiming to be uninterested in the conversations. She stands by my side, so close she almost imprisons me from joining others. But Christie is full of life, engaging, and captivating. She would do well in those situations.

There is the matter of her marriage. That shouldn't be an issue. The way she refers to her husband sounds as if she is ready to leave him immediately. She abhors the pitiful slob. Whereas our relationship is blissful. When next we are together, I will propose.

Pulling into the parking lot of my condo, an unexpected surprise awaits me. I see my future wife sitting in her Mercedes. Upon seeing me, she slowly emerges from her vehicle. Her smile isn't as bright as usual.

"I have a surprise for you," I say.

"I have to talk to you," she says as her smile fades. "This isn't easy."

"Huh?"

"I need to end this."

"What," I blurt, not believing what I heard.

"I've decided to reconcile with my husband."

"We had something…something special."

She looks down and then up at me. "No, ours was pure lust. Nothing more."

I open the box, presenting the ring. "I was going to ask you to marry me."

Patting my chest, she says. "You'll find someone." She turns and walks to her car.

"Wait," I cry.

"It's over," she says, reaching into her purse for keys.

My jaws tighten, clenching my teeth. Glaring at Christie as she enters the car, my heart pumps faster. I race to her.

From inside, she looks at me and locks her door. A fearful expression replaces her half-hearted smile. In a futile effort, I try to open the door.

"No one does this to me," I scream. "Not even a slut like you."

Watching her drive off, the thought reverberates in my mind. "No one does this to me." Snapping the box shut, my thoughts turn to showing her I am very much desirable.

"Meagan will accept my proposal," I mutter.

I pounce into my car, jetting out into the street, ignoring a blaring horn. I race towards Meagan's apartment, assuring myself of her loyalty. She idolizes me.

Parking on the street in front of her building, I walk to her place, regaining my composure. Inside, I see a piece of paper flapping on her front door. My curiosity grows as I approach.

I read the note in disbelief.

> Dearest James,
> I've decided to take a position with a new company in another city. The hardest part of this decision was making it without you.
> Lately your thoughts have been elsewhere. When we've been together, we are no longer talking. God knows I've tried. I can't be in a relationship where watching TV is the only source of communication.
> I know I am probably to blame as much as you. But I don't think there is any future for us.
> I've never loved anyone as much as I loved you. I don't think I'll ever find another like you.
> With loving regrets,
> Meagan
> P.S. Please don't try to find me. I need to move on.

My body slumps against the wall. I shake my head. "No, no. This can't be happening to me."

* * *

I rub my cheeks which feel burnt as a slight wind blows against them. Earlier this morning I shaved a week's growth. For this past week, I didn't go to work. I just laid in bed, unable to rise. Finally my boss called me and reprimanded me for my behavior. The elusive position of directorship won't be in my future any time soon. I'm lucky to have kept my job.

It's raining. My windshield wipers are on. I wait for the person I dubbed as Todd to arrive at the dry cleaners. He is a creature of habit, as I was. My weekly pickup is in the trunk of my car.

The package—the curse that turned my life upside down—lies in the seat next to me. Its wrapping looks as beautiful as the day it was left for me. My fingers trace the edges of the fateful note.

Maybe Todd's luck will be better than mine. It's ironic, but I hope he will be fortunate in finding that special lady for this ring—somebody truly worthy to wear it.

Meagan—angelic Meagan—was that someone, but I blew it.

Saturday Writers 2017

Sugar and Spice
Tara Pedroley

"Come on Sugar, just one more kiss."

I pulled away, turning my head. My long jet-black ponytail slapped him in the face.

I wanted to keep kissing Tave. I really did. But I knew I wasn't ready to get serious.

Tave Wilson and I met in third grade, when his father was transferred to Brimleigh. They moved into the house down the street.

We walked home from elementary school together, talking about our teachers while sharing a banana left over from lunch. In Middle School, we rode the same bus, sitting with our own friends, and then walked home from the stop together.

Now in high school, he had his license to drive. We rode to and from school together. We were neighbors and friends. Until, one afternoon during our sophomore year, he dropped me off in front of my house and...kissed me.

"Sugar," he said after the kiss, my mouth hanging open in shock, "I want you to be my girlfriend. I've always liked you."

I wasn't sure what to say at first. Tave was the only guy in my grade, in my neighborhood, I could share a mushy banana with and trust that he hadn't just picked his nose. That was pretty much it. I trusted him.

Tave never let me down.

We began dating, sharing kisses, holding hands, and showing a different type of affection. One that was more than just friends.

His beautiful green eyes, blond curly hair, and honest genuine smile lit up my day, whether in the morning before school, or driving me home in the afternoon.

I was attracted to him. He was very special to me. I just wasn't ready to go past second base with him.

We were too young. I was growing up way too fast and wasn't in a hurry to let go of my innocence—my purity.

Over the summer, Tave and I took turns pushing each other on the tire swing in his backyard. The grass tickled my ankles. It hadn't been cut in months.

We'd walk up to Brea's Diner to sip root beer floats and munch M&M's. We shared everything.

Just before starting our junior year, while walking back to my house after a stroll down to Kermier Park, we noticed a moving truck parked in front of the Simmons' house. A tall, shirtless guy about our age, with thin, caramel-brown hair combed to the front and dark blue-jean shorts, approached us as we passed Tave's house.

Barefoot, he removed his sunglasses and flashed us a friendly grin. I noticed how crystal clear his blue eyes were.

"Hello!" he nodded.

He and Tave exchanged handshakes, while my hands remained tucked under my crossed arms.

I gave a nod and a smile.

"I am Roche. My family and I just moved in."

"Welcome to the neighborhood," I said in a small, yet nervous, voice.

"Thanks. You guys happen to go to Beauford?"

"Yeah. We start Monday. You enrolled, yet?"

He shook his head. "Not yet. Mom and I are visiting the school tomorrow."

"You riding the bus?"

He scoffed, rolling those blue beauties. "Yes, unfortunately. I don't have my license, yet."

"Aww, man," Tave punched the air. "That's like a necessity around here. Once you're in high school, you don't ride the bus anymore. Otherwise, you're considered a geek."

Tave's comment didn't seem to faze this new guy. He blew it off with a shrug. "Guess it could be worse. I could be *walking* to school. It's okay. I plan to get my license before fall, so I won't have to stand outside in the cold waiting for the bus. Until then, I'm a geek."

I nodded, thinking about how smoothly that answer was delivered.

Tave pulled me closer to him, politely saying farewell to the very good looking young man.

"Well, it was nice meeting you. See ya at school."

Roche nodded, giving me a wink. "See you guys."

As we walked, I looked back and saw the beautiful blue-eyed guy glance over his shoulder, flash a very sweet smile at me, then turn back around.

Goosebumps went up and down my arms.

The first day of school, I accidentally ran into Roche in the hallway on the way to English class. He'd already made a few friends with some varsity cheerleaders—not girls I chose to hang around with. Given his looks, flirtatious smile, and great stomach muscles, no girl in their right mind would turn down a chance to spend time talking to that beautiful face.

Closing my locker and turning to walk down the hall, I ran into Mr. Popularity himself.

He smelled of fresh cotton, and a hint of cologne. I found myself inhaling his scent as he approached.

"Well, hello, neighbor." That pretty face with the perfect smile, at just the right time.

"Hi."

"Can you show me where room 202B is?"

"Sure—hallway A. It's on my way to class. I'll walk you."

"So, where's your beau?" He winked, playfully nudging my elbow.

I managed a smile. "He has gym this period, so he's on the other side of the building."

"The other day when we met..."

"Yeah?"

"You never told me your name."

I cleared my throat. "It's Sugar."

"Sugar?" he raised his thin brown eyebrows.

"Yes. It's really Shenandoah, but my dad's always called me 'Sugar' for short."

"Ah. Well, my name is short enough." He winked.

We stopped where the halls intersect, and I gave him a wave. "Your class is down the hall and to the left."

He flashed that grin, the one that had the ability to break hearts, and said softly, "Thanks, Sugar."

I stood there for a moment, watching his stone-wash jeans hug his backside so comfortably, as he casually strolled down the hall and disappeared into the classroom. I barely made it to English class in time, but I made it.

I met up with Tave in the hallway just before lunch. He said he had to leave school early. He wasn't feeling well.

"I think I just need some rest. I'll be fine."

"It's ok. I'll ride the bus. No big deal."

"You sure?"

"Yeah. I'll be fine."

"Thanks, Sug'." He pulled me close for a kiss.

Later on that afternoon, I got on the bus. Route 17 only had six students going home, so the ride wouldn't be as long as the morning route. Many students stayed after school for activities and sports. I wasn't one of those students.

"Well. Sugar Blackwell," the bus driver greeted me. "I am shocked to see you riding the bus! My, how beautiful and grown up you're looking."

"Thank you, Mary. Tave isn't feeling well. I told him I'd take the bus."

"It's good to see you, Sugar."

"You, too."

I moved to the back—my stop being one of the last. The plastic seats made the backs of my legs sweaty, sticking to them, even though my brown and red skirt should've been plenty long.

Roche climbed the steps. I saw him look at me, sitting at the back. Those beautiful blue eyes lit up. I can't explain how good I felt inside. That smile of his would be the death of me.

"Hi, Sugar. What a nice surprise." He gestured to the seat with his Algebra book. "May I?"

I moved my backpack to the floor.

I could still smell his cologne, although it was faint. The leg of his jeans touched my bare shin.

We began to talk about where he was from.

"Alverton," he said. Alverton was a small, upper-class town just forty miles from Brimleigh. He loved his old school, Alverton Heights.

He had a sister, Cadence, who was away at college.

"My father got promoted and had to transfer locations. We like it here, so far."

Our conversation flowed so well that I didn't notice when others got off at their designated stops.

Reaching our stop, I was shocked at how fast the ride home had been.

"Sugar, do you mind showing me the park? I just want to know where it is. You know, a quick tour of the neighborhood?" He flashed me that smile, and I felt my heart grow weak.

He has no idea how charming he really is.

"Sure."

Kermeier Park was pretty empty, except for a few middle-schoolers sipping juice boxes at the top of the jungle gym.

We laid our backpacks on the grass and sat on the swings.

"I love the swings," he said, pumping his legs back and forth. He gripped the chains tightly as he swung higher, saying, "Cadence and I used to have contests about who could get the highest."

I pumped my legs as well, trying to get as high as Roche. I felt the wind lift my ponytail off my shoulders as I came closer to the ground. Our swings would pass each other, never in the air at the same time.

We still managed to converse, our words buzzing past each other, making every other word inaudible.

We swung for a while, allowing time to fall away, leaving reality behind.

When the middle-schoolers grabbed their bikes and headed home, I stopped pumping my legs, letting my body come down to the ground.

I dragged my blue tennis shoes against the rocks, slowing my swing.

"We should head home."

He began to slow his swing down, too. "Oh. Yeah."

We sat a moment—our swings still, our bodies side by side.

"Thanks for showing me the park, Sugar." The smile, yes.

I nodded. "You're welcome."

The blue in his eyes looked like someone had painted them—like watercolors.

Then, it happened. The simple world I knew, ended.

Roche leaned over and placed his lips on mine. Before I realized what was happening, I was responding to him. We were kissing.

Weren't we? I had never kissed anyone else but Tave before. His was the only mouth I had ever allowed on mine.

This felt different. It felt heavier, more intimate. It was like someone had added hot sauce to a very bland steak.

His mouth tasted different. His lips were smooth and not sticky. His chin felt warm as it pressed against mine. I wanted to keep it there. I wanted to keep feeling this heat, to keep tasting the fire on my tongue.

This wasn't real—it wasn't happening.

I was too young for this.

My breath was heavy, my heart like a drum, the beat getting faster and faster.

This felt good, but unfamiliar. My palms, pressed against his chest, were beginning to sweat.

I closed my eyes, only seeing black. My skin felt warm. I felt like my body belonged to someone else.

I wanted to back away, to open my eyes and go home. I wanted to pretend this wasn't happening.

But it was.

I felt my legs tingle. His fingertips caressed my cheeks.

This was more than just kissing. I was feeling my innocence slip away.

I opened my eyes and saw those beautiful sapphires staring back at me.

I never felt this way when kissing Tave. He was routine. He was safe. He was comfort. His kiss was like eating a bowl of your favorite soup that sat on your belly like a warm hug.

This kiss, however, was fire. This was…not just in my heart. This was in every other part of my body. The parts that thought too much spice would feel strange. Unwelcome.

But how I felt right now, kissing Roche, was not unwelcome. It made my mind race with adventurous thoughts. Thoughts that drove me down a road toward bad decisions. My body craved his lips against mine again.

He pulled my face back to his face, his lips pressing harder against mine.

The back of my neck began to sweat, I felt his hands on my thighs. Everything I thought I would never find myself wanting, I wanted right now.

And I realized that I no longer wanted to be pure.

From Gluttony to Temperance

Feast of Gratitude
Susan Gore Zahra

Garlic, rosemary, and lemon aromas smacked Frank Herman in the face as he rounded the corner to the teachers' lunchroom. His triathlon training diet was difficult enough to maintain, but it was Ash Wednesday, and he had the added challenge of limiting himself to one meatless meal. He was sure the herbs and lemon were slathered on chicken or pork or something disgustingly unhealthy. He was equally sure who was sabotaging his training regimen, and that there would be more temptation in the lunchroom.

Frank's desk was buried under t-shirts to be distributed to the intramural volleyball teams. Had there not been a bone-chilling winter downpour, he would have eaten lunch out in his car listening to motivation CDs. He couldn't risk missing training time by coming down with a cold. He steeled himself to ignore the lure of pleasant aromas.

Robin Fuller sat behind a plate piled with rice and chicken dripping in gold and green sauce. A plastic box of assorted homemade oatmeal, chocolate chip, and sugar cookies sat open beside her plate, as it did every day. Robin finished gnawing the last shred of meat from a thighbone, licked her fingers, and wiped her mouth with a paper towel. She pointed to the empty chair across from her.

"Have a seat."

Frank looked around. Josh Stevenson had cordoned off his territory with stacks of math papers he was grading while nibbling a protein bar and gulping from a giant-sized coffee mug. Several female teachers took up another table, talking and laughing about their plans for yet another baby shower for some staff member. Emily Duncan, the unsociable social studies teacher, sat with two empty chairs across the table and two eyes daring anyone to come close enough to pierce her cloud of perpetual gloom. Frank took the seat Robin offered and tried not to inhale deeply enough to be tempted away from his training and fasting.

"Cookie?" Robin pointed to the box.

"No, thanks." Frank pulled the bowl of brown rice, black beans, baby greens, red cabbage, raisins, and almonds from his cold pack. He and his wife had agreed that their one meal on fast days would be lunch so that he wouldn't have every kid in his P.E. classes running laps the whole period as punishment for looking at him the wrong way. They also agreed that this would be his last attempt to qualify for the Ironman triathlon in Hawaii before they started a family.

"So, how is life going down in the gym?"

"Running smoothly."

Robin laughed. "Still quick with the puns, I see."

Frank and Robin had attended Our Lady of Sorrows grade school together. She was bone thin back then. Teachers fussed over her and tried to supplement her meager lunch of half a bologna sandwich and a carrot stick or two with something from their own lunches. He figured her family must be really poor. Then in fifth grade, her mother died. After that she started bringing whole sandwiches, bags of chips, apples, and cookies, like everyone else. By eighth grade, Robin started to fill out even more splendidly than some of the other girls. They went in different directions after grade school. When they met again as teachers at Winningham Middle School, it was clear that she had continued to fill out, although somewhat less splendidly. Frank was not sure whether her boxy shape was a result of middle-aged spread, or something he had overlooked during his adolescent fascination with bosoms. Whatever her body shape, Frank was impressed with Robin's strength and energy whenever they collaborated to convert the gym into a theater, a party room, or a display area for the science fair or the art exhibits Robin's students produced.

"Healthy lunch, I see. Keeping up your training regimen, eh? You are the only person I have ever met with the self-discipline to compete in a triathlon. Will you make it to Hawaii this year?"

"That's my goal."

"Want some chicken? It's lean protein."

"No, thanks. I see you've forgotten Sister Mary Joan's rules for Ash Wednesday."

"How could I forget anything Sister Mary Joan drilled into us? Especially Lenten guidelines for wimpy Catholics. She was the last of the real nuns in her long, black habit, clunky shoes, and love for the full forty days of fast and abstinence."

"I doubt she ever forgave them for limiting the ban on eating meat to Ash Wednesday and Fridays instead of all of Lent. Remember in eighth grade, when we were getting ready for confirmation, how she inspected lunches every Friday and confiscated any meat she found? She replaced it with dried up PBJ sandwiches, and recited her tale of PBJ every day of Lent from the time she was born."

"And every day of Lent for her mother even before she was born." Robin paused to pick out a chocolate chip cookie, then added, "When we were younger, Sister Mary Joan slipped some of those confiscated sandwiches to my brother and me, meat and all."

A buzzer sounded, signaling classroom teachers that they had ten minutes to return to their rooms. Frank and Robin had their planning periods after lunch and lingered a bit longer.

When the other teachers had left them alone, Robin said, "Do you know what my mother died of?"

Frank shook his head. All he could recall about her mother was a lot of whispering and head shaking among the teachers and women of the parish.

"Anorexia. It was several years before Karen Carpenter died and anorexia became the disease of the month. Mom never kept more than a minimal amount of food in the house. Dad worked odd hours at the electric company, so he didn't help much. If he brought home something good, like a pizza, she threw it out. There were some awful rows about that. She gave away our cat after she found my brother eating the cat's food. After she died, people brought in food. Neighbors, Dad's family, ladies from the parish."

"I didn't realize." Frank was stunned.

"Remember Mrs. Eckels, the lady who ran the fish fries that drew crowds from all over the metro area? She taught me to cook. I don't know which I loved more—cooking, eating good food, or hearing Mrs. Eckels tell me that I was wonderful and worthy of her time and attention.

"The way I see it, I spent the first ten years of my life fasting. Now I just say thank you with every bite I take."

Robin took a cookie, then nudged the plate toward Frank. He took an oatmeal cookie. It looked as though it might also contain carrots, which he had intended to include in his salad but forgot. He realized he had also forgotten another of Sister Mary Joan's rules, and stopped a moment to recall.

Bless us, O Lord, and these, thy gifts...

Fat Farm
Larry Duerbeck

Dedicated to Roald Dahl

Everything is custom-ordered and de luxe.

The chairs, the beds, even the golf carts, and golf is as active as the spa gets. The beautiful, manicured and much made-over private eighteen holes host carriers of special make and jolly nature.

Massively buttressed and sprung versions of Humvees, brightly painted and polished, every cart features super snack bar and beverage station and balloon tires. A lot of science went into their not crushing the grass, especially when parked on the for-guests-only greens. Each "carrysomuch" all but waddles its flabby way, its flabby weight, around the course.

Exclusive of driver (human driver), the blubber buggie—as one half-wit, pardon, one half-ton wit named them—sit, braced and squat, handcrafted for a maximum of four and a minimum of 1600 pounds. At least and, as is always hoped, much more. Foursomes prove quite the sight.

Yes, dining is the thing. For the guests. They are fed and coddled, soft as eggs. Here is a typical "Menu for Today," stolen at random.

Tuesday
End Overnitems – 6:00 a.m.
Eye Opener Room Service – 6:00 to 9:00 a.m.
Breakfast a la Carte(s) – 9:00 to 10:30 a.m.
Brunch Brought 2 U! – 10:30 to noon
Lunches Various – noon to 2:00 p.m.
Low Tea, a House Speciality – 2:00 to 4:00 p.m.
High Tea, featuring Prime Rib – 4:00 to 6:00 p.m.

Appetizers and Thick Soups – 6:00 to 8:00 p.m.
Dinner – 8:00 to 10:00 p.m.
Desserts – 10:00 to ?
Club Meetings, Catered, Time – Ad Lib
Clubs Include:
Clean Plate Kingpins
Scalebreaker Sweeties
Witching Hour Wonderland with
Buffets Internationale – midnight to 2:00 a.m.
Begin Overnitems – 2:00 to 6:00 a.m.

So, dining is the thing. For the guests.

Therefore, at this spa, no swimming pool shimmers in the sun, no volleyball net flutters in the breeze, no horseshoe clangs in the quiet. There appear, however, billiard and card tables. Napping is encouraged, reading accepted, television tolerated.

Massages, though, are enthusiastically mandatory—deep, muscle fiber-breaking massage.

You see, to the owners of this exclusive spa for demanding gluttons, meat is the thing. Rest assured that this coddled, massaged and well-marbled meat, whether fresh or frozen, well…

Everything is custom-ordered and de luxe.

The Assist
R.G. Weismiller

Kirk Woods cringed when he heard, "Now playing for the Lions, Samuel 'Sparky' Ferguson," over the speakers. The Lambert High School fans, bored with the runaway score of the season's final basketball game, jumped to their feet and chanted, "Sparky." Kirk realized the consequences of the announcement—no Lion could score until Sparky did.

Kirk's hope of capturing an elusive record would have to wait until the new player scored. No one in the history of the school had triple doubles—at least ten points, ten rebounds, and ten assists—in each game for an entire season. So far, in his senior year, Kirk had achieved this amazing feat. One basket separated Kirk from fame in his final game. Somewhere in this building, a banner would sway from the rafters, displaying his accomplishment.

Tonight, his shooting mimicked the winter weather outside. Some shots were too strong, bouncing off the backboard without touching the basket. Others rimmed in and out of the basket. The pressure of the quest, more than the physical pace of the game, fatigued him. While his entire body ached, he desired one last shot.

The banner waned in comparison to his ultimate goal—wearing a college uniform next season. This season, he'd pushed himself to a level where his performances could be noticed by colleges. His first choice was State—a childhood dream. Tonight, that wish could become a reality. In attendance, a college recruiter from State sat next to Ricky Jennings' promoter. Ricky, a teammate, bragged how his parents had hired a promoter to land him an athletic scholarship.

When Kirk approached his parents about a promoter, they said they could not afford one. Unsure his talent could earn him a basketball scholarship to any college, they encouraged Kirk to pursue an academic scholarship. Then, he could earn a spot as a walk-on on the basketball team. Regardless, Kirk wanted the basketball scholarship. With a recruiter sitting in the stands, Kirk aimed to secure the triple doubles in the game to impress him.

Sparky, a special needs student, donned the black and gold uniform of the Lions for the first time. During his freshman year, he tried out for the team, but his name did not appear on the roster at the end of tryouts. Refusing to let the setback dampen his enthusiasm for the game, he became the manager of the freshman team. In that role, he became the team's biggest fan. He greeted each player with a high five as he handed them a towel. After each three pointer swished through the net, his towel waved wildly in the air. He celebrated each victory and sulked after each loss as if he were a part of the team.

Sparky's nickname stuck with him after someone suggested he was the inspiration for the team—the "sparkplug." His undying passion earned him the position of student manager for the varsity team the next three seasons. The coach rewarded Sparky with the chance to be on the hardwood tonight as a player.

Each summer, Sparky played basketball in the Special Olympics, displaying the same enthusiasm he demonstrated as the team's manager. The team he applauded throughout the high school season saw every one of his games. Kirk and his teammates cheered when Sparky scored and reassured him after each missed shot. During those games, Kirk met Sparky's parents and grew fond of them.

Five minutes remained when Sparky bounced onto the hardwood. The lopsided score assured the Lions of a victory. Since their opponents, the Wolves, had little chance at a comeback, their coach put in their reserve players, comprised of sophomores and juniors vying for a starting position next season.

Dressed in their red and white uniforms, the Wolves brought the ball down the court. Ricky intercepted a pass intended for an inexperienced sophomore and drove the ball down the court. Sparky jetted down the court past Ricky and waited outside the top of the key for a pass. Ricky ignored him and scored with a left-handed layup.

Immediately, Coach Webster, who looked more like a football coach, signaled for a time out. He glared at Ricky who'd just scored his twenty-sixth point of the game—his season's best. Ricky barely tried to hide his smirk as he prepared himself for a tongue lashing.

"Jennings," the coach growled. "What part of teamwork doesn't a ball-hog like you understand? Gluttons don't make good teammates. You're on the bench." He tapped a sophomore, whose skills were considerably less than Ricky's, on the shoulder as the replacement. "For four years, Sparky has been supporting you. He deserves this chance tonight. If no one has grasped the concept of team play, you can observe it from the bench."

Timidly, the Wolves' seldom used players brought the ball up the court. Outside the three point line, they passed the ball around the perimeter without attempting to score. Kirk knew they were trying to avoid having the ball stolen again. The defensive pressure of the Lions was minimal since the Wolves were out of shooting range. Finally, after a minute, one of Wolves feebly shot the ball and it ricocheted off the backboard. Kirk jumped to snare the rebound and held the ball, allowing the Wolves to return to defend their basket. He dribbled the ball down the court. When he reached the three point line, he looked at an unguarded Sparky. Kirk flung the pass to him. Catching the hard pass forced Sparky off-balance. Hurriedly, he took the first shot of his high school career. The ball floated over the basket.

Kirk looked at Sparky and pointed to himself, taking the blame for the poor pass—a good throw would have allowed for a better shot. The ball landed in the hands of a surprised Wolves' player. He pushed the ball up the court and was fouled as he scored a layup. To the dismay of Kirk, the "mercy rule"—designed to give teams, losing by more than twenty points a chance to terminate the game sooner—permitted the clock to run as the fouled player stepped to the free throw line.

Kirk handed the ball to a teammate and yelled to his team as he waved his arms. "No fouls. We have won the game. Let them score. No fouls." Time became his enemy. He needed every remaining second to allow Sparky to score and to give himself one last opportunity for immortality in the school's history.

Kirk brought the ball down the court once again. At mid-court, a defender confronted him. He dribbled to his left, taking the defender with him. With a quick turn he dribbled to his right, eluding the defender. Another Wolf rushed to stop Kirk, but he sidestepped him and passed to an open Sparky. His shot hit the rim and the ball flew straight into the hands of a tall, lanky defender.

The Wolf sprinted up the court, weaving through a scattered defense of black and white uniforms. Kirk knew the player would have to run into him and be fouled if he attempted to score. Kirk stood firm. The impact knocked him to the floor. The referee blew his whistle, signaling an offensive foul. As the scorekeepers recorded the infraction, Kirk ran to the free throw line, determined to set the record. The second referee stood outside the in-bounds line, pointing to where the ball would be thrown in. Kirk sighed. There were no free throws for offensive fouls.

Thirty seconds remained. Kirk's aspiration faded as each second ticked from the scoreboard. He studied the opposing team as he dribbled the ball past mid-court. The opponents switched to a zone defense. Kirk felt confident he could score against this defense. Even if he missed, he was sure he would be fouled and be sent to the free throw line to redeem himself.

The senior glanced at his coach for instructions, pleading for the green light. No signal from the coach to deviate from the original plan. Kirk sighed as hope oozed from his body. The coach expected him to pass the ball to Sparky. This possession might be Kirk's last opportunity to score. If Sparky missed again, the Lions may not retain possession for the rest of the season.

Kirk caught a glimpse of Sparky's parents, occupying their usual positions—Mr. Ferguson sat on the edge of his seat, His mother clasped prayer-hands in front of her chin. Kirk recalled the brief conversation he had with Sparky's dad before the game, assuring him Sparky would play. "It's set, Mr. Ferguson. In the last few minutes of the game, the coach will put in Sparky." The picture of a proud dad's smiling eyes haunted Kirk as he glanced at Sparky, who waited for the opportunity to score. In his heart, Kirk knew

Sparky deserved another chance for a basket. But, time was fleeting for Kirk.

Kirk bounced the ball between his legs. His body tilted forward as he sprinted to the top of the key. Three defenders rushed to stop him, leaving Sparking unguarded. Kirk bounced the ball through a narrow opening between two defenders. Sparky caught the prefect pass. With his feet planted in unison and his shoulders squared to the basket, Sparky aimed.

As the ball left Sparky's hand, the crowd hushed. Kirk rushed to the basket for the rebound—ready to tip the ball in case of a missed shot. The ball swished through the net. The crowd erupted before the voice over the speakers announced, "Sparky Ferguson for three." Thunderous clapping, wild screaming, and shrill whistling deafened the gym.

A desperate Kirk stood on the balls of his feet, anticipating the steal on the throw-in under the Wolves' basket for the last opportunity to score. A deflated Wolf wandered to retrieve the ball which rolled away from him. Ten seconds remained as their guard picked up the ball and held it. The crowd counted down the final seconds of the game. The referee failed to deliver the five second count for delaying the game. The buzzer sounded—game ended. Kirk's heart sank and his shoulders sagged as he stared at the ominous zeroes on the clock on the scoreboard. His chance for a basketball scholarship vanished.

Students bumped Kirk as they rushed to congratulate their hero of the moment. Perched on the shoulders of his teammates, Sparky whipped his uniform shirt in the air with his usual frenzy. Students held their hands up, wishing for a return slap. A beaming Sparky reached out to as many as he could. Fists pumped into the air as the repeated chant of "Sparky, Sparky" echoed throughout the gym.

Kirk looked over at his coach, who stood clapping his hands. Sparky's dad placed his hand on the coach's shoulder, bending over to speak to him. The coach nodded, acknowledging Mr. Ferguson. Sparky's mom wiped the tears streaming from her face. Kirk forced a smile to hide his long face as he muscled his way through the crowd to honor Sparky. Kirk raised his hand towards Sparky, perched on his make-shift throne. Grinning, Sparky grabbed it with both of his hands.

"You're the man, Sparky!" Kirk screamed.

"I am the man!" Sparky yelled, raising his arms in the air.

Kirk watched the crowd parade Sparky around the court. He felt a hand on his shoulder. He turned to see the recruiter extending his hand. Shocked, Kirk shook the hand.

"Son," the man shouted over the jubilant celebration. "I would like to talk to you about an opportunity at State. Coach Jennings contacted us about your amazing season. That's quite an accomplishment. But there are some things more important than scoring points. Giving up a school record for that assist is the kind of player State wants."

"Aren't you here for Ricky?" the senior, still stunned, asked.

The recruiter grinned and winked. "We have more than one scholarship available."

Freddie and the Pot-Roast Puppy
Phyllis Borgardt

Pot-Roast was thrilled to be adopted, as seen by his wagging tail.

He had heard person after person say, "Oh, my goodness look at that fat Shih Tzu. Who would do that to a puppy?" Pot-Roast thought, *someone who over loved me?*

He had been enrolled in the Adoption Care Center for Animals when Granny Smith moved to her care center. She had given money to the adoption center to make certain Pot-Roast had enough food and treats to keep him in the life-style he was accustomed to.

Grandma Hanner smiled as she paid her dues to free Pot-Roast. "I know one little boy who is going to love you so much." She tucked the puppy under her arm, and left the center.

Three-thirty was the time that Freddie was out of school. He found Grandma Hanner waiting on the side walk. Freddie waddled down the stairs as fast as his chubby legs would carry him. He heard the unkind taunts, "Bye, fatty. Hope you have lots to eat tonight."

He tucked his head down and trudged ahead—one heavy foot at a time.

"Freddie, I have a wonderful surprise for you," said Grandma. She smiled broadly and placed Pot-Roast down beside Freddie's fat foot. Quickly, Pot-Roast began to sniff and sniff and sniff Freddie's shoes.

Freddie did his very best to lean over and pick up the round puppy. The ground was too far away and his tummy was too large. The boy smiled and shrugged his shoulders.

"That's right, Freddie. You and Pot-Roast have a lot in common. Both of you have been loved so much with food that you have a hard time reaching. Soon, you will be loved with a new plan and your life will change."

"I hope it's not exercise."

"It's fun-er-cise."

"Ok, as long as it isn't exercise. I don't do exercise."

"Pot-Roast used to sit on a pillow beside Granny Smith all day long. Granny Smith fed Him little bits of food as they watched television. Pot-Roast grew and grew sideways. He grew to be a round, round puppy."

"That sounds good to me. I like Granny Smith's philosophy. She's my kind of person."

"She over-loved her little puppy, but he wasn't able to run and play with his puppy friends."

"That sounds familiar to me. Maybe they weren't his friends."

"He would never know. Let's mark our calendar for the day we started fun-er-cise. We begin by taking Pot-Roast for a walk. Just a block or two today. Tomorrow, four blocks. Soon he will be so very trim. What do you think of our plan?"

"If it makes him healthy and happy, it will be a good plan. Maybe he could play in the dog park. He would have friends in no time. Let's have a snack now."

Grandma Hanner handed him an apple and Pot-Roast a low-cal treat.

"Grandma, that's not what I had in mind. What about the chocolate-fudge cake in the fridge."

"Oh, I gave that to the lady upstairs. She loves chocolate."

"She's not the only one."

"Freddie, we are about to change the way we see things. Are you on board?"

"Somehow, Grandma, I'm not certain Pot-Roast and I have a choice."

"Oh, Freddie you will have so many choices. Do I want an apple or do I want an orange? Do I want to walk to the park or to the school playground? There are so many choices to make."

"Grandma, I get the point. We are a team—the Pot-Roast Team."

"Our motto is down with gluttony and up with trim. This program will make my doctor happy as well. You see, we may add years onto Grandma Hanner's life."

"That's worth everything. You are the only one who cares about two overweight friends." He strained his toes to reach her cheek and plant a well-deserved kiss.

From Greed to Charity

Deceit
Heather N. Hartmann

Allie Fields pulled her wireless earbuds out and let them dangle around her neck as she fished out the apartment key from her shoe. She stood and jammed the key into the lock and turned. Anticipating Frank to still be asleep, she was startled when she saw him fully dressed, out on the deck, pacing, phone to ear.

Crossing to the kitchen, she kept her eye on the patio door. Allie filled a glass with water and downed it. She licked her lips and raised her eyebrows at Frank as he slid the door open.

"How was your run, darling?" Frank asked.

"Uneventful. You're up early." Allie set her empty glass in the sink.

"Important call."

"Seemed like it. Another tax emergency?" She closed the distance between them and skimmed her hands up his chest and around his neck.

Frank's hands found her waist and pulled her hips to his. "Always. April 15th is only eleven days away. I swear people would die without my services."

"I'm sure they would. Speaking of your services, when are you going to file my taxes?"

"I told you I would get around to it." Frank stepped back. Her arms fell down his chest to her sides.

Allie watched annoyance blaze in his eyes. She had been asking him since receiving her W-2. He always brushed her off. "If you don't have time, I can just take them to my regular guy."

"Get the paperwork together for me and I'll take them to work."

"Okay. Give me a minute."

"I don't have a damn minute. That call put me behind. I have several clients lined up for today. I have to get going." Frank pulled on his suit jacket.

"Okay, I'll bring them by your office." Allie bit her lower lip, uncertain if she should attempt to kiss him goodbye. She had witnessed these moods before.

"I'll let you know if that works for me."

"Okay. . ." Allie rolled her eyes at his back.

He walked toward the door, stopped briefly, his back to her. "Bring them by. Leave them with the receptionist."

Before she could respond, her cell rang. "See ya then." Distracted by the ringing, she ran across the room to pick up the phone.

"Hey, Mom! How's the beach?" Allie heard the lock click and flicked her eyes toward the door to make sure he was gone. "That's great, Mom." Sighing, she sank to the couch.

"What's wrong, honey?"

"Oh, I don't know. I think my relationship with Frank has about run its course."

"You've been dating for almost a year now. Are you sure you're not going through a rough patch?"

"I'm sick of his moods, and his evasiveness."

"I told you, you need to be more direct with him. Tell him what you want."

"I just feel that if I have to do that…then why bother?" Allie reached up and pulled the earbuds off her neck, tossing them on the coffee table.

"Well, that's a good question. Why have you been together this long?"

"He's pretty good in the sack."

"Allie, seriously. I don't need to hear that. You're still my little girl."

"Not so much, Mom." Allie smiled knowing her mother was blushing on the other end of the line. "I hate to say it, but I've about had it with his moods. I swear, sometimes it's like I'm dating a high school girl."

"If that's the truth, Allie, maybe you should end it sooner than later."

"I'm going to think on it."

"Okay, honey. Feel free to call me as late as you want."

"Sounds good. I love you. Have fun on the rest of your vacation."

"Love you, too."

* * *

Allie threw her newest Vera Bradley bag over her shoulder and locked her Mustang. Frank's office only had street parking. She wasn't great at parallel parking. Lucky for her, the area was often dead. Walking across the road, Allie studied the tall brick building set amongst the many rundown structures. Frank had told her that the company had built in the warehouse district because it was the new up and coming thing. Allie figured the owner was delusional.

In the ten months they had been dating, Allie had not once seen a client in his office. However, she also had never been past the receptionist desk. Frank always greeted her in the lobby.

Plastering on a smile, she pulled open the door and walked in. Her smile faltered when she found the lobby empty. Placed on Maisy's desk was an at lunch sign.

Not wanting to wait around, Allie called Frank's cell. When it went to voicemail, she decided to go into the office and ask for him. She opened one side of the double doors behind Maisy's desk. Allie stopped in shock. Hundreds of boxes were shelved from floor to ceiling, forming a hallway. She blinked twice and glanced back into the lobby, searching for another door into the main accounting office. "Maybe the owners only converted the parts of the warehouse they needed," Allie whispered. When she found no other door, she decided to move forward. Allie felt her heart double in speed. She focused on controlling her breathing as she tiptoed into the warehouse. Frank's muffled voice reached her ears. Sighing in relief, she took two confident steps forward and rounded the corner.

Abruptly, she froze, her hand flying to her mouth. Ice cold sweat dripped down her back. Diagonal from her and by a set of boxes, Frank and two men stood around a man tied to a chair.

Allie stepped back, out of the men's field of vision but stayed to see what was happening. Who was this guy? Frank, her boyfriend, the boring accountant, had a gun and a man held against his will? She leaned forward, peered around the boxes and listened to what Frank was saying.

"I'm a generous man, Steve. I've allowed you a year to pay me back, but what have you done? That's right, accrued more debt. Doubling down is a fool's game, Steve. I need to hear one good reason why this bullet shouldn't end up in your brain."

"Please, Mr. Netto, please. I can pay you back. I can. I just need a little more time."

Frank backhanded Steve. The man's head flew back and rolled on his shoulders. "You've been singing that same old tune for months now."

"I know. . .but I promise I can get. . ."

"La de da, la de da. . .," Frank sang out.

"Mr. Netto, I have a line on some big money coming and all I need is. . ."

Allie jumped in shock and bit her tongue as she stifled a scream. Realizing her eyes were squeezed tight, she peeked them open. Steve's body slumped to the side, the back of his head blown to smithereens. Vomit rose up hot and furious. She took two steps back, swallowing her bile.

"Greed's a fool's game. The man had it made, but he couldn't resist placing that last bet." He holstered his gun. "Get rid of him."

Allie jerked up straight and bee-lined it back to the receptionist office when Frank started her way. She made it to the outside door, hand poised to push it open, when Frank said her name.

Turning, she beamed her best smile at him. Her heart galloped in her throat. "Frank, I was just leaving."

"What are you doing here?" Frank asked, looking around.

"I. . .I was bringing by my taxes. When your receptionist wasn't here, I figured I'd come back later." He squinted his eyes and studied her. "I tried calling your cell. You didn't answer. Anyway, I was on my way out to lunch. I figured I'd come back by after, and…"

"Enough, Allie." Frank stepped closer to her, reached out a hand and cupped her chin. Angling her face toward his, a bead of sweat dripped down her spine. "You're pale. You feeling all right?"

"Actually, no. I think I'm coming down with something. I better get home." She pulled back, but he didn't release her. Allie's eyes felt as big as saucers and her breathing was rapid.

"Why don't I take you home?" He removed his hand from her chin to check his watch.

"No!" At his stunned expression, she tried again. "I mean, that's okay. I've got my car, and plus you told me how busy today was going to be for you." Shit, he wasn't buying a word she was selling. His eyes focused intently on her. She had to get out of there alone. Had to make him believe she was sick. The door to her back swung open, and Allie practically fell outside.

The receptionist had returned. "Hiya, boss. I've got the roast beef sandwiches as requested. Hey, Allie. Didn't know you were coming by today. I didn't buy any extra."

"Impromptu visit. I'm not staying. I really gotta go. Call you later, Frank." Allie leaned up, planted a quick kiss to his cheek, and bolted out the door. Almost to her car, she jolted when a hand laced around her upper arm, turning her.

"You forgot to leave your taxes." His hand lingered around her arm, but released when she pulled away.

"Oh, yeah! Duh. Here." She opened her bag and pulled out the paperwork needed to file her taxes.

"I'll get this ready and bring it by for your signature tomorrow. I have something to take care of tonight. I won't be over."

"Okay." She knew she sounded a little too eager.

Frank squinted his eyes and studied her. "You've got some color coming back. Good."

Allie tensed when he leaned in to kiss her. She responded in kind, but when he pulled away, she felt the bile return. Swallowing her vomit, she nodded good-bye and crawled into her car.

She pulled away from the curb and controlled her speed until she was out of his eyesight. Allie pressed the gas pedal to the floor and hit the roof release. She needed air, desperately.

* * *

The beat cop wrote down her story and told her he would be back, leaving her in the interview room. Allie stood, facing her reflection in the two-way mirror. Her hair was disheveled. Her skin pale. Her eyes bloodshot. She paced the room waiting for the officer to come back.

A middle-aged man in a brown suit opened the door. "Ms. Fields?" He walked into the room.

"Yes, that's me" She returned back to the hard metal seat.

"I'm detective Clark, Randy Clark. I wanted to talk to you about your police report."

"Have you arrested him yet? Who was the guy he killed? What about the other men? Do you. . ." Allie's rapid fire questions were interrupted.

"Ms. Fields, I've asked that we hold off on sending units until I've talked with you."

"Because you don't believe me?" Allie pushed away from the table and stood.

"No, because I do. And because you said the shooter's name was Frank Netto?"

Allie sat back down and leaned forward. "Yes. Frank Netto. Probably Franklin, but honestly, I don't know that for sure."

"Well, I can tell you around here we call him Frankie Netto."

"You guys know of him? Then why is he still out there?"

"Because, ma'am, it's really hard to arrest *The* Frankie Netto, without hard evidence against him."

"What do you mean '*The* Frankie Netto'?"

"Ma'am, Frankie Netto is the head of the local mob. We haven't been able to get any hard evidence to stick. Every time we have a lead, the evidence or the witness goes missing."

"I've been dating the head of the mob?" Allie fell back in her chair, scraped her hands down her face and looked the detective square in the eye. "Well, how do we bring the son of a bitch in?"

Golden Shower
Larry Duerbeck

Who'da thunk it? Me, an environmentalist!

A cool day in the Irish forest—not virgin, but distinctly old growth—and I, alone and a tourist from the Midwest, had just emptied my pub-primed bladder. The kidney stream jetted between some big, old, half-buried slab of rock and the base of a majestic oak among oaks. High pressure attention felt great and I was drawing in the old firehose when—"Stop! Stop!"

An excited voice carried up to me, thin and piping. While I zipped up, a drenched leprechaun zipped out of the crevice. "Just laid my poor head down for a wee nappie and this happens. I told the bishop when I finished this fine great forest for him, I needed a good dose of shut-me-eye."

He dried out while he spoke. "Oh, agh. The smell, the stink!"

Perfume of blooming heather arose. "Now you'd be after telling me—what parish claims you?"

"Parish? I'm Lutheran."

"Wurrah the day. Then you got it."

Little as he was, he seemed to shrink a little. An uneasy feeling crept over me. "It? What's it?" I seemed to shrink a little, too, here and there, in chilly fear.

"My pot of gold, you daft loonie! All yours. I told the bishop I'd find me a spot to sleep in and planned to sleep until a Protestant pissed on me. And when that happened—Oh, I'm an idle, a boastful, a thoughtless nipperkin. And when that happened he'd, lucky Protestant, he'd have my pot of gold into the bargain. He happens to be you."

I noticed that his lips moved first. Then, as if by magic, his delayed words emerged from a different time than mine, translated themselves, and I understood him. Sharp-featured and sly, he grew more so. "I offer you a trade. The pot of gold back for all your lusts made good. Tended to, my fine stinking waterspout of a man. Begorrah! A rare gargoyle you'd be making. Now imagine all your lusts, if you would be so kind, and tell me—"

I interrupted. "What year is it?"

He jumped. "The year? Why, it's sixteen-sixteen, the year of our dear and Catholic Lord, is it not?"

"The year is two thousand even. In what we call the Common Era." I laughed as he gasped. "You've been asleep near four hundred years! I'll take the gold. Have the best of both. Gold buys off lusts, you know. It really buys off avarice."

"Well. That's how it is, then. Done and done." His tone grew reassuring, then confidential. "This magic business bit me in the backside. My loss is your profit. Make nary a mistake about that. You see, I turned over, at the Great Leprechaun Depot, my pot of gold for a treasure seed. It would grow into another pot of gold overnight, for me to come and get, dig up the next morning." Now I gasped as he laughed. "Laddie, that seed's been growing all this long time!"

So here I am, in the owner's office of the Sleeping Leprechaun Mine. Geologists can't account for it, say there's nothing like it. They've written papers. Veins and shafts of pure gold, reaching out. Almost as if they've been growing, like a root system. I put my first of ever so many millions into environmental preservation—old growth Irish forest preservation, to be exact.

But only the first, mind!

Greenback

Nicki Jacobsmeyer

As a dollar bill, I've been around the block. Several, actually. My roots began in Philadelphia where I quickly hit the streets and ended up at a cheese steak stand at South and 10th Street. My crisp cotton and linen blend suit stuck out among the other dirt rags. I rested in the vendors pocket for no more than five minutes, when a big spender businessman exchanged me for a Grant. Not any businessman, but a Comcast Executive. The higher echelon. It felt perfect to rub shoulders with a Tumi bi-fold wallet engulfed in imported silk trousers. A greenback could get used to this kind of living.

I burned a hole in the executive's pocket come quitting time. After a brutal day at the office, the time had come to blow off some steam. Nothing a few fingers of scotch couldn't cure. The bartender at Ravens Lounge fondled me before she slipped me into the tip jar—easy money. She wanted to get back home to Michigan this weekend. Nothing said the Fourth of July like Traverse City's very own National Cherry Festival. She didn't mention that to Mr. Big Spender, didn't want to turn him off. She needed all the green she could get.

I made it to Michigan in one piece after a non-stop flight from the east coast. God's country. I hadn't seen a taxi in over an hour nor heard any shouts of profanity ringing in my ears. I could feel the scalding July sun soaking through her pocket and I felt restless. Soon enough, the echoes of the festival's Rock 'n' Roll band bounced off the trees in the park. I heard her stomach growl and knew my time had come to see the sights. She reached the Cherry Pie Contest Table and pointed to her entry choice. The aroma of homemade pie engulfed my senses as she pulled me out of her pocket. To my surprise, the klutzy baker dropped his creation all over me. There went my pristine motif. After a thorough cleaning, I still wore cherry stains. The next boy who needed change back from his pie didn't care. A dollar is still a dollar, stained or not.

The boy held me like a rare jewel, sprinting away from the pie stand and staring at George Washington's cherry stained teeth as he zigzagged through the crowd towards his mother. He never took his eyes off me, so he didn't see the divot in the ground, and went tumbling down. His mother ran over to him, slapping her chubby hands up and down his grass-stained jeans and fussing all the while. She swept him up and carried him away to safety, leaving me to lie on the grass like a piece of trash. I laid there trampled by everything from Timberland boots to Jimmy Choos. A brave soul risked his clean fingers and plucked me off the ground. He shoved me in his pocket before my owner came searching. He had enough now for a can of Meister Brau from the Speedway gas station on the way home. His luck ran out with the local town chicks and he soon stumbled off to his truck.

My next owner, a college student from Northwestern Michigan College, drove a beat up compact car filled with his rowdy buddies. His purchase at the Speedway didn't consist of a cold one, but a full tank of gas, Mountain Dew and bag of Doritos. They were getting the hell out of dodge and hitting the open road. The Windy City would be promising. It was every college guy's dream—beer, drugs and women. Not necessarily in that order. In Chicago that night, they scored big with a local selling dope in the back alley of a club. The college guys emptied the cash in their pockets and pooled together enough dough to fit the bill. The dealer had a smug look on his face. He enjoyed ripping off the tourists who never realized they were paying double, even triple, the real cost.

The drug dealer walked north with a spring in his step towards his boss's office. He reached the Howard Red Line Stop and casually looked around for any trouble. The building adjacent looked quiet enough, but trouble always lurked nearby. He smashed me into his pocket, and I prayed I wouldn't fall out. He might not be a saint, but his pocket seemed like the best alternative to the kind that walks these parts. His boss, Dwayne, sat waiting for my owner, and he looked like a mad bulldog ready to attack. After he ruffed the man up for being late, the dealer begged for atonement by sharing his last high price sale. His boss looked so satisfied, I thought he might plant a wet one on his cheek. Instead, Dwayne slid the action of his Glock 19 and fired a single nine millimeter through his underutilized brain. That was that, problem solved. No one paid attention to the sound of a gunshot; it was the neighborhood's lullaby playing through the dark hours of the night. All the commotion shook me up. I don't usually see this kind of action. Benjamin's knew about this life, but not me.

Dwayne pulled out a little baggie of powder from his pocket and dumped its contents on a piece of glass resting on the table. He took the razor blade sitting nearby to make four-inch-long lines. Then he took me out, rolled me up, and snorted the lines of cocaine. Finally, he packed up his shit and left, while wiping his nose. I agreed that the time had come for crisp fresh air. We weren't so lucky. The air outside was laced with weed and the iron smell of festering blood. Dwayne got on the Red Line, switched to the Blue Line and ended up at O'Hare Airport. I relaxed, relieved that he was finally getting us out of trouble and hopefully going to chill out. He marched over to the ticket counter and bought a First Class ticket on American Airlines. Destination: Las Vegas. Oh, no, not Vegas, baby!

It was almost dawn and Dwayne didn't skip a beat. He got off the plane and went straight to a strip club. He was a glutton for cheap pleasures. The girls looked like they were winding down from a night of lustful eyes and endless lap dances. A girl named Roxie caught my owner's attention. Roxie performed her pole dance as he drooled on himself. He pulled me out with the remaining stack of greenbacks and laid me on the table. It's amazing how your life can change in a matter of minutes. One minute, I belong to a cracked-out businessman who works in the hood of Chicago's dark side, and the next minute, I'm nestled between two robust melons sweating like a sinner in church. Isn't life grand?!

Roxie moved me to her g-string as she eyed the clock—8:00 a.m., quitting time. As she waved goodbye to my former boss, she stumbled down the backstage in her three-inch stilettos. Liquor was a necessary evil for a pole-dancer. She would never have made it through her shift if she hadn't taken those shots. She hobbled to her station, removed the makeup that screamed stripper, and changed into a nice floral sundress. She promised she would show up this morning, and she didn't want to disappoint him again. She swore she was done with this lifestyle and going back to school to study fashion and design. Which was partly true. She was wearing Victoria's Secret. No one knew that it had hung from the clearance rack. After Roxie finally looked presentable, she grabbed me and a few others and put us in her purse. Off I went, on another adventure.

She pulled up in the parking lot, already regretting her promise. She didn't belong here; she wasn't going to fool anyone. She walked up the stairs and tried to avoid eye contact. She looked down the aisle and saw her father mount the pulpit. She gave him a shy smile and his eyes filled with wonder. She had finally graced him with her presence and looked put together. Roxie took a seat towards the back of the church to avoid undue attention. She glanced around to see if she recognized any parishioners and to her relief, everyone was a stranger. The organ played, cueing the ushers to retrieve the offering plates. Roxie panicked. She watched as the others put bills and checks on the plate as though they had more where that came from. She glanced down at her purse. She struggled to make ends meet, but she could feel her father's piercing eyes. She casually opened her purse and pulled me out. I was still stained cherry red, wore traces of cocaine, and reeked of stale cigarette smoke and cheap perfume. She placed me on the offering plate and never looked back.

The members passed the plate down the pews and I wondered where I would end up next. "In God We Trust" is my motto. Everything will work out one way or another. An average greenback only has four years to live, so I have to make the most of my short life.

Going for the Gold
Susan Gore Zahra

Frank Herman was greedy for gold. Gold-painted plastic or well-shined brass would do as long as it was attached to a blue ribbon or a trophy pedestal. He had missed qualifying for the Olympic track team at the end of college by a few hundredths of a second. That may have been the only real gold medal he could have won, but there were plenty of other shiny rewards to be had. Frank was determined to win as many as possible, including his holy grail, the Ironman Triathlon in Hawaii.

The second bedroom in the tiny house he and his wife rented had shelves crammed with trophies on two walls. Plaques and ribbons adorned the surface above the desk. Frank stroked the ribbon from the Ironman qualifier race he had won last weekend. Two years ago he qualified, but he had pulled his hamstring as he crossed the finish line and crashed down on his right knee. His hopes of going to the real Ironman in Hawaii that year were as smashed as his bloody kneecap.

When he told Nicky he planned to spend the next year getting back into shape and try for Hawaii in two more years, she packed up and left. Before their wedding, they had agreed to save ten percent of their income so they could buy a house and start a family after he made it to Hawaii. Nicky saw him miss qualifying three years in a row. She began to complain about her biological clock running out before he made it. What if he never made it?

Nicky came back when Frank agreed to put the ten percent they saved during the next two years into separate bank accounts—his to save for the Ironman trip, hers to give her the freedom to hire a lawyer if he continued to pursue the Ironman instead of parenthood.

With his goal only six months away, Frank was determined to meet Nicky's deadline. He had saved enough money to take Nicky with him to Hawaii for a second honeymoon after the race. With all the romance the islands have to offer, they could get that family started.

They began to look at houses online, searching for the right neighborhood and dreaming about the style and size. There would be more bedrooms for children and an extra room for trophies. Although Frank agreed to stop Ironman competitions after Hawaii, he could continue competing in swimming, biking, and track events on into the Senior Olympics. Some day they would need space for their children's trophies.

Frank picked up his backpack, stuffed with the t-shirt and athletic pants he wore to teach P.E. at Winningham Middle School, and grabbed his bicycle helmet. He used travel time as training time whenever possible. He headed toward the kitchen, where Nicky was fixing her breakfast, to say goodbye.

"Oh, my God! Frank! Frank!" Nicky screamed.

Frank raced to the kitchen, where Nicky stood staring at the TV, her breakfast smoothie in hand, tilted precariously close to pouring out on the counter.

"What?"

"Damien Carter." Nicky pointed to the TV screen showing yellow tape cordoning off a mall parking lot. "Isn't that the kid on the high school track team you used to spend so much time with when he was in your class?"

"Yeah?"

"He's dead."

"What? How?" Frank dropped his backpack and helmet.

"Shot. Last night. His dad was shot, too. He's in the hospital. Critical."

"Shot! Why?"

"Don't know. A neighbor says they went out jogging together over in the Mercer Creek neighborhood. They were near that mall at the edge of the new subdivision on the other side of the creek. Somebody just started shooting." Nicky set her smoothie on the counter as she started to reach out to Frank.

Frank grabbed his backpack and pulled his car keys off the hook by the door, leaving his helmet on the floor. "School is going to be hell. I better get there early."

Memories of after-school sessions with Damien flooded Frank's mind as he drove. On Saturdays, Damien's father came with him, and they learned side by side. Damien had Olympic potential that Frank had nurtured solely to earn vicarious gold through his student's success. He continued to cheer Damien from the sidelines when he could make a track meet without disrupting his own training regimen.

Principal Margot DeVault steered teachers into the library as they arrived. She informed the staff of what had happened to Damien and reminded them that eighth-grader Ricky Carter was his brother.

As she assigned Frank and other teachers to cruise halls between classes and during planning periods, she told them, "Emotions will be running high in kids who are already walking bunches of mood swings. Let's try to keep them from hurting each other."

Teaching P.E. allowed Frank to run off some feelings while helping students to do the same. The hardest class was last period, when he had to stare at the empty space usually occupied by Ricky Carter. His best friend, Ben Montgomery, stood next to the emptiness, his face ashen except for red splotches around his teary eyes.

Nicky was in the kitchen when Frank returned home after school. He watched her through the window before he opened the door. She kept her hair blonde, although it had darkened during the seven years they were married. He suspected she was covering a little gray around the temples, near the crow's feet that appeared when she smiled. She smiled less and less as the deadline for Frank's Ironman approached. Now she looked as though she had been crying.

Nicky looked up when Frank walked through the door carrying a pizza box and a grocery bag. "What is that?"

"One sausage and bacon pizza with thick crust, a six-pack of Bud, and ta da!" Frank pulled a carton of rocky road ice cream out of the bag.

"That isn't exactly on your training diet."

"It was on our menu the night we made love for the first time."

Nicky began to sob. "There's something I have to tell you, and now you're being so romantic and sweet, and I am so scared."

Frank set his packages on the counter. He wanted to hold her, but found himself holding his breath instead, bracing for another shock.

"They commandeered the library for some extra counselors. Damien had so many friends! I watched them going in and out all day."

"It was pretty awful at our school, too." Frank struggled to wait for Nicky to say what she had done.

"There are five kids in his family in a house about the size of ours. And it's hilly there, with steps up to the porch. There's no way they can get his dad in and out in a wheelchair. Or maneuver in a tiny bathroom like ours. Then there's the hospital bills and Damien's funeral." Nicky gulped in air.

"And?" Frank felt his chest tighten.

"And I donated my lawyer money to the fund they set up. I don't know yet whether I can stay with you or leave. If the only thing that is important to you is that Ironman crap, I don't want to stay. I don't want to keep waiting for a baby. Now you remembered our first time together like you really want me instead of some effing medal. . ."

Frank could no longer hold the iron grip on his own grief. He pulled Nicky into his arms and wept with her until the rocky road ice cream began to ooze out of its box onto the counter.

"I need to tell you something, too. I donated three-fourths of the Ironman account to the fund for the Carters. I kept some so we can go somewhere. We can take our time together, relax, and start our family. We can even go to Hawaii if you want. But not during the Ironman races. No more triathlons."

Frank continued to hold Nicky. He stroked her hair, the only gold he would ever need.

Saturday Writers 2017

Ghost Light
Sarah Angleton

I suppose you want to know about Annie. There are many here who might answer your questions, though the others may not answer honestly.

But I will.

The newspapers don't exactly have it wrong, not everything, anyway, but the reporters weren't here. They didn't breathe in the scent of fresh-baked bread in Annie's kitchen the night it happened. They didn't hear the thump, thump, thump of her walking stick on the wooden deck out back as she made her way out of the house into the woods.

All they saw was what remained—the half-washed dishes in the sink, the tower in the corner of the room made from boxes of lemon-lime soda.

They don't know Annie like we do. They don't even write of her as if she's still alive, because they assume she's not.

They may be right. That's one piece of information I don't yet have. But let me tell you what I do know.

It all started with a light in the woods. You know, those ghost lights that flicker off in the distance? People attribute them to swamp gases or UFOs. Others speculate they're spirits guiding the living to their deaths. Except, most of the time spirits don't do that.

Annie had just baked bread and set it aside to cool for the morning. You can imagine the warmth of the kitchen, the lovely yeasty scent making your stomach rumble and flooding you with a sense of security and peace, with vague memories and with deep longing.

I'm sorry. I've lost the thread of my story. I was talking about the night Annie went missing. She'd begun washing the dishes when she looked out the window and saw one of those lights. The woman doesn't scare easily and she wasn't frightened, just maybe a little unnerved. And too curious.

It's her curiosity that led her to discover me in the first place. Despite how I might seem to you now, I'm not generally a nosy or talkative man. Maybe the odd appearance once in a while, but sometimes you just can't help that.

I was never much of one for haunting the living. They've got enough to worry about, I always thought. And it makes no difference who I share my afterlife with, if that's what this is.

I liked Annie. She's got a quiet gentleness about her. In her late sixties perhaps, though sometimes the ages of the living confuse me. I would put myself around that age, too, in appearance. In reality, my age is much more difficult to pinpoint. But I have seen occupants of this house come and go. Annie is the first to have seen me, though certainly not the first to see any of us.

I wonder if that's what compelled her to seek the source of the light. Perhaps she thought she'd found another of us. She likes us. Says she'd be lonely without the spirits in the rickety old house. She calls it rickety, but really it's well-maintained. The fella who lived here before Annie was a handy sort of man. He buttoned up the place pretty well, made some changes to it, modernized it. Some spirits grumbled, but not me. I don't mind seeing change, and feel privileged to be able to do so. Life is easier than when I lived it. In some ways.

Annie has been a friend to us. She hasn't screamed or uttered incantations.

And that's why I had to do something about her.

We're not a gruesome bunch, most of us, anyway. The afterlife, this form of it, neither alive nor fully passed on, can get a little tedious when you spend it with the same ten or twelve spirits all the time. Actually, I think we're pretty lucky. This has been a place of misfortune for the living over the years.

There are pitfalls and rattlesnakes and, back in the day, a fair share of mountain lions and bears. Randall got shot during a stagecoach hold-up on a road less than a mile from the house, before there was a house, and before there was much of a road.

He's sore about it. "Died before my time," he still grumbles, even though it's likely been centuries. He had a young bride waiting at the end of that trip. He followed the trail and found her, but there's only heartbreak in that. He backtracked and found us instead.

I don't have such a good memory of what happened to me, at least nothing that would have pulled me from this spot, I suppose, not even toward a different kind of afterlife. I know I have bloodstains on the only shirt I can ever wear, which also bears a bullet hole. I don't know why I was killed, or who did it. Maybe I'm here because I'm supposed to try to figure that out, but whoever shot me would be long gone by now. Maybe in his own woods somewhere, holed up with fellow spirits, all forgetting their own tragic stories.

I've never worried about my death much, though. After the first many years, it's hard to know precisely how many, a settler built this house, cleared out a bunch of the wood and lived here with his wife and family until she died of consumption. The widower married again right away, and that's when I experienced my first haunting.

The dead wife, Roberta, stayed here with us. A brave thing to do, you ask me. She watched this other woman raise her children, four little tykes who resembled their father and loved their stepmother fiercely. One day, Roberta got angry enough to appear to her husband's new wife, threaten her with eternal damnation. The new wife was fool enough to believe Roberta had the authority to dole out such punishment.

The family left, but soon after, the husband returned with a priest and a wild-eyed woman that jingled softly when she walked. I suppose your kind don't put on shows like that anymore. You ask me, what you do is impressive enough without all the nonsense.

For days the priest and the medium took turns mumbling prayers and incantations, calling Roberta's name. I'd never experienced anything like it. None of us had felt such close contact with the living since before our own deaths. It was like someone had awakened our senses. Colors became more vibrant, sounds more distinct. I drew in the fresh scent of woodland flowers, not initially able to identify the sensation, and then grasping onto it like a life preserver adrift in the vast sea of my misty thoughts. I caught glimpses, then, of other things, images of people I had loved and forgotten. I can no longer recall them, but I know they were there for a glorious, fleeting moment.

That's what this strange half-afterlife is like. The longer I'm here, the further from my former self I get, and the dimmer everything becomes.

Roberta left us after a few days with the priest and the medium. Where she went, I can't say.

One moment, she was talking with that jingly woman, then somehow, through her, sending warmth and love to her children, addressing their bewildered father, a radiant smile on her previously sullen and plain face. Then she was gone.

It's scary, that end. Those of you who still count yourselves among the living may not understand that. You fear death, but assume after it comes, there'll be no more transitions to fear. That's not true. Smile or no smile, Roberta was here. Then she wasn't.

I'm not anxious to be a wasn't.

Surely, you can understand that. It remains my only genuine fear, this sudden vanishing, but hunger overcomes fear, haven't you found? And that's what this is, hunger. Or I might more precisely describe it as desperation, or as terrible, unquenchable greed. Since Roberta, we spirits have haunted every person who has ever lived in this house.

Many have moved out, their sanity barely intact, leaving the complicated spiritual history of the place for the next unwitting resident to sort out. But others seek the aid of experts, such as yourself, those who allow us, for a brief time, to possess their consciousness, to breathe in the scent of the fresh bread, to witness the splash of miniscule bubbles bursting above the surface of the lemon-lime soda that stings the tongue with its fresh acidy taste.

The game we play is a dangerous one. None of us, since Roberta, has ever disappeared. We're careful. We enjoy the contact, the boost of energy, the likes of which we enjoyed when we had living tissue that would tingle for the joy of it. We have to be ever careful not to trip over the edge into the unknown. But even you living can surely understand, the reward is more valuable for the risk.

So you see why I had to get rid of Annie. She isn't like the others. She's not a medium who can speak to us in a way we can communicate back. She sees our presence as a blessing and chooses to live in peace with us, whispering to us, her words reaching us as if muffled by a feather pillow. When she walks through us, she giggles, as if the sensation tickles her innards, and utters, "Excuse me."

It's a quiet life here with Annie. It's a life of faded memories, and forgotten sensations.

Each day she bakes bread I can't remember how to smell, and pops open a can of her favorite lemon lime soda. I want to taste it so badly, I'm pulled helplessly toward the experience, a June bug bumping my head again and again into the porch light.

Your senses are like muscles, did you know? They grow more uncoordinated and weaker the longer they're unused. And once in a while, the frustration of that grows so powerful, there's a twitch, a burst of light, the kind that attracts the living, even leading a helpless old woman into a dense wood full of the kinds of dangers that lurk in the darkness of night.

I don't know how long it's been. The police have come and gone, along with volunteers carrying flashlights and determined expressions. They're not coming around anymore, and now you're here to find out if the house itself has any notion of where you could find whatever remains of Annie.

But the house has no notion, nor do any of its spirit occupants. Annie's not with us. Perhaps she found the light she sought and made that transition we all still fear. Perhaps a new homeowner will move in soon. Maybe this one will be intrigued by the legends of this haunted cabin in the woods, and will be a medium, one who channels the desperate dead, and bakes fresh bread, and drinks lemon lime soda.

POETRY
Lust and Chastity
Gluttony and Temperance
Greed and Charity

Saturday Writers 2017

Back Pocket
Bradley Bates

The salamanders came out from hiding. In the spring and fall,

when the ticks did not exist, I would hike a half mile down to the creek,

and find black four-legged amphibians with lemon dimes marked

across their bodies, and I still don't understand how the camouflage

works to keep their small dragon smiles safe. I spent four years

of my youth in the country with ten acres in the back pocket of my

trousers to spread across the landscape in correct latitude

and longitude of my being out in the middle of nowhere, and I would

spend my time trekking by faith of belonging not of the world but in

the world finding time expressed correctly in the sacred and

ominous tenacity of his lonely face. I brought him up to the family

house to show everyone, my Dad, Mom, and Sister, the creature

of light and darkness who belongs in all places at once.

Vindictable
Diane How

Do not have fear, rather deep respect
for the power of the sea
My crashing waves and giant swells
demand to remain free
Don't build your wall around my sands
I'll crush them to the ground
I own the beaches and the shores
as other sorely found
Just when you think you have control
when everything's divine
I'll reach my arms around your best
'til you recognize it's mine

Transfiguration
Larry Duerbeck

Lust.
    And Gluttony.
        And Greed.
      Oh my.
That's what I feel for you

Never such a living sinner
Bad as
Lust on honeymoon
Gluttony Thanksgiving Dinner
Greed with Christmas soon
Lust.
    And Gluttony.
        And Greed.
      Oh my.

Now I'm thrilled
My wish fulfilled
Begins for me
You feel these sins for me
Lust.
    And Gluttony.
        And Greed.
      Oh my.

Gluttons for Punishment
R.R.J. Sebacher

What lubricates and fuels America

Hard working fast food slaves

Vegetable oil and sweat of the short order cook

Grease defines our working class

Better known as the lower middle

Song beaten out with heavy steel spatulas

On flat metal griddles and sizzle of deep fryers

Beans—potatoes—rice and noodles fill soup kettles

From hot dogs and hamburgers it escalates

Chicken our national bird—oven for celebration

Sirloin and pork steaks on middle class grills

Stew—chowders—burgoo—chili—gumbo

Upper middle class tastes only the choicest

Stolen snatches of the richest tender pieces

Castle Watch
Cathleen Callahan

What care I the things they say,

or do not say,

of love moated by circumstance.

I could beckon the bridge of your arms

and enter

before their astonished eyes.

But care I whose heart I break,

if it be not mine,

what life I shove into the ditch.

And so, I call not

but stand afar,

watching the light move from room to room.

Love or Lust
Donna Mork Reed

I love him. I lust him.

I need him so.

Catching tigers by the toe.

Or dismembering daisies

One by one, we pull

Each petal to asund.

The wise, the old, they cast the stones

They accuse my desiring bones.

But I believe it is time

Our love was appointed by divine.

Peace out. Piss off. Pass the Deucey.

I'm in love. I'm not a floozy.

Saturday Writers 2017

From Wrath to Forgiveness

A Flash of Hope
Diane How

Lakeisha cursed to herself as she gripped the blank notebook with one hand while using the other to push a divergent black curl out of her face. The January winds whipped furiously as she waited for the bus to arrive. The English assignment, due Friday, wore on her mind. Normally, she'd be finished by the time she got home from school. Not this time. For two days she'd stared at the paper, the words refusing to bleed from her pen.

"What is *your* dream?" Ms. Lowery made it sound as if every student lived a normal life, complete with options and the financial support to achieve them. "College? Career? Travel? Write what you want to happen*" Does she have any idea what my life is like? NO!* The question seemed cruel to the new transfer student.

I have no dreams. Lakeisha lived in the real world, filled with responsibilities and hardships, drugs and booze, bill collectors and angry people. Her days left no room for dreams. With a mother imprisoned for selling drugs, and a father killed when she was five, the chance of having a successful career was improbable. College was out of the question. A high school education, if she was lucky enough to finish the year, would get her a minimum wage job.

Many of her classmates had applied to numerous colleges and waited anxiously to hear from each. Her goals? The first, survival, avoiding gang fights that erupted into gun battles at any given time. Walking from the bus stop to her front door involved risk. The second, keeping the electricity on. *Dreams? How am I supposed to write about such foolishness?*

There had been much controversy between the districts when the decision was made to transfer students from failing inner-city schools to academically successful ones in affluent neighborhoods.

At first, Lakeisha felt a tinge of excitement, holding out hope that she'd make new friends and learn useful skills. Hope faded quickly during the first week. The long commute added more stress to her day and limited the hours she could work.

Cliques of girls that didn't look like her, didn't speak like her, and didn't dress like her, whispered and giggled as she walked alone through the long hallways. Even the boys said lewd and offensive things, much like those in her old school, just in hushed voices.

Lakeisha knew why she'd been unable to complete the assignment. She wanted to tell the truth, not lie or pretend her future held magnificent opportunities. Dreams required more than just imagination. She wanted to respond to the snickers as they pointed to the same pair of shoes she wore every day. Her threads came from nearby dumpsters or Goodwill, hardly the place to find a dress for the upcoming prom.

It hurt to watch the students snub their noses at lunch menus and throw away perfectly good trays of food, knowing how many times she'd stood in soup lines waiting for a meal. Their spoiled, over-indulgent lifestyles sickened her. The anger boiled inside her head as she squeezed her pen. Suddenly, the words spilled across the paper. One page filled, she flipped the notebook and began another without pausing. The furor didn't stop until ink seeped to the edges of a dozen pages.

With trembling hands, Lakeisha slammed the notebook closed, pressed it against her chest, and glanced around to reassure herself of the private moment. The corners of her lips turned upward in acknowledgement of her decision. *I'm done! And I'm going to turn this in, no matter the consequences.*

Sleep evaded Lakeisha as she tossed and turned in bed, bits and pieces of her essay inching through the protective wall that normally kept her worries at bay. *Did I share too much? What if I have to read it out loud? Would it be worse than it already is?* Fear rose in her throat, and she jumped up from the bed. *I should rewrite it.*

She picked up the spiral-bound notebook and studied the cover that was filled with her favorite words. Words like dauntless, temerity, indomitable. Words never spoken in the world she lived in, but so inspirational to Lakeisha. Somewhere in the recesses of her mind, a quote from the late Dr. Martin Luther King, Jr., emerged. "Take the first step in faith. You don't have to see the whole staircase, just take the first step."

The frantic doubt that had unnerved her earlier, settled down to a vibration. She placed the unopened notebook on top of her coat, convinced the words had needed to be written, and now they must be heard. *I'll be a voice for others.*

* * *

Lakeisha held the papers tightly on the twenty-mile ride to school. Silently, she repeated her conviction. *I have a voice. I can make a difference.* It took hold, and by the time the bus arrived at school, she held her head a little higher than normal and smiled as she strode down the busy hallway.

"Sorry for the thumbprint, Ms. Lowery," Lakeisha mumbled as she laid the assignment on the paper-free desk, aware the rest of the class had submitted their stories electronically, not scribbled on lined paper.

"Don't worry about it." The teacher smiled as she accepted the paper and stuck it in her drawer, out of sight. "They're still trying to get a computer for you. Hopefully, soon."

Her words rang like an empty promise, one she'd heard for months. *I'll be gone before it gets here.*

The essay lingered in the back of her mind the rest of the day and throughout the weekend. Her emotions rode the wave from excitement to fear. One minute, proud of her courage. Then next, kicking herself for lowering the wall. Upon arrival in English class on Monday, Lakeisha was greeted by Ms. Lowery.

"Before you take your seat, the principal would like to speak to you."

"Mr. Hackmann? Why? I didn't do anything!" The announcement rattled in her brain. *Oh, crap. My essay. They're going to send me back to my old school.*

"You can put your books down first." Ms. Lowery looked at the blackboard as she spoke.

Lakeisha left the room on trembling legs, stopping at the water fountain to sooth her parched throat. A bright light shone on the metal object, her mouth agape at the brilliance as she searched for the source in the windowless hall. Suddenly, the place she'd dreaded walking down every day took on a significance she'd not previously considered. *My ancestors were never allowed to walk this hall, much less quench their thirst from this fountain.*

The unexpected affirmation filled her with renewed courage. Changes were made by brave people who dared to speak up. *I have a voice. I can make a difference.* She repeated the mantra as she walked through Mr. Hackmann's office door.

"'Good morning, Ms. Washington. Please have a seat." The tall, gray-haired man gestured toward a round table aside of his massive oak desk. He reached for a file folder and joined her. "How are you today?"

"I was fine, until I got called to see you. What did I do?" Lakeisha's voice was sharp, but respectful.

"I understand you wrote this essay." He passed the lined papers to Lakeisha as he spoke.

"Yes, sir. I did." Lakeisha straightened her back and looked directly at Mr. Hackmann, prepared to defend her assignment.

"Ms. Lowery was kind enough to share your story with me and my staff."

"And?" Her question blurted out more defensively than she'd intended.

"Your words stung. Painfully." He furrowed his brows and shook his head side to side, looking down at the floor. "I've always prided myself on being in tune with my students."

Lakeisha stirred in her chair, unsure how to respond.

The man drew in a long breath that filled his chest, then looked at Lakeisha with moist eyes. "I'm sorry. I was wrong. So very wrong." He choked as he pulled a handkerchief from his pocket and dabbed his eyes. "You have shown me how much I have to learn, how much we all have to learn."

"You're not mad at me?" Lakeisha tucked a curl behind her ear and leaned forward.

"Of course not, Ms. Washington. You were brave enough to share intimate details of your life and by doing so, you educated me and my staff in more ways than reading a thousand books. I want to ask a favor of you."

"A favor of me? What could I possibly do for you?"

"Share your story with the entire school. Every teacher and student needs to hear what you have to say." Mr. Hackmann raised a brow and waited for her response.

Lakeisha paused, her eyes flashed toward the door. "Share with everyone? Do you really think that's a good idea? I'm not very popular with my classmates."

"Teenagers can be hurtful, but I've seen the same students rally to support injustice when an issue is brought to their attention. Everyone needs a reminder of the things we take for granted. Your essay delivers a lesson they won't soon forget. I hope you will give them a chance to show you."

* * *

The gymnasium buzzed with questions regarding the school assembly.

"So, what's the assembly for?"

"Just Black History Month. Boring."

A voice loud enough to be heard across the room drew Lakeisha's attention.

"What's *she* doing up there?" One of the students glared at Lakeisha who sat on a folding chair a short distance from the stage.

You're not going to rattle me today. This is too important. Lakeisha directed her attention to the hundreds of students taking their seats. Ms. Lowery worked her way through the crowd and settled into the chair next to her, gently touching her arm with a reassuring nod.

Mr. Hackmann called Lakeisha to the podium. She stepped forward, forcing her shoulders back and raising her chin.

She inhaled slowly, repeating her mantra in silence then began. "I'm Lakeisha...Jackson...a transfer student from Roosevelt High." She glanced down at the ink filled pages for reassurance, then raised her head and continued. "I've been asked to share my story with you today." Quiet murmurs buzzed the room.

"More than 50 years ago Dr. King addressed the sacred obligations of the Constitution and Declaration of Independence in his speech, I Have a Dream. His words inspired significant changes, changes that I'm privileged to experience today, just by being in this school." Lakeisha paused, searching the room for reactions. "He also spoke of the 'tranquilizing drug of gradualism.' I didn't understand what he meant until recently.

"He was saying that while America has made tremendous strides, there's more work to be done. Ms. Lowery assigned an essay, 'What is your dream?' I've been asked to share my response. This is what I wrote." Lakeisha spoke slowly, deliberately as she read her essay, allowing the words time to penetrate. When she finished, Julie, the cheerleading squad captain, stood and clapped slowly. Joshua, a football quarterback, followed, then another and another. Soon the entire audience joined in a deafening applause.

Mr. Hackmann stepped to Lakeisha's side, a smile spread across his face. In a hushed voice, easily drowned out by the cheers, he said, "Thank you for taking the risk." He nodded toward the assembly that continued to cheer. "I think you've made some new friends. Can you forgive our ignorance?"

"I can do that." Lakeisha stepped away from the podium, moving toward her seat.

The principal stopped her and motioned to the students to sit. "Ms. Washington, we are grateful for the wisdom you've shared with us today. Ms. Lowery has something for you."

Her teacher came forward carrying a package. "Lakeisha, this laptop is a small token of our appreciation for your eloquent presentation. I think I speak for the entire school in saying you've touched our lives in ways that will continue for years to come. Thank you."

Lakeisha's eyes widened, and a smile spread across her face as she accepted the gift. "Thanks." The room exploded in another round of applause. *Maybe I did make a difference.*

American Neighbors
Susan Gore Zahra

Jeers and cheers erupted behind custodian Ahmed Hadzic. He slammed the dumpster lid shut and ran toward the students clustered around a pair of fighting boys. Elbowing his way through the crowd, Ahmed found Ben Montgomery and Ricky Carter starting the school day by trying to beat each other senseless. This was the third time that Ahmed had seen the former best friends locked in battle since Ricky's brother was killed and his father injured in a shooting nearly two months ago.

Ahmed grabbed the boys by their shoulders and tried to pry them apart.

"Stop! You stop, now, or I kick butts with my bionic leg."

Ben backed up, holding his left arm defensively in front of his face as Ricky raised his right fist. Ahmed stepped between them. "You want to punch me? You mad at me, too?"

Ricky lowered his fist.

"Now you both say you are sorry. I don't care who start fight. Both of you." Ahmed stepped back, again holding the boys by the shoulders. "And shake hands. Good."

Ahmed turned to the cluster of middle school students. Principal Margot DeVault and a few teachers stood watching at the edge of the crowd.

"All of you, just as bad. These are your friends and you encourage them to hurt each other. You two. You say you sorry and shake hands." Ahmed went among the kids, pairing them off to make peace. He came to Chad Woolsey and Summer Bennett.

Chad turned to Summer and leered. "I'll be happy to shake your hand."

Summer clutched her violin case to her chest like a shield. Ahmed stepped between them.

"You disrespect this young lady. You shake my hand." Ahmed gripped Chad's with the full strength of the soldier he once had been. He turned to Summer.

"I'm sorry," she whispered before Ahmed could extend his hand.

"That's fine. You go on, now. School will start soon."

Teachers steered students toward the building. The P.E. coach guarded Ben and Ricky's backpacks while they followed his instructions to run two laps around the field before entering the building.

Principal DeVault approached Ahmed. "Nice work. The students really respect you. I would appreciate your not threatening to kick butts, though."

Ahmed smiled. "Yes, boss."

Ms. DeVault started toward the door. "Oh, congratulations on becoming a citizen. I'm looking forward to your talk with the eighth graders this afternoon."

"I would rather break up fights." Ahmed waved and headed back to the dumpsters.

As the eighth graders filed into the library at the end of the day, some hollered, "Way to go," or, "Congratulations, Mr. Ahmed." Ben came up to offer him a high five. Ricky slouched in toward the end of the line and nodded in Ahmed's direction.

Ahmed told the students he and his family were originally from Bosnia and had immigrated to St. Louis three years ago. He described improving his English and how his son, only five years old when they arrived, had learned so quickly that he helped his parents with their homework. He told the students all the things he was required to learn, and quizzed the students on American history and government.

Emily Duncan, their social studies teacher, asked the students if they had any questions. A girl in front of the group asked what Ahmed's job had been. He told them he taught Yugoslavian language and literature.

Chad Woolsey asked, "So why aren't you a teacher here, instead of just a janitor?"

"You want to learn Yugoslavian? You tell Ms. DeVault you want to learn Yugoslavian. Then I teach while we sweep halls together, eh?" Ahmed enjoyed hearing the students' laughter. He missed teaching.

Another boy asked why Ahmed and his family left Bosnia. A girl asked why he taught Yugoslavian instead of Bosnian. Ahmed had hoped to avoid those questions. His son was content, so far, with hearing about their family coming to America to see the great Mississippi River, and someday the Grand Canyon. It would not be much longer until his son would want to know the whole truth.

Ahmed decided to practice telling whatever of the truth he could before his son asked. He rested his hands on the dais with his fingers interlaced so that no one could see how he dug his right thumbnail into the web between his left thumb and forefinger. If he pressed hard enough in the right spot, the pain would distract him from the pain of remembering. Sometimes, when a story on the TV news or the smell of exhaust fumes hanging in the air took his mind back to the war, he dug his thumbnail into his hand until he bled without relief from the painful memory.

"Bosnia was once part of Yugoslavia, along with Serbia and some other countries. After the leader, Tito, died, Yugoslavia fell apart. All the countries wanted to be independent. There was war. Serbia invaded Bosnia. When they come close to our town, I go in Bosnian army. That is how I lost leg." Ahmed could not tell them about the agonizing pain ripping up from his foot to his back when the medic dropped Ahmed after being shot himself. Nor could he speak of the terror when he realized that his lower leg was so mutilated that he could not stand; he would have to crawl to get help, or die in the forest.

"They bombed our town, destroyed our home. My wife was going to have baby. A friend help her escape to Croatia. When I find her, she was in Germany with her sister and mother. My son was almost two years old." Ahmed knew he would never be able to tell his son about the unspeakable horrors his wife's sister and mother endured in the prison camps before they were reunited with his wife.

"There was massacre in Srebrenica. All of the men and boys in family were killed." Ahmed looked at Ben and Ricky sitting on opposite sides of the room. They had been inseparable, laughing and teasing each other much like his two nephews. His nephews were near the same age as Ben and Ricky when they had been executed and shoved into the mass grave with Ahmed's father and brothers. He dug deeper into his hand.

Ricky raised his hand. "Do you hate those people from Serbia?"

The pain in Ahmed's left hand began to abate. He shifted to press his left thumbnail into his right hand before he could answer.

"When I hear about my family, yes, I hate Serbs. I hate Bosnian army for not running them out. I hate United Nations for not stopping war. Most of all I hate myself for still being alive. I want to go back to Bosnia to get revenge.

"I start to pack my suitcase. My wife see me and say, 'Look at you. You still need physical therapy and you limp. How you going to run around mountains shooting people? You have son, now. We need you here.' So we save money. My wife's family, they stay in Germany so they can help us a little bit.

"We move to nice house in St. Louis city. One day, I hear neighbor talking to his kids over back fence. I can tell he is Serbian. I decide I will not speak to him. That's okay. He don't speak to me, either.

"One day, I kick soccer ball around with my son. The ball goes over fence. My neighbor threw it back. My son say, 'Thank you.' My neighbor say, 'You welcome.' So I think maybe it will be okay to say hello when we are out in backyard, but that is all for a year or so.

"Neighbors on sides of our houses have nice chain link fences, all painted silver. Between our houses is old fence, just rusty old wire like you make tomato cages. It is coming loose from skinny, metal posts. One post is leaning into neighbor's yard.

"One day, I am digging in vegetable garden. My neighbor come out and start to poke at fence. He ask is this my fence. I say no. I think it is his fence. We don't know whose fence, but somebody is going to get hurt. So we decide to fix fence. I get rope to pull on bent post from my side while neighbor push from his side. Rope breaks and I fall down on my butt. My neighbor try to jump over fence to help me up, but he fall on his belly. He can't find his glasses, even though they have big, black frame. We lying on ground laughing. Then I give him his glasses, and we help each other up. My neighbor say, 'Do we really need this fence between us?'

"I say no. We spend day tearing down fence. Then we have barbeque together."

Someone in the back hollered, "Did he fight against you in the war?"

"Yeah. What if he was the guy who shot your leg off?" Ricky added.

Ahmed could not tell Ricky he knew his American neighbor was not responsible for the loss of his leg. During a battle to push the Serbian army away from his town, Ahmed found himself face to face with a Serbian classmate. They had been friends and had offered plum brandy toasts at each other's weddings. They had gone hunting together. He could not tell the students of the chill he felt when he saw the man's cold, blue eyes staring at him over the barrel of a gun. The man was a good shot. Ahmed knew if his classmate wanted him dead, he would be dead, not walking around on an artificial leg. Ahmed wished he had a steel nail instead of a thumbnail to dig into his hand. He took a deep breath.

"I don't ask my neighbor about war. He don't ask me about war. I see he has scars, too. Maybe I shot him. Today he is my neighbor. Today if we fight for our country, we fight side by side."

The students were silent. Some looked down at the floor. A few girls were teary. Ms. DeVault thanked Ahmed for telling his story as the dismissal bell rang.

Ricky shuffled around in front of Ahmed until Ben approached. "Hey. So. You know. This morning."

"Yah."

"You okay?"

"Yah. You?"

"Yah."

"So. Thought I'd shoot a few hoops before I try to figure out that math assignment. Wanna, you know?"

Ricky shrugged. "I don't…Well…maybe. See how I feel when we get to the corner, okay?"

Ahmed watched Ben and Ricky walk out side by side. Alone in the library, he looked down at his hands. The grooves he dug with his thumbs were red and deep, but he had not drawn blood. Maybe someday he would not awaken his wife and son with his screams. Maybe he would stop having the nightmare, stop dreaming his American neighbor's dark eyes and horn-rim glasses are staring at him over the barrel of a gun.

The After
Jeanne Felfe

The stark white page stared up at Marlene as if daring her to write. Daring her to breach the divide between anger and forgiveness. Her pen hovered over the page, but the words would not flow. She leaned back, releasing a quivering sigh. There would be no bleeding onto the pages this snowy day.

She was a farce, a charlatan, and all her words of wisdom to her three million followers on living in forgiveness only deepened the wrath churning in her guts. How could she have been so naïve as to believe she had anything to offer those seeking a better way, when she herself could not find a path out of the darkness that enveloped her soul?

The *We Are Family* ring-tone from her cell phone yanked her to awareness. Looking at the caller ID, she froze. *Can I even speak to her, can I, after what she did?*

No…never!

She sat, unable to move, unable to reach even her finger to push one single button and cancel the call. *A textbook case of stalled animation?* Grinding her teeth, she waited for the last, final ring to fade and go away…*go and don't call again. Why can't she leave me alone? All her fault. This is all her fault.*

Wrapping her hands around a now cold mug of tea, her gaze drifted to the cover of her latest book, which had arrived only days earlier—"Living in Forgiveness After Life Cheats You." "Ha!" She slammed her hands on the table before grabbing the book and throwing it across the room with a guttural scream.

Jumping from her chair so abruptly it clattered to the floor, Marlene raced upstairs to her office closet. She hefted a box of virginal books, carried them outside to the fire pit, and dumped every last one in, shiny covers and all. She lit a match and held it the edge of the top book, then stood back, rubbing the sharp ache in her chest with the palm of her hand. She breathed deeply, the ragged edges easing as the flames rose. *That's where these lies belong.* Watching the blaze lap at the bright orange covers, she sucked the resulting smoke deep into her lungs, hoping beyond hope that she would drown in the toxic fumes.

* * *

Marlene lay her head on her pillow, having resisted sleep for as long as possible. She dreaded that twilight moment when the demon of sleep overtook her thoughts and dragged her straight into hell. It was the same every night, with only minor alterations. First, the giggling of small children—Nathan and Matt—intent on experiencing a new discovery, tricked her dreams into a false sense of security. This would quickly be followed by a loud pop and then red. Red everywhere. Red and brains streaking down the canary yellow walls between and over the toy truck and car decorations. Although she'd never actually seen it, this is what her tortured brain conjured. When she jerked awake—as she did every night—sitting up covered in cold sweat, she realized the primal scream blaring in her ears had been hers. Again. Night after night.

Her therapist called it post-traumatic stress disorder and gave her pills. They didn't help. Nothing did. Although easier was a relative term, it had *seemed* easier with Hank. Maybe it was because she'd had Nathan to look forward to. Or maybe it was because she'd never seen the place he died. Had never sat in the same room playing with toys. It hadn't been a room in her best friend's house. Best friend—such a different meaning now in the after.

Marlene threw back the covers and crawled out of bed, onto bones that felt old, brittle, used up. Sleep could wait till she died, which she hoped for more with each passing day. She sunk into the familiar cushions of the sofa and draped her warm, fuzzy, blue blanket over her, tucking the hem beneath her chin. She rested her head on a tiny pillow that had once belonged to Nathan—his woobie—which had gone everywhere with him, except for that day.

The shrieking *It's My Life* of her agent's personalized ring yanked her to a glazed semi-awake state. She swiped answer but didn't speak.

"Marlene? Are you there? Marlene?" Trinity's voice became increasingly insistent, like the crescendo of a musical scale.

Marlene forced words to form, but they held no energy. "I'm here."

"I hope this is a good time. I need your approval on your tour dates so I can get them scheduled before your book hits the shelves."

"Cancel. All of it."

"What?" The silence that followed consumed the entire room. When Marlene didn't respond Trinity continued. "I know this has been a rough few months, Marlene, but it's time to get back out there. It will do you good."

"I'm not going on tour. I'm a fraud. I simply can't do it anymore."

"You know you love being on sta—"

"Loved," Marlene interrupted. "Past tense."

Trinity's heavy sigh leaked through the phone. "But...you have a contract. The publisher is likely to sue you if you don't—"

"I don't give a flip!" Marlene screamed and pressed the end call button.

The phone rang immediately, and she answered without looking to see who it was. "I told you I don't give a flip!"

"Uh, Marlene?"

The recognition of the voice slammed her brain around her head. She reached to disconnect, but the voice stopped her.

"Please don't hang up," said the voice, husky from crying. "Please, please, just talk to me," it continued between sobs. "It's been long enough."

This was the one person she needed most to talk to, and the one person she absolutely couldn't without losing what was left of her sanity.

"I loved Nathan. You know that. It should've been me," the voice continued when she didn't answer.

"It shouldn't have been anyone, Renee, least of all my little boy. He was all I had left of Hank. How could you have been so careless?" The words she'd held in her heart for three months dislodged in a torrent through the airwaves, followed by a rush of fresh tears. Who knew there could be so many tears in one person?

"I thought Jeff had it locked up. I never would have left the kids playing in Matt's room alone if I'd known."

"You were my best friend. I trusted you to keep my child safe," she hissed through clenched teeth.

The sounds of Renee's anguished sobs assaulted her ears. She couldn't do this, couldn't hold up the woman who had been her best friend for twenty years while she herself was falling apart. "I can't do this."

"Wait! Don't hang up. Please, Marlene. Are you ever going to forgive me? It's what you teach."

"Not anymore. I quit. I'm a charlatan. I have no clue what it takes to forgive someone, I just know that I can't. Not this. It's too big." She hung up before Renee could respond.

* * *

Six months later, the spritely tweeting of birds teased Marlene from a deep sleep. She stretched and rolled to her side, allowing a tiny smile to creep onto her lips. *I slept? For the first time in nine months, I slept.*

She slid out of bed and drew back curtains that had remained shut since the after. Slipping on her robe, the one she'd worn when she got the call that forever broke her life, she padded down the stairs and into the kitchen. After making a cup of tea, she picked her book up from where she'd thrown it six months earlier, and carried it out to the deck.

Taking a deep breath, she rubbed the shiny cover, and flipped it over, her brain still unable to recall a single word she'd spent over two years writing. She knew she'd written it—after all, her picture was on the back. So she must have. In the agonizing months after Hank was blown to bits by a road-side bomb in Fallujah, she'd grown both a baby and a book idea.

She opened the book and read the random page her finger landed on, words vaguely familiar in the way a dream might be:

Life isn't what happens to us. Life is what you do with what happens to you. Forgiveness only comes once you've stood in the fire and allowed it to burn you to your core. You must forgive yourself for needing to forgive.

Marlene grabbed a blank notebook and wrote for the first time since the after. The words that flowed weren't her usual style. These words came to her in the voice of a small child...Nathan's. Within an hour she had written the bones to a new children's picture book she titled "Don't Touch That."

Staring at the words, a light entered her heart, and she could see the bright colors of spring that before had simply been gray and...drab. She picked up her phone and dialed.

"Trinity? It's Marlene. I need a children's picture book artist. Now."

* * *

Marlene stood on the porch of the house next door to hers and looked at her watch, noting that it was eleven months, eleven days, eleven hours, and eleven minutes since the after. Her hand trembled as she reached for the bell, but the door burst open before she could press it.

"Marlene? Oh, my gawd!" Renee burst into sobs and swept Marlene into a crushing embrace without waiting for a response.

Marlene melted into the familiar arms, holding the new book between them, feeling a lightness in her chest that hinted at hope. When she pulled away, tears of a different sort leaked down her cheeks. These tears contained the seeds of a new way to live. Because she'd been here before, she knew the hole in her chest would never completely go away, but that it would diminish to a dull, ever-present ache. An ache her new book promised to assuage.

"Can I show you what I've been working on?" Marlene asked, holding out the mock-up with an artistically rendered picture of Nathan and Matt on the cover, playing in a sand box. They were surrounded by pictures of fire, a snarling dog, a stranger in a car, other child dangers…and a gun.

Renee gasped. "That's…come in?" she asked with a tentative shrug.

Marlene rewarded her with a slight smile as she stepped through the doorway and into a new chapter. A new beginning.

Forgiveness
M.L. Stiehl

As I consider my life, I remember the many times I've been hurt or disappointed. Most pains were small and did not last very long—nor became a lasting problem. Yet, one exception I remember well.

My best friend and I were fussing and fighting over some small disagreement at school—I don't remember exactly what. It was a menial thing, but seemed important at the time. It should have been a quick argument, but we drug it on so long that it became a serious problem separating two good friends.

Eventually, we let the anger and frustration grow to the point where she slapped me on the face. The sting was not as surprising as the shock. I was dumbfounded. What should I do?

I knew I wasn't going to hit her. That wasn't my style. Yet, I couldn't just stand there.

It was then I remembered a Sunday school lesson I had heard while young. I turned my head to reveal the other cheek and said with sincerity, "Hit me again." I braced for another blow.

But my request took her by surprise. Her eyes opened wide— she had no words.

After what seemed a long time, she recovered and responded, "I'm sorry. Please, forgive me. I won't hit you again. Ever!"

Now it was my turn to be surprised. I asked myself, *Why should I forgive her? Hadn't she hurt me?*

But I knew I had been just as guilty—fighting with her, trying to make her feel bad. And I could tell she was really sorry. So after a short pause, I grabbed her, and we hugged, tight and long.

"I forgive you."

It never happened again. We closed the subject.

As I continued down the path of life, though, I never forgot the incident, and it never happened to us again. It changed us—cured us, if you will. Probably because that's what those lessons are meant to do—to show us the path to being what we were intended to be.

We stayed close friends for many, many years after that. When the subject of our disagreement came up, we laughed about it, as good friends should.

The last time we saw each other, I said, "We should always remember the lesson we learned, so we don't ever go through anything like that again."

I guess lessons learned in our youth sometimes stay with us always.

And the act of forgiveness is its own reward.

Could I Have This Dance?

Tammy Lough

"Could I have this dance?"

I looked to the right and saw a tall, broad-shouldered man sporting a great big smile. He wore a St. Louis Blue's hockey jersey and blue jeans, so I knew one thing for certain, he bled blue, and so did I. Standing to take his outstretched hand, I could not help but mirror his expression.

Once we reached the dance floor, I realized he requested "Could I Have This Dance" for its title before placing himself out of my line of vision. When the song began to play, he had delivered his "line." The music, soft and gentle, allowed us to hold a conversation. By the time the song ended, my intuition had told me we were falling in love. I didn't know if it was his constant smile and the way he threw his head back when he laughed, the protective hold around my waist, or how I felt in his strong arms, but I knew.

We danced every song that followed, taking a break for a quick drink and then back to the dance floor. We could not get enough of each other. Every slow dance that followed, he held me a little tighter, and I fell a little deeper. After that evening, we saw each other or talked on the phone every day for over three years.

We had dated several months when he told me he had a special surprise. He said to be ready at 6:00, dress warm, and expect to be treated like a princess. That evening, when I heard a knock on my door, I knew it was Steve coming to pick me up for our date. Instead, a man dressed in a black tuxedo, holding two-dozen red roses, stood on my doorstep. He placed the bouquet across my arms and escorted me to a white limousine parked in front of the house. My handsome prince sat inside and flashed his biggest smile. Holding a bottle of champagne in one hand and two fluted glasses in the other, he nodded his head at a box of chocolate-dipped strawberries. I scurried into the limo and had my arms around him in two seconds flat.

He wore his favorite hockey jersey, and we traveled in style to a St. Louis Blues hockey game, and then to dinner at a popular downtown restaurant. I stayed on a high all night. It was my first ride in a limousine, a hockey game with up-close-and-personal seats, and snuggling with the man I loved with all my heart.

Steve always had something up his sleeve, and being a true romantic, he often showed me that I was on his mind. Many days, I found a greeting card in the mailbox, a surprise package, or a bouquet of flowers with a "just because" note. I had to be the luckiest lady in the world to find such a loving, funny, and compatible partner who let everything roll off his back. He had a kind word to say about everyone and treated others with utmost respect.

He surprised me one evening close to Christmas in our second year together with a carriage ride through Winter Wonderland in Tilles Park. As the horse and carriage driver were halfway under a long archway of sparkling lights, he asked him to stop. Steve turned to me and reached for my hands. He spoke from his heart about how much he loved me, and his greatest desire was to spend every single day for the rest of his life proving it to me. He then proposed, and I accepted. He slid a beautiful diamond ring onto my finger. My feet didn't touch the floor for days. Talk about being on Cloud-9!

When his mother became ill and diagnosed with terminal stomach cancer, his sisters, along with Steve and I, respected her wishes to remain in her home. We all took turns caring for her. Hospice care took over near the end of her life and a day didn't go by that Steve wasn't pulling up a chair at her bedside, telling her stories to make her smile, and reminiscing. We lost her on Christmas Day.

The next year, in mid-November, Steve complained of severe stomach pain. I pleaded with him to see a doctor, but instead, he carried rolls of antacids in his pocket and chewed one after another. I became greatly concerned, but he would shush me and say he needed to eat a better diet and give up the spicy foods he loved.

Thanksgiving rolled around, and I asked what time he would like to eat dinner. He wondered what I thought about feeding the poor at a homeless shelter instead of celebrating with a meal. That is how we spent Thanksgiving. I reflect on that day often and how wonderful it felt to give to those who have nothing. It is one of my most memorable experiences.

He told me one day he had another surprise for me and to get all "gussied" up. He took me to a fabulous restaurant in St. Louis where we chose our steak from various cuts of meat brought to our table. The waiter presented us with a delicious meal, and I noticed Steve left most of his food uneaten. We arrived at the fabulous Fox Theater to see *A Christmas Carol,* and I noticed he looked pale and kept laying his hand on his stomach. I suggested we skip the play. He refused to cut the evening short, but spent more time in the men's restroom than in his theater seat. At one point, 15 minutes passed, and he did not return. I found him standing against a wall in the lobby and watched as he buried his face in his hands. I walked over, put my arms around him, and he agreed to leave.

He walked me into my house, and within minutes, I saw him double over in pain. I led him to my car, helped him inside, and drove to the emergency room. The date was December 22nd. The doctor ordered blood tests and discharged Steve home for Christmas, but re-admitted him on December 26th for more tests, a liver biopsy, and exploratory surgery. The incision went from breastbone to pelvis, and one morning the entire surgical site split open and required frequent packing with antibiotic gauze. He never complained about the pain. Not once.

On his 44th birthday, January 16th, his doctor entered the room and asked Steve if it were all right if he spoke in front of me, or should I step into the hallway for a few minutes. Steve grabbed my hand, pulled me close, and told him to start talking. I remember the doctor taking a deep breath before telling us the diagnosis. Pancreatic cancer. He said cancer had spread all through his stomach, liver, spleen—Steve held up his hand and asked how long he had to live. The doctor answered three to six months. Closer to three. Steve looked at me and said, "Niagara?" I shook my head, yes.

We had talked about honeymooning at Niagara Falls, and we were both ready to pack, jump in the car, and take off. But within days, as he healed from the surgical wound separation, his cancer pain became unbearable. He required more and more morphine, falling in and out of consciousness.

The intensive care nurses and staff were more than professional. They took care not only of Steve, but me as well, asking if I were comfortable and if there was anything they could do for me. When I hadn't been able to sleep for three nights in a row on the cot beside his bed, the nurses talked me into going home and getting some rest. Finally, I agreed.

"Don't worry," Steve's nurse told me, nodding in his direction. "He'll be fine. And, if there is any change in his condition, I will call you." Being an intensive care nurse myself, I felt a strong need to stay with him. I took his hand—he had lapsed into a medication induced coma—and told him I planned to leave for a while, but would return in a few hours. I kissed him good-bye and said how much I loved him. With reluctance, I drove home and went to bed. At 3:20 a.m., the phone rang. He didn't want me to see him die, so he waited until I left. I know he did. Classic Steve, always thinking of other's, even when he is the one suffering, and dying.

After the funeral service and a period of grieving, I entered the volunteer registered nurse program in the intensive care unit where he had received expert care from his doctors and nurses. It was a time of healing for me. I felt by volunteering to care for these patients, it gave the nurses a helping hand. Also, for the first time serving as a registered nurse, it awarded me the ability to give patients extra care their regular assigned nurse wouldn't have the time to devote. I could sit at the bedside of a patient who needed to talk, wash an elderly lady's hair who felt self-conscious about her appearance when the family visited, give a warm, soothing bath and shave to a patient who otherwise may have only received a warm washcloth wiped over his face. Not that the nurses chose not to, they simply did not have the extra minutes to devote.

The time I spent volunteering in the intensive care unit, giving back to those who gave so much of themselves, helped me to accept Steve's death. I will never forget my love for him, but will go on living, loving, and paying it forward.

Classic Steve.

Final Betrayal

Donna Mork Reed

The day you fell on the floor, I laughed a little. You were such a big, rambunctious dog, full of life and love. Even at 100 pounds, you still acted like a puppy, romping around in pure joy that always made us smile. This time something was different.

You were an unplanned purchase during a mall trip one evening. Your long black fur got on everything, and your spotted pink tongue was usually the only feature to be seen in most photos. You loved your stuffed toys, but never chewed them. You loved to ride in the car, even the long four-hour trip to Grandma's farm. You walked down the gravel road and jumped into the deep side of the creek, fearless and so happy. But you always came running when we called.

When my back went out and I spent three long, painful weeks lying on the couch, you never left my side. All I had to do was reach my hand down over the edge, and you were there, sleeping beside me. When Dave got cancer, you remained by his side through the long months of chemo and radiation, side effects, and surgery. With the long slow recovery after surgery, you adjusted your normal trot to meet his hesitant steps. A brief walk to the mailbox and back replaced the walk down the street, but you never complained.

We had good times walking through the woods. You didn't care what we did or where we went as long as we were together, our pack. You trusted us with everything. Your food. Your shelter. Your safety. Your life.

The day you fell, I thought, how cute. The big dog slipped on the floor and fell down. My laughter soon subsided when I noticed you did not get up. The trips to the vet were hard. You did not protest, trusting as always, as we carried you out to the car and took you there, then carrying you in from the car, and repeating in reverse order for the trip home.

When, after three trips, the doctors concluded you had cancer, worse than what Dave had, in that it had spread and there was no hope for you, our hearts broke like an icicle falling from the edge of the house, hitting the driveway below, and shattering into a million various sized pieces. No amount of king's men or king's horses could ever restore our hearts again.

The last drive to the farm was so hard. You knew we were going to Grandma's. I wonder what you thought. Maybe you thought you would feel better and be able to swim in the creek again and run through the front field. Or maybe you knew time was drawing near and this would be the final trip. I don't know what you thought, but I know you trusted us. And therein lies the final betrayal.

We pulled into the vet's parking lot twenty miles from the farm and went inside. The vet offered to come out to the truck to make it easier on you. We cried and held onto you as if we could stop your soul from leaving by sheer will. We could not. When the vet gave you the shot, you looked into Dave's eyes one final time, always trusting, always loving. And then you were gone.

I beg you for forgiveness even now, months later. No matter how much I know you were hurting and that it was the right thing to do, I beg you again. Please, forgive us! You loved us. You trusted us. We euthanized you. Hell, say it plainly, we killed you. Or rather, had you killed. The horror of it bores into the core of my being.

I hope you will forgive us, because I cannot forgive myself for this final betrayal.

The Thief Who Stole the Coals of Hell
R.G. Weismiller

Hell's overlord, a Yakuza Kumicho named Taizi Saito, dispatched his hounds from its deepest abysses to pursue my wretched soul. From the lavish settings of Tokyo to the sultry slums surrounding Bangkok, they trailed me for committing an unforgivable transgression—stealing the glowing, red coals of hell—Saito's rubies.

Sloth abetted Envy, initiating my demise. I entered the business world as a legitimate gems courier, delivering precious stones to wealthy clients throughout the world. Their extensive possessions of exotic cars, exquisite goddesses, and majestic estates forged my envy. But my compensation prohibited me from acquiring those indulgences. Transporting stolen jewels became an enticing proposition. Its lucrative rewards always carried risk.

Greed afforded Gluttony, nurturing my descent. My appetite for the finest flourished with each illicit transaction. Suites from Savile Row and the finest Italian shoes supplanted my pauper attire. The world's best food enticed my taste buds.

Lust tempted my soul and captured my heart. The daughter of evil seduced me with her svelte figure, long dark hair, and bewitching eyes. Saito's infatuation for rubies provided an opportunity to meet his daughter. I desired Jasumin from the very moment my eyes saw her. Her beauty and mannerism wooed me as never before. That night, in my hotel room, she lured me into a forbidden love. I surrendered my soul and heart to the siren.

Saito forbade his daughter from being with a Caucasian—making ours a forbidden relationship. Captivated by Jasumin's beauty, I vowed to overcome any obstacle barring us from being together. I searched the ends of the earth for the rarest of rubies that would delight Saito. Jasumin arranged for me to deliver the gems at Saito's infamous dinner parties, providing an excuse for us to be together in front of her father without arousing his suspicion. Once, when she did not attend one of the parties, devastation overcame my disappointment. Unbeknownst to me, she waited for my return in my hotel room. Switching on the lights, I saw a bruise on her angelic face.

Wrath subjugated sanity. Outraged, I demanded to know who did this. She refused to reveal her assailant, telling me it was for my safety. Adamant, I pounded my fist against the nightstand, insisting on knowing who committed this sadistic act. As tears streamed down her cheeks, she confessed her father beat her as he had often done before. I swore to kill him, but she convinced me I had no chance of succeeding. The most feared man in Tokyo became my enemy.

Among the Yakuza, Saito enjoyed a reputation as a ruthless leader, utilizing fear as a weapon. For those who dared to displease him, he spared their lives only if they proved their loyalty in a ritual called yubizume—amputating one of the smaller fingers with a knife. It originated from the samurai warriors who needed to make amends with their peers. The severed finger weakened their grip on the sword, forcing the samurais to be more dependent on their colleagues for protection.

Jasumin suggested revenge, more rewarding than killing. While she slept, I devised a plan. For vengeance to be served, her father must be stripped of his prized possession—the beloved rubies. In the morning, I revealed my plan to her as I comforted her in my arms. In Bangkok, an unlimited number of unscrupulous jewelers would desire to fence stolen merchandise. With the profit, we would live the rest of our years in Europe. Due to my limitations about safecracking, Jasumin needed to secure the code to the safe. My expertise lay in smuggling and selling the gems. She smiled with approval, lifting her hand to her bruised cheek.

I approached Saito about a rare pink ruby. Jasumin's father was to have another of his famous dinner parties, notorious for its debauchery, which lasted until dawn. I informed him I would be in Tokyo at the time of his dinner party. Knowing his weakness for the precious stone, I was sure he would invite me to the dinner party for the delivery of the gem. His voice boomed with excitement as he extended an invitation to me. In the past, he allowed my briefcase to remain in his office until the gala was finished.

On the evening of the dinner party, sitting behind his desk in his office, Saito's face radiated as he drooled over the jewel. His bodyguards watched my every move. Jasumin was right—my attempt to kill her father would have been futile. As the transaction ended, I returned his enthusiasm with a facsimile of a smile, disguising the nervousness of my plan being successful. Doubt crept through my body. The image of Jasumin's bruised face kept me focused on the heist. His eyes danced with excitement as he opened the safe, placing his newest addition with the other rubies. Somehow, I wished I could see his expression when he discovered his treasures had vanished.

Late into the night, after the guests ate their fill of delicious food and overindulged in the delights of Saki and other spirits, Jasumin drugged the alcohol for the revelers and Saito's guards. A half-hour later, everyone on the estate slept with the exception of my love and me. With the surveillance devices turned off, I proceeded to the safe.

Using the combination from Jasumin, I opened the vault with sweat dripping from my hands and relieved the Yakuza of his jewels. But they weren't the only valuable items available. Hordes of yen tempted me. But the rubies filled my case, leaving no room for the cash. Closing the safe, I locked it. Upon my exit, I kissed Jasumin. She grinned, telling me of her anticipation of meeting me at the airport. She was right. Revenge was more satisfying than murder.

Waiting for Jasumin to arrive at the airport, I paced with Saito's former treasure. With every passing moment, horrifying images of her being caught by Saito haunted my mind. When passengers boarded our plane, my stomach sickened. A voice over the loud speaker indicated the final boarding call. My nerves calmed and my hearted leapt when I saw my love running towards me. She kissed me passionately and beamed about our success. We rushed to our seats before the door of the plane closed.

On the plane, she told me she had rented a house outside of Bangkok—a quiet place to hide while I sold the rubies. She named it our love nest as she nestled on my shoulder with heavy eyelids.

As she slept, I realized that I had accomplished my dreams. The sale of the gems could acquire the mansion and the cars I had sought. One of the world's most beautiful women rested next to me. Smugly, my success brought a grin to my face. Now, I enjoyed the status of being an elite.

After the plane landed, Jasumin received a brief telephone call. When she hung up, she giggled with excitement, informing me about a buyer she knew who just happened to be in Bangkok. He expressed a great interest in our rubies. I returned her smile, but cautioned her—jewelers in this part of the world were notorious for being unscrupulous.

At the house, a youthful, handsome Asian man—whom she introduced as Antoni—waited. He carried a briefcase similar to mine. I studied him as we shook hands. Although I couldn't establish why, he made me uncomfortable. When he asked to see the gems, I demanded to see his money first. He set his briefcase on the table. As he opened the briefcase, the amputated finger of his left hand exposed him as a Yakuza.

Betrayal shanghaied Pride. I felt a gun pressing at the back of my head. Jasumin spoke the dreaded words. "He is my lover, love."

As she walked around me, Antoni produced his pistol. A wicked smile appeared on her face. I was a mere pawn in her game—the necessary tool needed to transport the rubies across the Pacific. It never occurred to me there could be someone else.

They revealed how they had tricked Saito into believing I acted alone. On the night of the heist, Antoni waited until I left. He went to the safe and stole the cash, placing it in the briefcase he now carried. When everyone woke the next morning, Saito watched the video of me placing his rubies in my case. In a second video, an extra case appeared in my possession giving the impression I left with two briefcases—the gems and the money. Antoni edited Jasumin and himself from the videos. He convinced the Yakuza overlord to allow him to search for me in Bangkok. Rage blinded the father from suspecting his daughter.

Antoni grabbed Jasumin and passionately kissed the siren. Their desire caused them to take their eyes off me. Lunging at them, I knocked their guns to the floor. All three of us fell to the ground. Jasumin freed herself from the struggle as Antoni and I fought, punching and choking each other. When we separated, I sprang to my feet. Unable to find a weapon, I attacked my foe. Antoni screamed for Jasumin to shoot. Out of the corner of my eye, I saw her gun trembling and aiming to wherever I positioned myself. When she winced, I forced Antoni between me and the hand of fate. The weapon discharged. Her lover collapsed.

Stunned, Jasumin's pistol fell. She raced out of the house to Antoni's car. In her haste, she forgot the gems and the money. Exhaustion forbade me from a pursuit as I listened to the sound of the engine speeding away.

Remorse eluded me as I stared at the corpse. My apathy for the crime finalized the eternal damnation of my soul. This rite of passage converted me from a lover to a man capable of cold-bloodedness.

Now, Jasumin would metamorphose into a loyal daughter, confessing and pleading for the overlord of hell's mercy. The father would absolve his daughter. Rather than the amputation of a finger, her penance would be my life.

Saito would kill me, even if I returned his money and the gems. Jasumin's redemption depended on the capture of my soul. Time became a fleeting commodity for a marked man in Bangkok, especially a Caucasian. Opting for refuge in a seedy hotel near the Port of Bangkok, I planned on how to flee Asia—a continent where I could easily be identified.

With the door and windows shut, the ceiling fan in my hotel room failed to dismiss the sweltering heat. I opened the briefcase containing the gems. Their fiery color sparkled in the sunlight, seeping through the slits of the drawn blinds. Glowing coals of a fire mesmerized me. Saito's obsession with the jewels became apparent. Their allure had tempted his soul, dragging him into a lunacy beyond absolution.

My guns flashed at every sound outside my door. Whether the footsteps were light like children or plodding like those with a heavy burden, I was alert—barely sleeping. The pursuit of Saito's fallen angels in this hellish climate has expended my wretched self.

Redemption could be attainable. Amsterdam, my Purgatory, could pardon my transgressions. If I could make passage to that Dutch city, refuge would be possible. There, I knew enough jewelers who would buy these damning gems.

I elected to wait until predawn, when this city would be most peaceful, to find a corruptible captain who will provide a cabin aboard his cargo ship. Trafficking my distressed soul would appeal to them. I knew, for smuggler's blood flowed through my veins.

Hopefully, for the last time, I secured the briefcase, housing these damning coals of hell.

From Envy to Kindness

Saturday Writers 2017

The Threads That Bind
Diane How

My leisure retirement, often spent writing or accompanying my husband to a local casino, left a significant void in my life. I yearned for a sense of purpose. As I skimmed a list of volunteer opportunities in my local newspaper, my eyes settled on two words, *Story Keeper*. I paused to read more. *Story Keepers capture the meaningful moments of a patient's life.* The simple description intrigued me, as I'd always dreamed of writing life stories of other people.

As enticing as the opportunity sounded, the thought of volunteering with a hospice care organization weighed heavily on my mind. The pain of watching my mother die a slow, difficult death made me question my ability to keep my emotions under control. I wasn't sure I was ready for a task involving the potential death of a loved one. I cut out the contact information and let the thought simmer.

The clipping remained visible near my laptop for the next two weeks, tugging at my heart and urging me to act. Finally, I picked up the phone and called the manager of volunteer services listed in the ad.

"I may be interested in the Story Keeper position. Can you tell me more about it?"

"We're looking for someone to record the life story of a hospice patient for their family to keep as a legacy after the patient passes."

"Oh," I felt a hint of disappointment. "I'm not adept at electronic things, more pen to paper."

"Why don't you come in and talk further about it? It's a new position. We can work through the details. And while it doesn't involve writing, you never know where the journey will lead you. Maybe it was meant for you."

The charismatic manager's reassuring words urged me to take a leap of faith. I met with her to learn more. Within two weeks, I'd completed all the prerequisites: TB tests, study guides about working with hospice patients, and hepatitis injections.

It wasn't long before I was assigned my first visit. I studied the manual that came with the small, hand-held recorder. Since I was the first person to fill the position, training had been minimal. The anxiety and nervousness I anticipated never surfaced. Instead, an unexpected tranquility about the process made me excited to get started.

"The patient is hesitant to make the recording," my manager warned me on the drive to his home. "The wife is urging him to make the recording. I thought you should know before we get there."

The patient's wife greeted us at the door and invited us in. The man, already seated in a recliner, extended his hand and nodded as he studied my face.

My manager made introductions and a brief explanation of our visit. The man frowned and grumbled, pursing his lips. Then it was my turn to speak. I wanted to help him relax and feel comfortable about the recording.

"We're just going to talk today. I'd like to get to know you and your wife."

"Ok." The tense lines around the man's eyes eased.

"Did you grow up in Florissant?" I smiled and tilted my head awaiting his response.

"Jennings. I went to Corpus Christi grade school."

"I know that school. I attended St. Paul the Apostle. We were practically neighbors."

"I went to St. Paul's!" his wife announced with excitement. "Oh, my goodness! You're Diane Hootselle. I saw the resemblance to your mother when you first arrived, but couldn't place who you were."

My eyes welled with tears at the mention of my mother. I was unable to say anything for fear I'd start crying.

"I'm your grandmother's niece. We're cousins. I grew up two blocks from you."

I realized that I knew her parents well, but because of our age difference, our paths had not crossed, except briefly at funerals or weddings. The emotional journey over the next hour was overwhelming and rewarding. The wonderful stories about my mother, who was an only child, and her distant cousins with whom I had lost touch over the years, brought such joy to my heart, I left the visit feeling like I was given a gift, one that I would treasure for life and share with my siblings. I even learned that my grandfather saved my cousin from drowning in the Mississippi River when she was a teenager.

Over the next few visits, I recorded heartwarming and memorable stories told to me by the patient and his wife. From their heritage to their marriage and their many life experiences, we worked together to create a treasured gift for their children, grandchildren, and future generations. I completed the project and presented the audio recording to them on their 65th anniversary.

I've always believed that a common thread connects us all. That belief was again reinforced during my second recording— another male patient unsure about telling his story, but encouraged by his daughter to do it. As he talked and became more comfortable with the idea, he shared stories of bar-hopping with a group of friends when he was much younger. The stories sounded familiar, much like some told by my first patient. It turned out that my cousin's husband was one of this man's best friends with whom he made the tavern rounds. They had lost touch over the years.

The validation that I was exactly where I was supposed to be filled me with joy and anticipation for where my journey would take me next. And then, it happened. On my initial visit with another patient, the opportunity to achieve my dream presented itself. I remember it was a sunny Friday afternoon. A middle-aged woman invited me into the quaint, senior-living apartment. A bouquet of flowers scented the room. A young girl sat on the floor doing cross-stitch.

"This is my daughter. She likes to sew. Her grandmother taught her."

"Nice to meet you."

"This is my mother." The woman who let me in directed me to a robust woman who was busy rearranging a large stack of assorted papers and clippings.

I smiled and extended my hand. "It's so nice to meet you. How are you feeling today?"

"Fine." Her voice as firm as her handshake.

"Looks like you have some important papers there."

"When can we get started?"

The abrupt response surprised me. "It sounds like you're ready. I don't usually start recording on the first visit. It helps if we prepare for it by getting to know each other a little first. That way I can be sure we meet your wishes and make the best recording we can. Would that be alright?"

"What I really want…" she hesitated before continuing with tears in her eyes. "I wanted to write my life story, but I don't know where to start and I don't have enough time." Her eyes pleaded for understanding.

I felt the corners of my lips turn upward. I touched her hand in reassurance. "I love to write. I've always wanted to write someone's life story or help them write it." I drew in a breath while contemplating my offer. "Perhaps that's why I'm here. God works in mysterious ways. Maybe I can help you."

Her eyes beamed with excitement. "Really? Would you? I can't do it by myself."

"I'd be happy to. How exciting! I can't wait to get started."

"Will you take these with you and read them, if you have time?" She pushed the pile of papers in my direction.

"I'd be honored. How about 1:00 p.m. on Monday? Will that work for you?"

"Oh, yes. That would be fine." She reached for my hand and squeezed it. "Thank you."

"It's my pleasure. I'll see you Monday and we'll jump right in."

#

I spent Saturday reading the scribbled notes and brief stories, trying to place them in chronological order. The woman's parents had owned a 350-acre farm in South Dakota, and in the menagerie of papers, I found an essay written by her mother. It described the challenges of feeding twenty-five farmhands during harvesting in the 1900s. It was a piece of history that had been entrusted to me.

On Sunday, I received a call from the volunteer manager telling me that the woman had passed away. My heart ached knowing her wish went unfulfilled. I planned to return all the paperwork to the family, but before I could, I received another phone call from the hospice manager. "The family asked if you could help write the book for the patient. They want to meet with you to discuss it if you are interested."

A couple of meetings and two months of emails between family members allowed me to piece together the information. Additional stories were shared and incorporated by her children and surviving sister. The woman's wish had been fulfilled. I have no doubt that a greater force brought us together for that very reason.

The simple act of giving my time returned ten-fold, not in money, but in something much more valuable. I admire the people who share their life stories to create the audio recordings. They allow families to continue to hear their voice after they're gone, and by filling a void in their lives, they've filled the void in mine.

The Midwife's Apprentice

Bradley D. Watson

The woman woke suddenly from her sleep, her breath labored and her body sweating. She'd been doing that more and more often lately. The straw beneath her clung to her wet skin. She couldn't let go of how real the dream had seemed.

The smell of animals, hay, and perspiration filled the loft she'd made her home. It was the only place these people had to offer her, so she made the best of it.

She tried to make sense of the dream—this time it was a village. She was watching from above, as if she was a cloud, seeing the sun shine overhead, though its color was washed out in the vision. The village below was all dark, covered in shadow. She could make out black flames snapping into the air from the darkness—colorless flames. The screams of the villagers filled the streets, but louder in her head were the voices filled with evil. She strained like she did every time to understand them. The sounds were loud, muffled by the distance. Even as she woke, her mind still heard them for a while. Something was wrong—something bad was happening.

"Marda!" a voice called from outside. In her drowsy state, it took the woman a moment to clear her head. She remembered— Marda was the name she decided to use when she came here.

"Marda!" the voice repeated. "Get down here." It was the midwife calling. The one who had taken her in, giving her a place to rest at night. Larger towns had healers on their payroll or, at the very least, village-witches to help with childbirth. A woman was not, of course, allowed to practice real magic, but they could engage in the less powerful arts, providing help with childbirth, love potions, and other incantations that may or may not have had any true magic in them. Small villages, like the one Marda now called home, were not even large enough for that. So, they made do with a non-magical midwife.

She recalled last night. There had been two births lasting late into the night, and Marda had helped the midwife with both. She envied the women their normal lives—even the life of the one whose labor had been particularly difficult, the baby being turned wrong. It was a struggle, but Marda managed to save the baby and her mother. Exhausted, she had retired to her loft in the barn soon after.

"Coming," she called as she worked her way down the wooden ladder, her dirty feet clinging to the rungs as she descended. She stepped out of the stable.

At the back door to the little shack, the mistress stood, her eyes red, her face showing exhaustion, waiting for her assistant.

"Marda," she began, ushering her into the small shack. "Geldar, the blacksmith, brought his wife in after you went to bed. Fron helped me, so I didn't wake you." Fron was the midwife's daughter. She was a little slow and only able to help with easy childbirths. "I'm gonna get some rest now, so I need you to go down to the tavern and let Geldar know the baby is here. It's a girl. He'll have to name her."

"Yes, ma'am," Marda said, turning toward the village. She hurried down the street, her feet cold on the dirt roads, a chilly wind in the air. She passed children playing in the street and women laughing. She wiped a tear from her cheek and kept moving. A life like that could never be hers.

Marda entered the tavern quietly, her rags pulled tight around her. This was the only tavern in town and not a place where women came. The room was filled with undesirables. While respectable men, if they felt the need to get a drink, would go to the inn at the edge of town, this tavern, was a place for men who desired to let their drink take over.

Marda was all but ignored as she entered the tavern. Her mind, though, was already on fire—an unexplainable mental pain. As long as she could remember, something within her burned when she was near evil, and the men of this place were full of it. It took all she could do to ignore the discomfort and focus on her task.

The blacksmith, dirty and loud, sat with friends at a small table. Marda wasted no time. She headed toward the man to deliver the news and get this over with as quickly as possible.

The muscular figure saw her approaching.

"Well?" he slurred, trying to focus his eyes on her.

"You have a girl," Marda said, knowing that was not good news to a man like him. "My mistress wants to know what you want to name her." Marda was fully familiar with the feelings barbarians like this had about women and girls, and so prepared for the tirade that would assault her ears.

Geldar surprised her, though. Out of his chair with a speed that belied his inebriated state, the back of his fist slammed into her cheek full force, knocking her back to fall among the other tables. The men around laughed.

Marda had been caught off-guard. She felt rage fill her. The pain in her head, the exhausted state she was in, and the years of abuse and hiding overcame her self-control.

"Barbarian," she said through clenched teeth. Eyes aflame and without thinking, she lifted herself quickly to her feet, hearing the mocking laughter around her. With a sweep of her arm, power burst forth from her.

Geldar's eyes widened, suddenly sobered, as the force of the spell hit him, blasting him backward through the wall behind him. He fell unconscious to the ground. Gasps filled the room...then silence.

Her regret was immediate. Not for the man, but for herself. She had managed all this time to keep what she was secret, for women were not allowed to practice high magic. And though her life here was hard, her mistress had at least been fair with her. Something she had not found in other hiding places through the years. Now there was nothing left but to disappear again. To move from town to town until she could find another place to hide...another place to conceal what she was...a woman with power.

Saturday Writers 2017

Envy Never Dies
Donna Mork Reed

"I think this room will look great in mocha," Sandra said, spinning in a slow pirouette.

"Mocha?" John said.

"Yes, a deep, rich brown, like coffee."

"Why didn't you just say brown?"

"Oh, John. You men are so limited."

I laughed. Sandra and John had moved in three months ago, and though I liked them, I found myself becoming more and more envious of Sandra. She had everything. Everything I ever wanted. Everything I had ever hoped for. She was young, beautiful, and so energetic. And she had John. I once had a boyfriend, but it hadn't ended well.

Sandra laughed and ran out of the room, John chasing her. I went to the window and watched them pull out of the driveway, obviously headed to the local home improvement store for paint. I liked mocha. Sandra was right, this room would look great in mocha. She was also talented with decorating. I let out a sigh, my envy growing in my very core.

Two days later, the room looked incredible. Sandra lit a scented candle to assuage the paint smell and placed a potted plant on the table in front of the window.

"There! It's perfect."

"You're perfect," John said, wrapping his arms around her and nuzzling under her hair and kissing her neck.

"He's right, Sandra. You are perfect," I said, reigning in my frustration.

"Oh, don't be silly. I'm not perfect," Sandra said, giggling at John's antics. "That tickles!"

"Would you guys get a room or something," I said, plopping on the couch in order to block the visual onslaught of romance.

"Let's take this somewhere more comfortable, eh?" John pulled on Sandra's waistband, guiding her out of the room and into the bedroom they shared.

I stared at the mocha walls and felt a tick of anger. What was wrong with me? I liked the color. It was so much better than the drab white this room had been for decades. Yet, the anger grew. I felt like lashing out.

I stormed to the window, looking out as the curtains blew in the breeze. Soft smells of spring wafted in, waging their own personal war with the fresh paint odor. Fists clenched, I stared at the framed photo of the loving couple, Sandra and John. I was beginning to loath those names. Rage welled up, a boiling volcano about to burst, and in a flash, I slapped the faces smiling back at me. The frame flew off the credenza and landed with a crash onto the hard oak floor, glass shards sparkling in the sun.

I stood in shock. I didn't mean to do that. I quickly left the room, going through the doorway just as Sandra and John came racing in from their room.

"What happened?" John asked.

"Oh, dear. The curtains must have knocked it off. I'll get the dustpan." Sandra left the room, intent on her task.

John stood staring. He seemed to be calculating the angle of the picture, the distance from the window, the length of the curtains. He looked around. I jerked my head back, hoping he hadn't seen me, or he'd begin to suspect my discontent. At last, he grabbed the trash can as Sandra returned and swept up the mess. She placed the photo in a drawer.

"I'll pick up another frame tomorrow. Now…I believe we have some unfinished business?" She pulled at the hem of John's shirt, leading him back into their room.

As the weeks passed, I felt myself sinking into depression and anger. I felt distant from my housemates. They didn't seem to notice whether I participated in their discussions or stayed in my room. I wallowed in my darkness.

One day, Sandra came in from the store and ran into the

bathroom. I was moping around the house, aimless and sad, as usual of late.

"Yes!" I heard her cry from the bathroom. Minutes later, she came dancing out with a small wand in her hand. I didn't know what it was, but she seemed very happy, more so than her usual joyful annoying self.

John came in that night, and Sandra body slammed into him, nearly taking him off his feet.

"Well, there's a welcome home I won't soon forget," he laughed, Sandra hanging from his neck.

"John!" she beamed at him. "We're pregnant!"

He gasped, then hugged her and swung her around.

Lost in their news, they didn't even say hello or acknowledge me. Maybe they knew better. Why bother sharing your news with an old lady who could never have children? Enraged, I knocked the candle off the credenza, the glass holder breaking apart.

They both turned in shock.

John stared. I didn't care if they knew it was me. I wanted them to know. That's right, perfect happy couple, your housemate hates you.

Instead, I was the one who was shocked.

"What the hell?" John said. "The window isn't open this time. Candles don't just fall on their own power,"

"Damn right!" I yelled. "It was me! What of it?"

They didn't say a word to me. Instead, Sandra said, "John, don't be silly. I'm sure it must have been sitting too close to the edge, and with all of our jumping around, we probably just vibrated it off. I'll get the dustpan."

She left the room. John looked unconvinced.

I stood in shock. "No, it wasn't a vibration. It was me! ME!!!" I threw my arms up in front of his face. He didn't move. Anger welled up and I lashed out. My hand flew through the air, and through his face, making no contact. I staggered back, staring at my hand.

John glanced around as if he'd noticed something but did not make direct eye contact with me, as if I wasn't even there.

I turned and ran out of the room into my boudoir and stared

into the mirror, but only the empty bed behind me appeared in the reflection. I reeled back and went to sit on my chaise lounge, but it wasn't there either. Instead a twin bed sat against the wall with a framed print, "Be Our Guest," hanging over it. This wasn't my furniture. What had happened to my furniture?

I shrank into a corner and tried to come to terms with this new reality.

A week later, John put the finishing touches on a crib in my room. MY ROOM! As much as I wanted a baby, I wasn't prepared to be shoved completely out of my home, the only place I'd known for decades. I knocked the stuffed animals off the changing table.

John turned and looked at the animals on the floor. Then, he turned and walked out of the room, leaving me to seethe.

I heard the perfect couple actually arguing. This made me both happy and sick to my stomach at once.

"I love our house, John. I want to have our baby here. The school district is perfect."

"I just get a bad feeling about this. Things keep falling and moving on their own. I have never really believed in ghosts, but I am afraid this house is changing my mind on the matter. I think this place may actually be haunted."

"Don't be silly. Ghosts don't exist."

"I'm telling you, something isn't right in this house."

The argument went on for days, coming up at odd times—in the middle of the night, at dinner time, before work.

I decided to keep up my end of the bargain. John seemed to know I was here. I would keep reminding him I was. I tossed the animals down again and again. I even managed to knock a frame off the wall one day. His keys disappeared and turned up in odd places.

Sandra had to finally admit John was right. Something was definitely going on in the house.

One day, in a rage, I followed Miss Perfect Sandra as she took a load of laundry to the basement. On her way upstairs, I stood, barring the door and let all of my anger and hate seethe out of me. She gasped and staggered back, falling down the stairs and landing heavily on the floor below.

"That's right, San-DRA. This is my house! How dare you come

in and take over? GET OUT," I raged.

Sandra pulled herself up and hit the light switch, but the bulb wouldn't come on. She pulled out her cell phone and with shaking hands, flipped the flashlight on. She limped up the stairs, clutching the banister with a white knuckled grip. At the top of the stairs, she spun around and slammed the door shut, sliding the lock into place. As if that would stop me.

I followed her to her room where she made a call.

"We need to do something. You were right. Before the baby comes. I won't let anything hurt my baby. ANYTHING." She spoke into her phone, but her eyes were staring through me. It was a look I had never seen on her perfect happy face—a haunted look. I smiled at the apropos term and returned to my room. I had gotten to her this time. She was afraid.

Two days later, John and Sandra answered the door together. A short, fat woman dressed in black came through the door with a large bag.

"Thanks for coming," John said, exhaling as if he had been holding his breath for days.

"I come when I am needed," the woman said in a spooky voice. I wondered which of us was the haunt. She walked around the room, nodding and mumbling. "Ah, yes. You have a very angry spirit here." She stopped in front of my bedroom door. "Here. This is where I feel it the strongest. Hmmm." She spun and retrieved her bag. She pulled out what looked like dried weeds, lit a candle, and crumbled the plants into a shallow ceramic bowl. Using the candle, she lit the detritus until it emitted a gray-black cloud of smoke. She swayed around the room, holding the bowl in front of her, thrusting it up into the air, then down to the floor, into corners and over doorways, chanting something I couldn't understand as she went.

I leaned against the doorframe, arms crossed. This chubby visitor was not going to scare me.

The air became thicker and harder to breath. I fanned my hand to dispel the smoke. When the woman arrived at my doorway, she stopped and continued waving the smoking item around the frame and several times thrust it right at me, even through me.

It burned. First my eyes, but then my skin. I coughed and

stepped back. Seeming to sense me, the woman followed me into the room. I backed away and then scurried past her, but nowhere in the house was safe. Everywhere I went, the same choking smoke filled the air, getting thicker by the moment. I couldn't see. Everything was burning. I expected my skin to peel off.

I knew jealousy and anger. And now, I knew fear. How could one fear for their life when they were already dead? I wasn't sure, but I knew I had to escape or I would surely succumb to the noxious odors.

With a screech, I ran straight for the back wall and into my yard. I looked around like a wild animal, already feeling the relief of fresh air. Then, I saw it. The playhouse. I dashed into the small building and hugged the walls, thankful for a safe haven. I heaved and gasped and slowly recovered my senses. Fine. I could stay here. I went to the window and stared at the house.

Yes, this would do nicely. I'd bide my time here, and someday soon, I'd make a new acquaintance. Maybe Little Sandra or Little John-boy would come to play in the house in the backyard. And I would be their new friend. Chase me out of my own home? That's okay, I thought, rubbing my hands together in anticipation. I'll have my revenge soon enough.

The Legend
Heather N. Hartmann

My name is Ella James, and the last place I thought I would ever be is in the bed of Ray's pickup truck. Now, don't let your mind jump. I'm not with Ray. I'm alone. Hiding out, more accurately. Letting the dark hide me from my friends who are sitting only a hundred yards away around the pine-stinking bonfire. Well, only one of them is my friend. My best friend, Paige.

Paige has been dating the quarterback on the varsity football team for six weeks. The story actually starts eight weeks ago when Paige made the cheer team. Paige always yearned to be popular. Yet, never quite made that rank, until recently. When Paige made the cheer team, her life suddenly catapulted into the popular world. Being the best friend that she is, she dragged me along, and for reasons unknown, they tolerated me.

Not that they didn't always make sure to let me know I wasn't as good as them. That I wasn't a cheerleader. That I didn't have a boyfriend on the football team. That my size-six jeans weren't quite small enough. But, because I love Paige, I put up with it. Not to mention, I was sitting at the popular table during lunch. It was worth being told I shouldn't eat my favorite mozzarella sticks.

It didn't take long for Ray to pounce on Paige. It's known around school that Ray likes to hit on fresh meat. He holds the record for scoring with the most cheerleaders. At least the legend says.

I'm still pretty sure the word girlfriend to Ray means sex. As far as I can tell, he is pretty bad at being a boyfriend. When Paige screwed up a landing on the cheer team and got benched for the rest of the game, he was nowhere around afterward to console her. It took her three games to be put back in. And whenever she wanted to talk about it, he would just "kiss her worries away," as he said.

Since they've been dating, making out has become a top

priority in Paige's life. Against the lockers. At parties. On the side of the football field. In his truck. In his bedroom. I was worried, with a twinge of disappointment, when Paige told me she let him go all the way. It had only taken Ray two weeks to take Paige's virginity.

Since Paige was over the moon about taking that step with Ray, I found myself caught up in her joy. She was the first of the two of us to have sex. I wanted every detail, and she obliged.

Their make-out sessions only intensified from there. At our locker I would be forced to look away from their PDA. I always became flushed just watching. When Ray would pull back, he would smile at me and say, "Hey Red," before strutting down the hall to class. And, it had nothing to do with my burnt brown hair.

In all honesty, the "Hey Red" was usually the most Ray talked to me. I found myself flustered around him, turning into a stupid giggly girl. It had nothing to do with me liking him. Every girl in school had a stupid crush on the QB of the varsity football team. But he was my best friend's guy, and I honestly didn't think of him as boyfriend material. But he still had a way of making me turn to mush.

The group sitting around the bonfire are all juniors, while Paige and I are sophomores. It's a big deal around school for us to have been invited to one of Ray's secret bonfires. Paige being invited wasn't a huge surprise, she was his current girlfriend. But my being invited made front line gossip.

The legend says he throws a bonfire, at an undisclosed location, at end of every football season. Ray only invites his "top level friends," as he so nicely puts it. So, the real surprise came when he personally invited me to his secret bonfire. Not only was it a shock to me, it was a blow to the entire school.

After accepting, I went right away to Paige, who was applying lipstick at our locker mirror, and I asked how she managed to get him to invite me.

"What? I didn't. Awww! He is so sweet. He must have known how much it would mean to me if you were there."

"Wow. I guess so. I'm still surprised he didn't tell you to invite me."

"Come on, you know better than that. The secret bonfire is by his personal invitation only. If I invited you, that would open it up to others inviting their best friends."

"Oh, well, that's true."

"See. And you have been worried he doesn't consider my feelings. He knew you coming would mean the world to me. So he asked you!" Paige turned from her locker and squealed before pulling me into a hug. "I better go find him and thank him ... proper." She said the last word with a wink as she ran down the hall.

When the night of the bonfire came, there was a total of thirteen of us invited. Five of his best guy friends, all football players. Five of the top cheerleaders, Paige and me. Ray picked Paige and me up personally, and the rest of the crew followed us out to a vacant wooded lot about an hour away.

The legend said that Ray's bonfires consisted of drinking, drugs, and sex. I knew they were wrong about drugs, because they all cared too much about the spot on their teams to jeopardize it with weed. Drinking, however, was more forgivable, if you didn't do something stupid like drive. But, that's why the secret bonfire was an overnighter.

I've never been much of a drinker. And as the shots started to flow, I found myself wishing I hadn't come. That is how I found myself lying in the back of Ray's pickup truck, wishing for morning.

It was pretty telling that nobody noticed I was gone. Paige had been right, Ray only invited me to make her feel better. To pass the time, I started tracing constellations with my finger and naming them. I've always loved astronomy. Just as my mind started to ponder the greater world around us, a shadow fell over my eyes. Glancing up, my heart skipped. I'd been caught by the man himself.

"There you are," Ray said.

"Here I am."

"What are you doing, Ella?"

"Looking at the stars."

"Oh, I love star gazing," Ray said, and then, to my horror, climbed in the truck and laid down next to me. My whole body tensed and my mouth went dry.

"Uh, yeah."

"What's your favorite constellation?" he asked.

"Um, I've always loved Ursa Major," I said, trying to sound smart. His arm was next to mine, and warning signs were shooting off in my head. "We should probably get back to the group."

"That's because of the big dipper, isn't it?"

"Well, yeah. It was the first group of stars I could ever actually see. Where is Paige?"

He went on, completely ignoring me. "I've always been a fan of Orion."

"Uh, yeah. That's a good one, too." Feeling I needed to get out of there, I made my move to sit-up. His arm slipped around my shoulders, bringing me back down. He slid on top of me. My breath caught.

"Ray, get off me. Paige is my best friend."

"Oh, Red, those cheeks give you away," he said.

Before I could evade, his lips came down on mine. Fierce, fast, demanding. His tongue slipped into my mouth. I managed to turn my head, and he just continued nibbling on my chin. "Damn it! Ray, get off." I pushed him back a few inches before he braced and stopped my progress.

"You flirt just as much as every other girl, and you're telling me you want me to get off?"

"I don't flirt with you." I gasped, mortified. "You just make me uncomfortable. You're my best friend's boyfriend, now get off me." I could see the anger come into him and braced for his verbal attack.

"What the hell. Make you uncomfortable? That's bullshit. You have wanted me since you started high school. I'm trying to make that a reality for you, babe. It's no big deal to me if I fuck a sophomore nobody."

"You're ridiculous. Now get off me." Waiting for him to move felt like an eternity. My heart was hammering in my chest as I prayed he would move. Finally, he rolled off, sat up, then climbed out of the truck. I took several deep breaths, my nostrils burned of his sweet and musky cologne. I managed to sit up and climb out of the truck. When I came to the fire, Paige was nowhere to be found.

"Where's Paige?"

"Over there, throwing up. What a rookie," said one of the cheerleaders.

I ran over to where Paige lay cloaked in darkness and shivering. "Oh, Paige, are you okay?"

"I think I've managed to puke out everything I've ever eaten my entire life."

She wasn't joking. Blue liquid from our cookie monster drinks sat regurgitated by her side. The odor radiating up was not the smell of chocolate chip cookies, as it had been going in. "Oh, honey. I'll get you some water." Pulling a water out of the cooler, I noticed

Ray flirting with the same cheerleader who called Paige a rookie. "Why don't you help your girlfriend instead of trying to get up everybody else's skirt? I'm sure she would like to go home."

"She's nothing but a sophomore lightweight," Ray said.

"You're nothing but a pig." I ran back over to Paige and asked her if she wanted to go home.

"Desperately." She took the water and drank half the bottle in one gulp.

"All right. Well, Ray won't take us. I'll text your brother, Carter." I pulled out my phone and sent the SOS message.

"How will he find us?"

"I'll turn on my GPS and he can track it with the app."

"Okay. Thanks, Ella. You're the best friend a girl could have."

"Um. I don't know if this is the right time, but I should tell you, while you were over here getting sick, Ray came on to me. I pushed him away and called him a pig and all, but still."

"I've had my fears that he's gotten bored with me," Paige said, moving to rest her head in my lap.

"Oh, Paige. Why didn't you tell me?" I asked running my hand through her hair.

"I was hoping I was wrong. I wanted to see what happened tonight before I became the crazy jealous girlfriend."

"What are you going to do?"

"If he doesn't already consider us broken up, then I am going to break things off. I mean, look, he left me over here to die while he hit on my best friend. And to think I gave it up for that jerk."

"I should go over there and give him a piece of my mind. Better yet, let's hire some muscle to beat him up."

"This is why you are my best friend. Thanks for making me feel better already," Paige said.

"Always. That's what best friends are for."

Envy's Hard Lesson
M.L. Stiehl

I woke up to the smell of head cheese. Yesterday had been hog-killing day, and today Grandma would work in her kitchen making the head cheese—all day. I didn't care much for head cheese, but it sure smelled good when she was making it.

Grandma would also make sausage that night. Unfortunately, I didn't know much about making either of those, so there wasn't much for me to do in the house.

"Where is Grandpa?" I asked Grandma.

"He's upstairs in the store building. The butchered hog is there, you know. They'll be using salt to cure the meat."

"If Grandpa's there, I think I'll go join him."

"Well, I bet you won't stay long. It's ugly, cold, and hard work—and no play. Not something for little girls."

I'd heard Grandma's warnings many time. She always tried to tell me things were not good for me. But I'm pretty tough.

Getting dressed quickly, I ate a little breakfast and headed out.

The store building was on the edge of our property. I ran across the yard and up the stairs. When I opened the door, I was almost knocked backward. Boy, did it smell bad. I had to turn around and take a big breath. After a moment, I made my decision and stepped inside.

The room was cold, but I had dressed warmly. Inside, light slanted in through the two side windows. The men were busy, rubbing salt into the huge slabs of meat. I was surprised to see that no one had gloves on, and their sleeves were pulled up to their elbows.

I moved over beside my Uncle Jay. "How come no one wears gloves and your sleeves are pulled up?" I asked.

"We pull our sleeves up to keep them from touching the meat," he answered. "Our hands are bare so we can feel the meat better—that way we can get the salt in every little crack."

"Ah," I said. I watched them work for a while. It looked like fun. And I didn't like being left out. "Uncle Jay? I want to do it, too."

"I don't know about that," he replied. "It hurts a little."

"I'm okay," I said.

Some children can be taught with words, and others with actions. Me? I was one of those children who had to learn for themselves. Not always a good thing.

My uncle gave me a small piece of shoulder meat and some salt. The salt grains were large, not like the kind we used in the kitchen.

I grabbed a handful and started rubbing. It was rough and began hurting right away, but I could stand it. I wasn't going to admit I couldn't do something they could. It took a while to finish my piece. I saw Grandpa and the others still working.

"Is this okay, Uncle Jay?"

He took a look at what I'd done. "No, not at all. You need to rub hard on both sides, and get a lot of salt in there. You need to make it feel almost smooth."

Oh, my goodness. I was already tired from what I'd already done, but I wouldn't quit. It was a lot of work, and at times I thought it was impossible to make it smooth, but I kept working.

I saw the men watching me with smiles on their faces. I knew they were laughing at me, a little girl trying to do men's work. They were used to me wanting to be wherever Grandpa and Uncle Jay were—they were always busy with new and interesting things that I'd never seen before—and sometimes it was something I was too little to help with. This was probably one of those times, and they were waiting for me to give up.

Uncle Jay asked if my meat was smooth yet.

"I don't think so," I answered weakly.

"Let me know when you get finished, and I'll get you another piece," he said with a grin.

Soon, Grandpa announced it was about time for lunch. That was the sign for everyone to find a stopping point.

Uncle Jay told me, "Come on, and we'll finish later." As he started toward the door, he stopped. "Hmm. I think yours looks pretty good." He patted the shoulder, as if giving it a final approval.

Once they rest of the group was ready, we headed to the house.

Grandma and the wives of those helping with the work were busy in the kitchen fixing lunch. The men were reminded to wash-up before they sat down. Warm water had been placed in a pan for that purpose.

The men went first. I washed my poor hands last. I could hardly feel them, they were so cold. And they were as red as my red crayon. But I wasn't about to say anything. I acted like everything was okay.

Grandma fixed me a plate. I ate in the kitchen while the men ate in the big dining room. I never ate with them. They spent all their time talking about hunting, fishing, and work on the farm—not much to interest a little girl. I did try to listen to what I could, though, so I could ask Grandpa and Uncle Jay about those things later. I always wanted to know what some of it meant. Often, they would answer my questions, but sometimes they'd just say, "I don't know." I'm sure that was only when they didn't want to answer. Some things were "better left for when you're older."

Grandma always told me, "Most of the stuff men talk about is just foolishness."

I didn't believe her, but I never argued with her.

When it was time to head back to the store building, I think Grandpa or Uncle Jay gave Grandma a special look, because she said I had to stay at the house and do some homework. When they said that was fine, I knew they didn't want me to go back. Normally I would have fussed, but my hands were so red and sore. I gave in.

I never told them about my hands. I guess they knew from the way their own hands felt.

After they left, Grandma and the women started on the dishes. "How did you like it?" she asked me.

I decided to fib a little. "It was fun—but lots of work."

She said, "Let's put some lard on those hands. That'll help them rest for the day."

I didn't stop her. It felt good.

I did casually mention that Uncle Jay had said I did a good job with my piece of meat.

Having learned how hard it was on my hands, I knew I didn't want to go back and do that job anymore. I could only hope they would get smooth and soft again.

After cleaning up the kitchen, Grandma smiled at me and said, "Tomorrow, they're going to prepare the hams so they can smoke them in the smokehouse."

I gave a sigh of relief. "I'm too little for hanging up hams and lighting the fire," I reminded her. "Anyway, I don't like the ugly smoke."

She laughed. She knew that I wouldn't envy the work they did with the hogs again.

"I'm through with the hogs for now," I told her. "But call me when they bring them in for us to eat."

Hazel Eyes
Susan Gore Zahra

April 19, 1995

Emily Duncan savored the vision in her rearview mirror while she slowly buckled her seatbelt. Danny Hogan sat in the back in a booster seat as he bobbed to the music of the Sesame Street CD she played. She could see his hazel eyes, so much like her own. Countless nights, her husband, Kyle, had cradled her face in his hands and murmured, "Someday we will have a child with curly hair and beautiful hazel eyes just like yours." Danny's mop of curls was rust colored instead of black like Emily's hair, but his eyes were a perfect match for hers. After multiple miscarriages and years of aching for a child, today Emily finally had her own hazel-eyed little boy.

Remorse crept into Emily's heart. It would be months, maybe years, before they could reunite with Kyle. Emily shook off the sadness and put her car into reverse. Danny's lousy excuse for a mother would forget about him in a matter of days. She and Kyle and Danny would be one happy family by next Christmas.

Luring Danny into her car had been easy. What kindergartener is not in love with his teacher? Besides, he missed his bus at least once a week. His reluctance to go home after school was a clear indicator that he was not bonded properly with his mother.

For years, Emily had greeted parents bringing their children in for the first day of school. So many of them didn't know the first thing about caring for a child, yet nature allowed them to have babies.

Danny's mother was the worst. She had tattoos on her arms, her neck, and who knows where else. Her nose was pierced, as well as four studs in each ear. Her lips were slathered in deep plum lipstick that made her mouth look bruised. She wore rock band shirts or lacy camisoles with ripped jeans and army boots. Her spiky tufts of hair were sometimes Kool-Aid red, sometimes bleached white, other times as black as a starless night. She reeked of tobacco smoke and something earthy.

When Emily called Danny's mother "Mrs. Hogan" on the first day of school, the woman corrected her. "I'm Tish. Just Tish." Yet Danny told fantastic stories about his father, the soldier; his father, the scientist; his father, the policeman. The poor child needed a father, and a stable, loving mother. Emily and her husband, Kyle, were ready. They had space in their home. They had gaping caverns of longing in their hearts.

Tish brought a toddler along to conferences. She ignored Danny and the snotty-nosed toddler with the droopy diaper as they ran, climbed, squealed, and shoved each other. At the last conference, she appeared to be pregnant again, still with no mention of a husband. Someone needed to rescue those poor children. Emily couldn't do anything about the toddler or the baby on the way. She could rescue Danny.

The therapist, whom Kyle insisted she see after the last miscarriage, suggested her students' parents might not be as unfit as Emily believed. Andrea had the nerve to suggest Emily was consumed by envy for women who were able to bear children. For over a year, Emily argued with Andrea. After she developed her plan to rescue Danny, Emily nodded implied agreement during her therapy sessions. She laughed at her silly attachments to students, never mentioning Danny. Andrea expressed some skepticism when Emily said she no longer felt a need to come in for therapy, and offered to refer her to another therapist to get a different perspective.

Emily already had her different perspective. She planned carefully. She always parked her car on the back edge of the staff parking lot, away from school office windows. She kept granola bars, packets of cheese crackers, and tiny boxes of raisins in her glove box.

A plastic bin labeled "school supplies" stowed in Emily's trunk was filled with a couple of changes of clothes and pajamas for both herself and Danny. The clothes were tucked beneath the quilt her mother made the first time Emily was pregnant. The quilt stitched with grandmotherly love would finally keep a child warm.

When she found Danny squatting beside a forsythia bush, trying to piece together a broken robin's egg shell, Emily was prepared.

"Hey, buddy! It looks like you missed your bus, again." Emily approached quietly, smiling.

"Uh, oh. Mommy's gonna be mad." Danny turned his sober little face away from the broken eggshell toward Emily. A bright yellow blossom nested in his unkempt curls.

Emily's throat tightened. How could that woman be angry with such an inquisitive child?

"How about I give you a ride home? You won't have to bother her to come pick you up."

Danny had smiled and taken Emily's hand. Now, they were pulling out of the exit farthest from the crosswalk, where the last of the crossing guards were ambling back to the school. They were on their way.

"I live at 725 Windswept Drive. The bus always turns at Casey's General Store," Danny said. He was such a bright child.

Emily reviewed their route in her mind. They would take I-80 out of town, heading west, across Iowa to I-35, and make their way to Tuba City, Arizona. The university job board always had postings for teachers in Tuba City. She kept a separate bank account and credit card, supposedly to save for graduate school. She had thought of everything.

"Ms. Duncan. That was Casey's General Store. You didn't turn there." Danny was no longer smiling or bobbing to Bert and Ernie's song.

Emily stopped at the light before the I-80 interchange. Glancing in the mirror, she could see Danny beginning to tug at the booster seat straps.

"Where are we going? Why didn't you turn at Casey's General Store?" His little face looked panicked. "I want my mommy. Let me out!"

Emily pulled a box of raisins, Danny's favorite treat, out of the glove box and reached back to him. "Don't worry, sweetie. Here's a little snack. You must be hungry."

Danny batted the box from her hand. "I want my mommy!"

Emily pulled through the intersection onto the westbound ramp.

"This is the big road! It goes to Meemaw's house. I want to go home!"

"Where does Meemaw live?" Emily felt her chest tighten. She

planned to stop in Des Moines for the night.

"Iowa. I don't want to go to Iowa. I want my mommy!" Danny's face was red as he strained against the straps.

Emily had planned for everything, except for Danny having family along her chosen route to Arizona. Except for Danny actually liking his mother.

Emily looped around the cloverleaf to turn back the way they had come.

"I'm sorry, Danny. I had a little brain burp and didn't see Casey's General Store. You help me watch for it this time, okay?"

As they approached Danny's house, Emily could see Tish standing in the yard running her hands through her neon pink hair, her bulging belly peeking out between her ripped jeans and an AC/DC t-shirt. Once Danny was released from the car, he bolted toward his mother. Tish whooped and squatted down to catch him as he leaped into her arms. She kissed every inch of his cheeks and forehead.

"Mommy! Mommy! Ms. Duncan had a brain burp and forgot to turn."

"She did?" Tish stood up to face Emily.

"I'm so sorry," Emily said. "He missed the bus, and I wanted to save you a trip out."

Tish leaped at Emily and embraced her. "Thank you! Thank you!"

Emily saw the flashing lights of a police car over Tish's shoulder as it pulled to a stop. A tall man with curly, rusty orange hair, and wearing a badge, stepped out of the car.

"Daddy!" Danny ran over and grabbed the man around his legs.

"Hey, buddy. What have you been up to, now? Mommy called me, all upset and crying. She said you were lost." The man extended his hand. "I'm Detective Dan Hogan, this little imp's dad."

"I'm ... I'm his teacher." Emily stammered as she shook his hand. "I got a bit lost bringing him home."

"Well, thank you for looking out for Danny. I'm happy to finally meet you—work schedule always seemed to get in the way."

After another round of hugs and thanks, Emily drove to the Casey's parking lot. She slumped over the steering wheel and tried to catch her breath as the magnitude of what she almost did crushed her. She pulled out her cell phone and hit a speed-dial number.

"Andrea? It's Emily Duncan. You're right. I need help."

May 26, 1999

Emily pulled the gift bag out of her car. She had settled into a new community when Kyle got a job transfer to Winningham. After a year of psychotherapy and graduate school to become certified to teach middle school, she began a new job teaching social studies. Tweens were more pimply and prickly than cute and cuddly, as her kindergarten students had been. She had no desire to take one home with her.

The one drawback had been the high fertility rate among school staff. There must have been a baby shower every month in the three years since she started teaching here. She had never attended one and never brought a gift.

Until today. Robin Fuller was special. Emily told no one when she became pregnant that last horrible time. She thought things might go well because she was ravenous instead of morning sick, but she didn't want to risk the looks of pity should she fail again. One day she found a plastic container of bite-size oatmeal cookies in her mailbox with a note: "Thought these might help, Robin."

When the miscarriage led to the unrelenting hemorrhage and hysterectomy, she told the principal only that she had emergency surgery. Robin showed up the day after she came home from the hospital with dinner ready to reheat when Kyle came home, and frozen, single-serving containers of homemade chicken soup, beef stew, and vegetable soup. She brought food every week until Emily returned to school.

The afternoon Emily stood weeping and barefoot in her sweatshirt and flannel pants out on the deck while snow swirled around her, Robin wrapped her in the afghan from the sofa. She stood silently with her arm around Emily's shoulder until Emily went inside. Robin brought towels to rub Emily's feet dry. She listened to Emily pouring out grief and despair after reaching the end of her struggle to bear a child.

Emily stopped at the door of the cafeteria, which was already decked out with pink banners and balloons. She took several deep breaths. She knew she was not ready to smile her way through the shower, not even for Robin.

Emily took her bag to the table piled with gifts. She tucked in the card with her congratulations and note: "Let me know when you are ready for company and some chicken soup." Robin would understand if Emily shed a few tears while holding a baby for the first time in years. She moved the tissue paper back for one last look at the quilt her mother had made for the hazel-eyed grandchild who would never be.

They Called Him Ducky
By John Marcum

Joe Medwick was a World Series champ in 1934. That was ten years before I was born. My first encounter with him wasn't until 1961. He was coaching and scouting for St. Louis University at that time. It was a far cry from his heyday with the St. Louis Cardinals' Gas House Gang in the mid 1930s. In 1937, his best year by far, he was the league MVP and the last Cardinal player to ever win the triple crown in baseball. He had the highest batting average at .374, most home runs at 31 and most RBIs at 154 that year.

I was a left-handed pitcher for Lindbergh High School in 1961 and played in the American Legion league during the summer months. That's when Joe first touched my life. I didn't even know who he was by sight. My father knew and told me after the game that he was in the stands that night. How did I learn he was there scouting me? Well, because the following spring I received a letter from St. Louis University (SLU) asking if I'd consider committing to go there on a full scholarship in baseball. It was all done on Joe's recommendation, and I started college there in the fall of 1962.

It was spring of the following year before I actually saw Joe out on our practice field. It didn't take me long to see how he got his nickname, Ducky. He was bow-legged, and when he walked he waddled like a duck. I was surprised by his size—well under six feet tall. His lesser known nickname was Muscles, and I figured that must have been what enabled him to be the outstanding hitter he was. By the time I met him, his physique had changed. He just looked like an average guy to me. He was unassuming, then, not flashy or boisterous. He spent his time watching hitters—instructing and encouraging them. Since I was a pitcher, we didn't interact much, but I knew he was watching. He had a keen eye for everything on the field.

In my sophomore year at SLU I hit my pitching stride. It had taken me six years, but I had perfected my curve ball and had a good changeup as well. I won five of the first six games I pitched that spring. Then the Missouri Valley Conference tournament began. It was a three day affair.

We skipped school on Friday, met early that day, and boarded a chartered bus that took us to Louisville, Kentucky. Our first game was late that afternoon, and our ace pitcher for that game was a senior. He pitched five innings before running into trouble. The opposing team had scored twice already. They sent me in as relief with two men on and no outs. I struck out the side and finished the game. I held them to the two runs already scored. With a few timely hits, we took the lead, and I got the victory with a final score of 3 to 2.

The next day I was the scheduled pitcher. After relieving four innings the day before, I pitched nine more that day. My curve ball was working well, and I won in a shutout, 2 to 0, while striking out ten.

Sunday at noon was the final game of the tournament. Our head coach went back to our ace pitcher and by the fourth inning, he was in trouble again. Three runs were in and more runners on base. We were down 3 to 1. Our head coach sent Joe over to talk to me. He said, "Listen kid, you've already pitched 13 innings in two days, and I don't want you to go in in relief if it's gonna hurt that arm. Coach wants me to be sure you're okay if we need you. So, you tell me now if you're too tired or your arm is too stiff."

I gave him a smile and said, "I feel fine." And I really did. At 20 years of age I was in the best shape of my life. They put me in and I held the opposing team to no runs and no hits. SLU came back in the eighth with three runs and I got my third win in the tournament. I had just pitched a total of 18 innings in three days and we won the tournament. My teammates carried me off the field. That's the day I got the nickname, Mighty Mouse. Thank God it didn't stick. I hated it.

The following year, 1965, I was the ace pitcher for SLU. My record that year was 9 and 0 in our conference. Then we played the University of Missouri Tigers in the regional playoff. They were then ranked #3 in the country. The winner of a two out of three series would go to the College World Series in Omaha. In the first game, I had Mizzou shut out 5 to 0 for eight innings, but through a comedy of errors, they scored four unearned runs in the ninth inning before I finally struck out the last batter for the win. The second game was close all the way, but we won it 5 to 4 also. It was the most emotional moment of our lives. The whole team went crazy. We chanted, "We're going to Omaha," over and over till we were hoarse.

A week later, we were in Omaha and I pitched the first game, winning it 2 to 1 and striking out 14 batters in the process. It was one of the best games I ever pitched.

The next day, Joe sent his wife, Isabelle, to talk to me in the lobby of the hotel. I thought it strange at the time that he would send his wife, whom I barely knew. But it soon became clear as she said to me, "John, I want you to know that you are a terrific pitcher, and no matter where your career takes you in the future, you can always be proud of what you have accomplished today. You were just voted first team, All American pitcher for this year." I was floored and speechless, and I realized she was relaying Joe's sentiment. He wasn't big on that kind of talk himself.

We lost a game the next day, but it was a two-loss-and-out tournament, so we were still alive. Then, in the next game, I came in to pitch the last two innings in relief and got a save in that one. Two days later, I pitched against Arizona State. They were the top seeded team in the tournament. They also had the #1 Major League draft pick—power hitter Rick Monday. I struck him out all four times he faced me in that game, but we still lost 6 to 2. It was my only loss that season, and we were eliminated from the tournament, finishing third. The following year we were ranked #3 in the nation.

That winter, Joe invited me to a Cardinal's football game. It was the first pro football game I'd ever attended. That was memorable, but the following spring he invited me to a baseball game between the Chicago Cubs and the Cardinals at Busch

Stadium. Joe was never a flashy guy. He picked me up in his ten-year-old rickety black Ford and we were off.

I'll never forget what happened next. Joe took a box seat on the third base line in the first row on the rail. Within minutes, there were cameramen mulling around. Then Leo Durocher, the manager of the Cubs at that time, walked over and started talking to Joe. Joe introduced me to Leo, and he said hello. Cameramen started clicking off photos. The next day, one of those photos was on the front page of the sports section. It was captioned something like, "Local ace pitcher looking ahead to a promising career." To this day, I believe that Joe set all that up as a publicity stunt for my benefit. I still have that photo of myself and Joe seated in the stands and Leo Durocher with his arms resting on the railing.

My senior year, 1966, I developed a sore arm that dogged me all that spring. The weather didn't cooperate, either. It was a cold spring and hard for me to get loose. I managed to pitch a no-hitter that year, even with the sore arm. My record was fair, but not like the year before, and we lost out on our chance to go back to the College World Series in Omaha. Two weeks later, during the Major League baseball draft, I was given a small cash bonus offer from the Chicago White Sox. I accepted it and played one summer season in Class A, and that fall in the Winter League in Florida. I won about half my games, but my arm never recovered completely, and the following spring, I didn't go back for spring training. I pitched locally in a semi pro league, hoping my arm might recover, but it never did.

In 1968, I got married and started a family. I held numerous jobs in sales and marketing over the years, mostly in the steel industry. I always remembered Isabelle's words and kept my head high. And as Satchel Paige once said, "Don't ever look back. Something might be gaining on you." I carried on. What else could I do?

Joe had a love-hate relationship with sports writers during his career. He could be crude and rude at times, on and off the field. Therefore, he had been shunned by the baseball writers and had to wait 20 years before he was finally inducted into the Baseball Hall of Fame in Cooperstown in 1968. He died in 1975 at the Cardinals spring training camp from a heart attack doing what he loved best, hitting baseballs. He was 63 years old. In 2014, he was among the first group of inductees into the newly formed Cardinals Hall of Fame.

I waited 30 years—and in 1995, I was inducted into the SLU Sports Hall of Fame. In 2000, my entire1965 team was inducted. Our SLU team is still the only one ever to go to the College World Series. I was finally selected to the Lindbergh High School Hall of Fame in 2004.

When I was ten years old, someone asked me what I wanted to do when I grew up. I said I wanted to play baseball with the St. Louis Cardinals. I diligently worked toward that end for over ten years. I eventually came close to that goal, and it was greatly due to the help of a St. Louis Cardinal. Reflecting now on all of my past accomplishments and awards, I'd have to say the best thing Joe did for me was to make it financially possible for me to earn a college degree. Aside from a lot of great memories, my education is the most important thing that's lasted a lifetime. I am proud to say I knew Ducky Medwick.

One Universe, Prepaid
Larry Duerbeck

The grave's a fine and private place,
But none I think do there embrace.
  —Andrew Marvell

I

"Life. And you're well out of it," said God, leaning back from the game table. His eyes kept trained across perfectly smooth, perfectly beautiful wood; aimed at a waiting soul.

"The time had come, I suppose." The soul blinked behind heavy lenses. "Tell me, please. Am I going to stay like this?"

"Oh, heavens no. You're like this now only because you are my especial case." God wriggled in anticipatory delight. "Of course," admitted He, "every case likes to think it's an especial case. But there aren't many even shade on you."

The two paused, each mulling in His (his) own way the scope and specificity of things.

God spoke. "It may come as a surprise, but I like to enjoy Myself. What befell you, from before birth to long after, was all in the law of mechanistic life. Nothing personal. Now it's all personal. I'll attend to you, to your outer man. I like the term clothing." He moved His hands, His fingers. "Stage effects only," noted God.

For the first time in a long time the soul took off his glasses to see better. Folded, they were laid to rest on the table. Soon, hearing aids followed. Then—"Go ahead. Take 'em out," advised God. "It's all right. Better hurry, though."

There they lay, full dentures. "Don't they look," the soul spoke through thirty-two baby yet now fully erupted and eternally adult teeth. He spoke, then laughed, then spoke once more. "They look like that chattering-teeth gag in the back of the pulps."

The soul laughed anew, God's grin deepened. "No teething pains for you, I trust and…We've just started." He flicked a finger.

Oxygen tanks and aspirator/ventilator/respirator equipment vanished. Without these encumbrances, the soul found he could undo his own straps and stand up from the motorized wheelchair, last in a long line.

"Sit down again," suggested God. "Won't you?"

With nary a look he sat, trustful only; tempting a no-laugh, rather tragic pratfall collapse. Instead, the wheelchair evanesced. The soul landed in a freshly dispatched, table-matching chair.

"Comfy?" asked God.

The soul's answer came in deep, profound stretches and first, fresh yawns. Soft effulgence grew to suffuse the room for glowing moments. Bathed by an internal welling of self-restrained, sublime brilliance—God giggled. "I've heard hymns—hell, oratorios less heartfelt, more profane."

Another pause while God and soul savored.

The game room brimmed a more luminous highlight, filled briefly with incandescent aromas of first garden at first bloom.

"For you. Sorry about that canned air you had to use, all those years."

II

The soul spoke. "I must thank You for all Your Godsends. My parents, first of all. I always felt my birth, what came out, I was a betrayal. Oh, but they were great. Then those many things that helped my life and work. So I could become the best proofreader possible."

"Best is right. Everyone wanted you, those writing in English. The biggest names across the board. You reigned as the *ne plus ultra*, uncorrupted by an era that elevated merely good proofreaders to secular saints," declared God. "But now it's time that you write for yourself."

"About what?"

God showed He could be discursive. "One of my subtler miracles came when I put the idea of TCM in Ted Turner's mind. For you."

"I loved Turner Classic Movies!" The proofreader blurted this out, then a second-take, much smaller-voiced, "For me?"

"Why not? Turner was nothing, compared to Gutenberg. You're a virgin?"

"Don't you know?"

"Well, yes. I do. But I thought you might like to engage in a spot of confessing. In some quarters confessing is believed to be quite the thing."

"Confessions and forgiveness," the soul pointed out. God only nodded. "So, yes. Little afterbirthy mess, I died an old virgin."

"Your life?" said God, brighter again. "Noble soul, I bask in your forgiveness."

III

God picked up the pace. "Your universe is all but prepared."

"My universe!" The soul sat up. "Really? That seems a lot of work."

"I'm God," reminded God. "You humans keep trying to rein me in. A universe to Me is—Where were you from again?"

"New York City. The big-house publishing crowd."

God shuddered. "A universe is like a grain of sand at Jones Beach. And I can always truck in more sand, if I choose."

Hooking His thumbs in His vest pockets, God chose silence. Suddenly:

"Well, have you written anything?"

"About what?" the proofreader asked. "If I'm not being redundant."

"Didn't they tell you? The seraphim, the cherubim, did no one in My immediate staff tell you?" God's tone, thunderstruck, struck thunder round the proofreader.

He bore up, undaunted. "Yes, sir. No one told me."

God sighed, breezes of balm and benevolence caressed the proofreader. "Ahhh-h-h, that's right…I kept my own counsel on this one. No files to keep, no reports to make. Just an Amanuensis, First Class. One copy, intended for a member of Saturday Writers Guild. If this writer ever wins, chalk up another for good old YOU KNOW WHO! Hmph. But the writer needs a check and, oh well. Where was I?"

"Keeping Your own counsel. Does the amanuensis know how to spell amanuensis, or which counsel to use. I could," the proofreader mused, "go over it. Help You around here."

"No need. Besides, we have other fish to fry."

"Cliché, sir." The proofreader arched both eyebrows and voice.

God thumped the table, from the sound a redwood trunk burst

asunder beneath His fist. "Of course it is! I like clichés! Why do you think I made so many, and why do you think I hear them so often?"

Before the proofreader could answer, God pelted on. "Why, do you imagine the fish and loaves were sushi and lumps of raw dough?"

The proofreader shook his refurbished head.

"Those fish? Served 'em up fried," grumped God. "Delicious. Now the universe I'm devoting to you is, shall be—"

God broke off. He eyed the proofreader. "I may use 'shall'?"

"With You? Unreservedly, yes. For You, triune or whatever, You alone in Your first and second and third persons, You resolve all problems of grammar, of 'command' and 'wish,' of 'intent' and 'simple futurity.' The only tricky part lies in all the quotation marks."

God turned to drill a hard, meaningful look into the amanuensis, hovering in the corner behind Him and to His right. Turning back, He directed a more liquid, kindly gaze over the wood. "Your universe shall be dedicated to you and your lustful desires."

"Oh my," breathed the soul in new, everlasting life.

"Who do you want to look like?"

"Whom," corrected the proofreader, as of old.

God snapped His fingers. "I never can keep those two straight. Thanks. Whom do you want to look like?"

The soul's reply was nothing if not prompt. "Errol Flynn."

God applauded; echoes boomed, rolling in waves like breakers aery. "One of life's finest throws of the dice. In his full manly attire I clothe thee. Robin Hood, Warner Brothers, thirty-eight. A great growth, a superb vintage. There you go."

There he sat. "Thank You!" Just the smile could fill a screen.

"Now Errol," prompted God. "Use your paper and pen to write the names—" God interrupted Himself. "I know what's inside you. What was inside you and what is still inside you. Write the names of the women you lusted after."

"You don't mean—?" The virgin pulled himself together. "Of course You do. You're God." Still he did not write. "These interludes are to be <u>con</u>sensual, though with the accent on the sensual?"

God at first looked affronted, and that takes some doing after Sodom and Gomorrah and Larry Flynt. The look passed to one of enthusiasm, "And how! I mean, so be it. Them." Another look, irritated. "So be they. Be they so." A smile of satisfaction graced His features. "Be they all…So."

"May I further change myself? Into the personification, the embodiment of each lady's lustful desires?"

God's assurances sounded casual and far reaching. "Sure, sure. Even the lesbians."

The proofreader started writing. God threw His mind as if He were a lowly ventriloquist throwing his voice. Watching not just names appear, but details and requests. Accusations of eavesdropping and voyeurism might have been leveled but then— He knows everything anyway.

God began lazily kibitzing. "You want to do that? With her?…And her? Ooh, kinky. She'll like that…Now you'll have to wait for her. She's not dead. Yet."

But soon God grew silent, distracted. The only sound came from the continuous skritch of pen across paper. Distraction led to fidgets and, "Anything else, Errol?"

"Yes, please. May I have another piece of paper?"

"You certainly may!" hooted God. "Try this. A spiral-bound notebook." He splayed His hands on the deal table. "It's been fun. But I have only a little of your time left to spend with you. Now. See, I'm scheduled to go design a few more fossils. Then they'll retrofit a crew of volunteer dinosaurs to match. Any questions?"

"There are writing teachers who say no happy endings in short stories. Not nobody, not nohow! What do You think?"

When God speaks in seriously angry tones, His tones display something striking to see. He chose His own, His chosen metaphor: Brow, massed storm clouds; Words, flashed lightning.

"Indeed! Do they indeed! What do I think? Seems to Me you've had more than enough unhappiness. Errol, I'll go them at least one better. I'll see 'em and raise 'em. I shall make it My business to give you a happy ending.

"Hah. You are in for not just a measly one, but at least two happy endings. First carnal, with every taste jaded, then one ending with no ending at all. The one you haven't even begun yet. For you? Heaven can wait. Let 'em sneer at that."

God dipped His right hand under the table. "But here's a weekend pass. A pass in, for you. All set." He brought His hand up and reached across a piece of parchment, one bedizened with signets and seals and ribbons.

"Capitalize the 'we.' So We can settle once and for all that betrayal bullshit for You. Capitalize that 'you.' Got it?"

The amanuensis nodded.

"Going to." The proofreader put down his pen, reached out to take the pass in a tender and shaking hand. He nestled it down beside his notebook, as though the tough sheep's skin were a fledgling fallen from nest. "Heaven? The parents? Thank You." He snatched God's more hastily proffered handkerchief, used it, saw His smile, and resumed writing.

"Keep that, too. I just put in for perpetual, as-needed, dry cleaning. Thank You. That's all I ever want to hear, and now I've heard it at least three times from you. Well, I'm off. To another enjoyment, playing in the mud."

After The End Notes

The amanuensis thought to title this short story "One Man's Vice Is…" The title fell, perhaps unhappily, overruled by Greater Authority.

God nevertheless promoted the Amanuensis, First Class to Secretary, Second Class—with further happy and conterminous endings and beginnings.

POETRY
Wrath and Forgiveness
Envy and Kindness

Saturday Writers 2017

White-Tailed Deer
Donna Mork Reed

Brown against brown, movement in the trees,

Nearly imperceptible. Shades and shadows drifting

Softly through the branches.

A white-tailed deer, nose to the ground, searches for
grasses and moss,

Edible remnants from winter's cold grasp.

Freezing, head up, the shape fades. She is invisible

Save black orbs peering out, searching for danger.

All seems safe. She moves on,

A shifting form against branching lines,

The fence of forest trees hiding her secure.

A branch snaps from somewhere beyond.

The figure shoots off, an arrow flying away

With only a white fletching showing which way.

I watch the flight in awe and admiration

All that remains is winter's vegetation.

It's Dumb to Pick Fights with Old Men
Cathleen Callahan

The old man gripped the stand
and the audience who didn't listen
but let him claim space your bodies used
because the movement said he was a great running man,
and you were, after all, part of the movement.

He trembled with arthritis,
you with desire.
He still had teeth,
yours were new.
He chewed on gruel,
you shook your head
at his tepid soup,
wanting to know
where was the heat?

He had lived sixty years more than you,
yet you stole the punch of his favorite line.

Fury straightened you both,
gulping each other down
belching each other back.
"Young man, why don't you wait
your turn!"
"Old man, it is my turn!"

Each of you
was essentially
two.

Imaginary Lashes
R.R.J. Sebacher

Now a diabetic sixty-five trading small talk with my podiatrist
To distract myself while he ripped off my left big toenail
He thought anesthetic might be unnecessary
He asked do you remember Deaconess Hospital
I said not really
Later in the parking lot it struck me

As a child I had been admitted
Diagnosis Spinal Meningitis
Later transferred to what we called the death ward
Run by a girl of seven or eight who told me she had beautiful
    red hair
Our frank discussions would have frightened most adults
Not to cry in front of parents our only rule

A cloth surgical cap covered her hairless head
Her mother made it with a Raggedy Anne and Andy print
"Because Raggedy Anne had beautiful red hair, too"
Sometimes we would race at night
Wildly down and around hallways
The like of my race car I have never seen before or since
Two metal yellow spoke wheels
Red seat suspended between
Donated toys, wheelchairs, crutches, it did not matter
Only the feel of speed and freedom
Abandon I had never felt and seldom since

She told me I could hold her hand—If I wanted
I wanted—How could I have blocked this all these years

Pale red lashes—bullwhip's slight curve at end
Ready to snap and tear apart
Already covered in my hearts blood
Flickering over black eternal pits
Centered in round green hillocks
Radiating simple joy and acceptance
Along with concern for the sad boy leaving her
Whose mother wouldn't take me back to visit

Now after reflection—it came clear
My subconscious had exacted wergild
For the crime of abandonment
In her last days or months
Judgment was right—symmetrical
Just recompense for my sin
Sometimes harsh and lonely
I had chased her perfect ghost till now

Believe me when I tell you
Knowledge is not freedom
As a child made viscerally aware
Watching my stepfather try
To compete with my father's ghost
No mortal could ever match
My mother's expectations
Perhaps in truth this was my bloodprice

Cleaning House
Cathleen Callahan

I'm letting the light back in,

cleaning house,
shedding the drapes
that sealed me in
to the dark dungeons of you,

welcoming light
through filigrees of lace
that tat moon and morning
to delicate designs,

waking
from dreams
free of you,

recovering the sunroom
in over-the-rainbow blues
on cushions now not sat upon
by you,

painting sooty corners,
changing browns to party-mint greens,
emptying junk drawers of your droppings,
cleaning house of you.

I'm letting the light back in.

Saturday Writers 2017

Forgiven
Cathleen Callahan

There was a time when I thought
the world would let me by
as good.

I did what was right,
skipping along the blade of life,
gathering bouquets
from those who counted deeds
as the harvest
of fulfillment and grace.

Unfallen, I winged
by fabric stitched into my skin,
fluttered above the point of my life,
unscathed by the blade
I hovered above.

Then I tore
the wings from me,
plunged and bled
and was
forgiven.

Now clothed in healing fabric spun
of nature's nest,
I love without regret
or shame for the passion of
my quest.

From Pride to Humility

To Trying Again
Donna Mork Reed

The years had not been kind to him. Matthew did show up, though Kathleen hadn't entirely expected him to appear, despite the fact it had been his email asking for this meeting.

"Kathy." He nodded awkwardly, looking unsure of the propriety expected.

"Matthew." She walked into him, giving him a hug like old friends. After a moment's hesitation, he returned the hug. She motioned to the coat rack, and he hung his thick, wool coat and red scarf on a hook. "You look good," she half-lied. She had loved him at one point in her life, and with love comes acceptance of the ravages of time and age.

"You look amazing," he said, giving her the once over, his eyes crinkling in appreciation.

"Your table is ready," the waiter announced, appearing out of nowhere and seemingly unaware of the tension in the room.

They both turned and followed him through the dimly lit dining area to a table by the window against the far wall. The soft, thick carpet offered a nice contrast to the view of the snow flaking down, adding to the already covered landscape. Kathy pulled the pink cashmere sweater closer, feeling the coolness emanating from the window.

"I was a little surprised by your email," she ventured, holding the thick menu unread in her hands.

He looked up from his, then smiled.

"Yeah, I guess you would be. Thanks for actually reading it. And for getting back to me. I wasn't sure you would."

"Of course. It's been a long time."

He smiled. "Only thirty or so years, give or take."

"Only," she chuckled. "Time flies, whether you're having fun or not."

The waiter barged in again. "Take your order?"

Kathy turned her attention to the menu while the waiter blathered on about the specials, his thin lips matching his ski-slope nose.

"I'll take the steak special, medium rare, with broccoli."

"Have you made your decision, miss?" the waiter asked, his eyebrows dancing up and down in impatience.

"I'll take the sea bass with garlic-roasted asparagus."

"Very good, ma'am."

The waiter took the menus and disappeared.

"I wanted to see you face to face. To apologize," Matt began, leaning forward, forearms on the table. His skin had age spots that hadn't been there the last time Kathleen had seen him.

"For...?"

"For our divorce, everything that happened. Time teaches all things, and I realize now that I was wrong."

"Don't," she put her hand out, covering his. "We were both wrong. We were too young and prideful to realize it, that's all. Water under the bridge."

He nodded. "I suppose you're right."

The waiter brought their dinner rolls and too-large salad.

"Would you like fresh ground pepper?"

"Yes, please," she said.

"No," Matthew said, at the exact same time.

They smiled at each other.

"I see some things never change." He motioned to the pepper being ground, nearly blackening her salad.

The waiter eyed her, sure she had forgotten to stop him, when she finally said, "Thank you, that's enough."

"You still like things spicy." Matthew shook his head in disbelief.

She nodded at his statement of the obvious. "Yes. Just, now that I'm older, I do have to moderate, sometimes."

"That's moderate?" he asked in shock.

She just smiled in return.

They ate a few moments in tolerable silence. The restaurant became noisier as more people crowded in to escape the weather, but they didn't seem to notice. The sky darkened with night setting in, but the outside was still lit by reflecting snow, giving the landscape a moon-like glow.

"Look, I don't know what to say. I just want...well...I thought, I mean...." He sat back in his seat, ran his hand through his salt-sprinkled hair, took a breath, then started again. "I heard about your husband passing. I'm sorry to hear that."

"Are you?" she asked, without malice, but true curiosity.

"Yes. Really, I am. I had many happy years with Monica. When she passed away, I was heartbroken. Almost as much as when you walked out."

"You left me no choice...," she started, defensive, her face tightening and eyes flashing.

He held up his hand. "I know, it's true...I'm just stating fact. You walked out, and at the time I was devastated. Now, I realize why you left. And I did love Monica, as I'm sure you loved Douglas. But now they have both passed on."

The waiter brought their meal. "Is there anything else I can get you? Some wine?"

"No, thanks," they said in unison.

He turned and walked away in what appeared to be a bit of a huff.

Matt looked at Kathy, and she answered with a shrug. Garlic and steam rose from her plate, making her tongue tingle. She took a deep breath in, enjoying the aroma.

He cut into his steak and chewed in deep concentration. Finally, washing down the bite with his tea, he continued.

"I thought maybe we could try to be friends again."

"Just friends?"

"Maybe. You know, whatever. You were my best friend at one time, remember?"

She smiled. "I remember."

"Remember when we went sledding at your mom's place.

And it was more ice than snow, and we slid right into the fence post?"

She smiled, her knee twinging in remembered pain as she had tried to push them away from the fence, but only managed to jamb her knee into the metal post, cutting through two layers of winter pants as well as the top layer of skin. "How could I forget? I still have the scar."

"And remember our dog, Ghost."

"He was one of the best dogs ever."

"Except the time he jumped up on the dining table in the middle of Christmas dinner,"

"Oh, my goodness. I about died. I grabbed him so fast and put him on the floor, your mother wasn't even sure she had seen what she thought she saw." She laughed. "He was something else."

"He didn't know he was a dog. He thought he was a person."

They laughed, and the tension began to drain out of Kate. She was surprised at how fast her defense walls went up when she thought she was past all of that. She focused on relaxing her grip on her utensils. It was nice talking with Matt.

They continued talking through dinner, sharing fun memories. The passage of time had lessened the bitterness of past pains, and divorce, and words spoken in anger.

"Can we try again? As friends. And if it becomes more than friends, so be it. And if not, that's okay, too?" Matthew asked.

Kathy looked at his face, so much older now, more wrinkled, and edged with gray hair that hadn't been there those many decades before. His eyes were tired, but kind and pleading. She remembered the blue eyes of youth, when they had looked into hers with so much love. He sat, looking at her now, so open and vulnerable, she wanted to jump up and wrap him in her arms, but that would be too fast. They needed baby steps.

She reached for the glass. It was a water glass but had a stem like a wine glass.

"To trying again. As friends." She held it up in "cheers" fashion, and he answered with a clink of his own, the sconces reflecting off the crystal.

Pride goes before a fall. But sometimes, in late fall, pride learns a few things about friendship and love and life, and it discovers it's time to set aside the pridefulness of youth and press on, accepting a gift of friendship.

Twice a Dark Moon Night
Tammy Lough

Nick Kozlov unsnapped the faux rabbit earflaps of his tan ushanka and lowered his chin deeper into the thick, fur-lined collar of his parka. The snow-packed coat was turning sodden as a downpour of rain mixed with sleet fell from a dark moon night. His black, steel-tipped work boots trudged through mounds of snow, robbed of their lustrous white sheen by the city workers' sprays of road salt. Brownish-gray clumps dangled from the hem of his trousers. He stopped under a yellow-lit lamppost to brush away, with insulated polar gloves, the brunt of freezing crystals before venturing back down the crowded walkway toward the bus stop, and home.

A protective glass enclosure shielded the waiting passengers from the onslaught of freezing rain. Nick hurried to a long, wrought-iron bench, a young man's Eagle Scout project that turned out damn good, and found it over-occupied. Again. Huffing, he turned and walked toward the protective awning of a used-book store. As he neared, the space filled with late arrivals bogged down with overloaded shopping bags. Nick hated Christmas and everything about it. Glass storefronts with over-sized windows, sprayed with canned snow, beckoned shoppers with sales displays featuring overpriced holiday attire, mannequins skating perfect figure eights near pine trees clothed in multi-colored ornaments, garland, and silver tinsel. Now that his Maggie had passed away, holidays were meaningless.

His body jerked sideways when, in his right ear, he heard the sizzling of a match-strike followed by the immediate smell of sulfur. A tall man, thin, with weathered skin, standing mere inches away, had lit the twisted end of a hand-rolled cigarette. For a second, Nick watched the red-hot tip jerk near his pressed lips like a bobber on a fishing line, bouncing to the stream of his words as he spoke to the woman beside him. He seemed unaware that the thin line of smoke weaving an upward trail triggered a constant, irritated squint to his eyes. Nick stared at the man's profile for a second longer and decided a punch to the man's kisser wasn't worth jail time.

The incident did jolt his memory to purchase cigars for his brother's visit the coming weekend. He preferred holiday time spent alone, but he tolerated the once a year intrusion, including Dmitry's incessant talking. It annoyed him to think of the imposition, and he felt his jaw tighten as his heart pounded in the hollows of his temples, warning of impending migraine.

Five minutes remained until the bus arrived, so he shouldered himself through the noisy crowd and inched into the alleyway. He surveyed the passing shoppers before turning his head to the sound of a snore and caught sight of a man lying on his left side two or three feet deeper into the passageway. The vagrant faced away from the howling wind, his spine rounded and his knees pulled upward to his chest in an attempt at warmth. He wore a filthy plaid jacket sewn with threads of yellow with green stripes pulled together so tight the seams warned of an impending tear.

Nick stepped deeper into the shadowed alley and stole another quick glance at the bustling walkway, but the passersby didn't pay him a first glance, much less a second. Not a sound came his way except the howling wind as it whooshed the city's stench into his nostrils, forcing tears to his eyes. He wanted to escape, but the memories that surfaced as he stared at the jacket held him in place like a bear trap. Before he considered his action, he swung his leg for momentum and planted the tip of his boot directly into the center of the vagrant's fetal-curved spine. No response. He geared up and kicked him again, more forcefully. The man attempted to unfurl, and Nick saw his face, ruddy and wind-whipped from the harsh weather. He stared as the shaken form tucked his shoulders up under his ears and shivered like a wet dog after a rain shower. His eyes pleaded for Nick to stay, pleaded not to be left alone in the shithole alley, even after the stranger's brutal attack. Sleet blew in with gusts of wind. Nick tilted his head downward to prevent further chafing of his face, gave the bum a final glance, then hurried to rejoin those waiting at the bus stop.

The sound of hydraulics, followed by a whiff of diesel fuel, assaulted his nose. The bus came to a stop in front of the shelter, and Nick pressed into the line of passengers, plodding up the steps. He flashed his bus pass to the blank-faced driver shivering in his seat, one gloved hand poised on the door control bar, anxious for the last passenger to board. The bus emitted a cooked-cabbage odor that reminded Nick of the orphanage dormitory from years past, as did that damn threadbare plaid coat worn by the homeless man in the alley. Seated passengers hugged red and green patterned shopping bags with colorful silver and gold handles, bulging with contents and invading a portion of the aisle. Nick bulldozed his way through as if the path were clear. He ignored the cursing and glaring stares from those whose packages he plowed into, causing several to topple into the wet, filth-ridden aisle. He found a seat halfway back that an elderly woman used to hold her oversized purse and bloated grocery bags. Nick lowered himself into the seat as she hurried to pull her food aside before he crushed it with his hefty bulk.

Nick and three-fourths of the passengers shaded their eyes when the bus made three forward lunges as pistons forced air into the engine's cylinders. Giant slivers of glimmering sunset pierced the dirt-caked windows. Nick squinted and watched as a truck in the oncoming lane slid and then recovered after hitting a patch of ice on the sleet and snow-packed road. Just as he released the breath of air he'd been holding, Nick saw a red, double-decker tour bus, driving way too fast for the weather conditions, enter a skid and head straight into the path of his bus. It was clear, if the driver didn't recover, the double-decker would T-bone him right where he sat. Nick braced for the collision.

#

Nick regained consciousness to the blare of constant ear-piercing sirens. He saw blurred red, white, and blue lights swirling across, and reflecting from, wet streets and storefronts. Bodies lay strewn from one side of the road to the other. He must have ejected on impact. He became confused when, as he tried to lift both hands to shield his ears from the piercing alarms of police, fire, and ambulances, he lost control of his right arm and watched as it fired off in hundreds of jerky spasms. He saw the look of horror on a fireman's face as he raced toward him, slowed to assess, then pivoted and ran to a victim he may be able to save. Nick grunted and attempted to roll from his left side to his back before realizing his legs and left arm were severed and he lay in a pool of blood and clots.

Before he lost consciousness, he saw the fireman point in his direction. A nurse rushed to his side and squatted. Her delicate hand rubbed his right shoulder and she looked pointedly into his eyes. Her lips, encircled with fine wrinkles, attempted a smile which only served to make her lips tremble. Nick attempted to move, but his body refused. Not even his eyelids followed the command to blink. He stared at the only thing he wanted to see, her light blue eyes and long, curled lashes…just like Maggie's. *Don't leave me. Please, dear God, don't let her leave.*

Then he heard a voice softer than cashmere. Never, would he forget the divine comfort of her words:

"You need care. I am here to help."

#

Multiple surgeries and physical, occupational, and speech therapies passed. Would he be able to find the man who invaded his dreams and made frequent appearances in his nightmares? He spent another dark moon, icy winter night searching in the snow and sleet with a biting wind whipping over and around his electric wheelchair, stinging his exposed skin. He rode past alley after alley, blowing into a sip-and-puff wand to stop his chair, or trigger a flashlight beam. False alarm. Another empty alley. He dipped his chin back into the fur lining above the top stop of the center-placed zipper on the heavy Goodwill-bought coat. He forged ahead to 23rd Street and Vine where he would cross at the light and ride up the other side before returning to his government-subsidized one-bedroom apartment and asking his caretaker to crank up the bedside heater.

The sun set with the hues of purple, pink, and violet-blue. Shadows inched into the alleyway, and as he peered inside the final one on this side of the street, he saw a body curled up against the wall, shielded from the drifting snow that moments ago mixed with sharp pellets of sleet. He motored the chair close to touch the shrunken form and triggered the flashlight. His vision blurred as tears pooled in his eyes and trickled down his cheeks. The man wore the tattered, yellow jacket with green stripes. The form moved, just a bit, and he saw his ruddy features, and knew he had found the man he sought.

Nick cleared his throat, controlled his shaky voice, and spoke the words he heard nearly a year past:

"You need care. I am here to help."

The Diva
Sue Fritz

"Harry. Harry. Look!" Delia pointed to the TV set. "That's the producer I was telling you about."

From the TV they heard: "So, Mike, you're producing a play in our little town. I think what many listeners want to know is, why? I mean, we're nothing like New York."

"Well, Tom, I like to offer my services to small companies and theaters to remind myself where I came from. And besides, you never know where your next big star is going to come from."

"Not this crap again. I'm going to bed."

Harry stomped to the bedroom, mumbling to himself. Delia sat glued to the TV.

The interview continued: "So Mike, what does your ideal star look like?"

"She would be tall and full chested, if you know what I mean. She would have long, blonde flowing hair. Her lips would be luscious. The kiss-smacker kind, ya know. But that's only if—"

Delia turned off the TV. She knew what she had to do to get the part. She spent half the night researching doctors and surgeons online.

When Harry walked into the living room the next morning, Delia was asleep on the couch.

"Hey." He nudged her to wake her up. "Hey!"

She popped up.

"You didn't come to bed last night. What's up?"

"Oh, Harry. Wait 'til you hear!" She told him about what kind of woman the producer was looking for. "I stayed up looking for surgeons."

"Surgeons? What for?"

"So I can turn myself into the kind of woman who will be his star!"

Harry rolled his eyes and headed for the kitchen.

"There's no coffee made," he growled.

Delia was already back to searching online. Harry stomped around the kitchen making his own coffee and muttering to himself again.

Several days later, Delia sat in the surgeon's office.

"Delia, what size are you wanting?"

"The bigger the better," she said.

"I think your frame will hold a double-D nicely. Now, they are a tad bit more expensive."

"That's fine. I've been saving for a vacation, but Harry never wants to go anywhere. Might as well use the money on me."

Driving home, she thought about the starring lead.

"I just know I'm going to get that part!"

* * *

"Harry, hand me my pain pills. Harry!"

"Get 'em yourself. You're the one who wanted this ridiculous surgery."

Delia downed two pain pills. She drifted off to sleep, telling herself that once she had the lead part, it would all be worth it.

A week later, Delia sat in another doctor's office. Her chest still hurt, but it was getting better each day.

"Delia, come right in."

She followed the nurse to the exam room and sat on the table while the nurse took her vitals.

"So, how have we been feeling?" the nurse asked her.

"Oh, I've been ok. I had breast enhancement surgery a week ago."

"Hmm... You know they aren't the same size, right?"

"What?" Delia exclaimed.

"Look in the mirror."

Delia got off the table and stood in front of the mirror. They did look lopsided.

"Well, the doctor said this might happen. He said the swelling on each side sometimes goes down at different rates."

"Ah," said the nurse. "Well, the doctor will see you soon."

"Do the injections hurt?" asked Delia as she climbed back up on the exam table.

"The doctor will give you a numbing shot first. Then he'll start plumping up those lips."

After her appointment, Delia drove home. Her mouth was swollen twice its size. *I hope this goes away soon,* she thought. *The auditions are only a week away.*

The Thursday before the tryouts, Delia found herself sitting in a beautician's chair. She stared at herself in the mirror. Her chest remained lopsided. The nurse was right. They must have put in two different sizes of implants. *I don't have time to have another surgery,* she thought. Besides, she could fix it with Kleenexes stuffed in the smaller side. But what was she going to do about her mouth? Her lips were huge. The swelling was going down too slowly.

"Good morning. How are we to…Oh, my. What happened to you?"

"What?" Delia said.

"Were you stung by a bee or something?"

Oh, great, thought Delia. *I got the newbie.*

"No, I did not," grumped Delia.

"Okay. Well, what can I do for you today?" the newbie squeaked.

"I need my hair dyed blonde, and then I need long, blonde extensions put in."

"Oh, that will be lovely."

The girl set to work mixing the dye to put on Delia's hair. Using a small brush, she started at the scalp. A half-hour later, Delia's whole head was covered in dye and foils. Ten minutes after that, Delia started screaming.

"It's burning my scalp!"

The young beautician rushed over. "Yes, it does that sometimes. It'll stop soon."

After what seemed like hours, Delia's hair was washed and dried. Then came the extensions. It was a long, painful, tedious process. When it was over, Delia had long, blonde flowing hair, but her scalp was as red as a lobster.

"That will go away in a few days," the teenie bopper of a beautician said.

The night before the audition, Delia studied and studied the lines.

"Harry, listen. How does this sound?"

"Like a load of crap."

"Oh, what do you know?"

The next morning Delia was up early. She stuffed her bra on the small side with Kleenexes, used a ton of concealer to hide the redness around her mouth, and put on a cap to cover her still irritated scalp.

"Perfect! Look out, lead role. Here I come!"

Harry drove her to the audition so she could go over the lines one more time. He followed her into the theater.

"You can send everyone away, Michael, darling. Your star is here!" Delia climbed the steps to the stage.

Everyone turned to look at her. Their mouths gaped open. She was quite the sight.

"I'm sorry. Who are you?" asked the producer.

"I'm your new star. I saw you on TV a few weeks ago. You described me perfectly…big chest, full lips, long, blonde, flowing hair."

"I'm sorry, ma'am. You must not have watched the whole segment. That was the description of who I would want if I wanted the play to fail. See, through the years, I have learned that talent makes the best star, not looks. I'm sorry you missed that part."

"You're sorry? SORRY?? Do you know what I have been through to get this part? My boobs used to be perfect, but now they are lopsided. I have a rash around my mouth, and look at my scalp!" She ripped off the cap and threw it at him.

"I did all this for you!" Delia lunged towards the producer. Harry ran up on stage and grabbed his wife, picking her up around the waist. She pulled the Kleenexes out of her bra and threw that at the producer, too. Harry dragged her to the car.

"I told you, you didn't need any of that. You were perfect the way you were." Harry started the car and headed home. All the way, Delia muttered to herself, "I'm a star, I'm a star, I'm a star."

Saturday Writers 2017

Hidden Treasures
Diane How

Julie Perkins shook her head in disgust when she passed a local newsstand and saw her picture plastered on the front page of the *West Coast Inquirer.* "Free-Lance Writer Robbed Twice in One Day." Black mascara streamed down her tear-stained face. It was just the type of photo the sleazy magazine loved to print, but not the kind of fame Julie imagined.

Her crisp November morning started before sunrise, while nosy neighbors still slept and streets weren't snarled in traffic. Other than a few boxes stacked near the door of her studio apartment, the room was bare. Julie sold the furniture and anything that didn't have strings attached to her heart when she received the certified letter informing her of her father's passing.

With a loud grunt, she hoisted a box of rejected screenplay manuscripts and spiral bound notebooks and carried them to the rusty '65 mustang that would take her back to Missouri, provided the tires didn't go flat and the transmission held up. "Shit," she moaned when she realized the key was in her hip pocket. She tried to balance the overstuffed contraption on the bumper with one hand. The minute she popped the trunk, a gust of wind sent papers flying out into the street. "Crap," she cursed and dropped the box into the trunk.

By the time everything was retrieved and the final boxes were loaded, sweat dripped down Julie's neck. Hot and exhausted, she rolled down the windows, put the car in gear, and took off. *Screw this town. I wish I'd never came here.* Tears stung with the painful acknowledgement.

As a child, Julie swore Hollywood whispered her name in dreams. She envisioned walking on stage to receive an award for best screenplay. She wanted fame and fortune. She wanted to be somebody special. Growing up in the rural Ozark Mountains didn't afford those opportunities. Julie was sure her mother, gone since she was twelve, would have understood. Her face lit up at the mention of the movie theatre in a nearby town.

Her dad, on the other hand, fumed and cussed, calling her a fool for chasing an elusive dream. "Everything you need is right here," he insisted. The more he talked, the more relentless she was to prove him wrong. Julie never forgot his hurtful words the morning she decided to go. "If you leave, don't come crawling back." Too proud to admit defeat, she never returned.

The man standing by the stoplight went unnoticed by Julie until he reached in the car and snatched her purse from the passenger seat. "Nooo!" she screamed. He took off down an alley with Julie following close behind in her car. "Stop!" The thief ducked between two buildings and disappeared. *What the hell am I going to do now?*

Julie circled back around, determined to find her belongings. Surely the man would dispose of her purse quickly. A trash bin caught her eye, and she threw the car in park, leaving it idle while she dug into the nasty metal container. "Got it." Pleased with her find, she brushed off her jeans and straightened her blouse, just in time to see her car drive off. "Son of a bitch!"

The sun glared overhead as she stomped her way to the nearest police substation. In her furor, she hadn't noticed a fellow reporter standing nearby, armed with a camera. "Don't you dare," Julie protested in vain.

"Just doing my job, trying to make a dime. You know how it is."

A park bench became home until the following day when police recovered Julie's stolen car. Wanting no more delays, she dropped the charges against the teenage joyrider, withdrew the last of her money from the bank, and with the warm California sun to her back, she headed east.

November winds had stripped the trees of their leaves. Still, the rolling Missouri hills brought nostalgia and a sense of peace that had escaped Julie for many years. She had cherished the mornings picking fresh vegetables from the garden and the endless hours in the kitchen helping to snap the beans, shuck the corn, and fry the chicken in preparation of the next meal. When the sun went down, Dad would come in from tending the fields and give her a big hug.

As the Bloomsdale exit came into view, Julie noticed the addition of a large truck stop. *Bet all the farmers love that.* She wound her way through the back roads, past quaint little towns, and across low water bridges, in giddy anticipation of seeing the two-story home that held so many treasured memories. She hummed to the music as the miles clicked away.

The euphoric mood imploded when the house came into view. Abandoned years before, the deteriorating home mourned for attention. Not a window pane survived the solitude. The roof barely provided shelter for intrusive squirrels. Even the front door succumbed to the gravity of its unattended wounds.

"Oh, my God," Julie moaned as she shook her head in despair. The words echoed across the barren yard. Gone, the prized rose garden her mother tended to as if it were an innocent child. Gone, the field that once bore acres of corn, now overgrown with weeds. Gone, the man who protected it all. Puddles filled her eyes and she blinked to clear them. In the distance, an image appeared. Frozen in disbelief, she watched the man walk toward the house. "Dad?"

His response, a faint whisper in the wind, wrapped around her and made her shudder. "Good, you're finally home. Follow me."

Still firm and in command. That's my dad. Julie smiled to herself. She reached out to touch him just as he disappeared and was met with the hard surface of the wood siding. "Dad?" Julie stepped toward the front of the house peeking through the collection of spider webs, brushing them aside as she stepped through the opening. Her father stood near the bedroom he'd shared with her mother.

"Should have given this to you sooner. Your mother wanted you to have it. I think it's what you've been looking for."

At the foot of the bed was a slat of wood, slightly ajar. She bent down and dusted off the area before removing the board. With both hands, she wiggled the old cigar box from the snug hiding place. "What is this, Dad?" She glanced up just as her father faded from view. "Dad! Don't go!" Julie clutched the box close to her chest and hurried outside. Her father was gone. She collapsed to the ground sobbing.

* * *

Dr. James Howell escorted Julie to the front row of the theatre just as the lights flickered, indicating the play was about to begin. She glanced at her handsome date and smiled. *Who would have thought I'd be here tonight?* She was tempted to pinch herself to be sure it was real.

It had taken five years, and although it was still difficult to admit, her father had been right. The treasure she sought had been there all along. Had he shared it sooner, he might have celebrated with her.

Inside the box had been a love story like none she had ever read. Unwed and pregnant as the result of a rape, Julie's mother had been stowed away at a convent and forced to place her newborn son up for adoption. After the baby was born, her family shunned her, as did most people in the southern Illinois town where she grew up. Isolated and distraught, she packed a bag and hopped a train into Missouri.

With no place to stay, her mother hid in the ladies room at the picture show in Ste. Genevieve until the theatre emptied. It served as a place to lay her head and her only source of food.

Julie's father, just a teenager himself, cleaned the theatre. He noticed the attractive young girl lingering nearby several days in a row. He became suspicious and confronted her. She begged him not to throw her out on the street. Instead, he took her home and provided her refuge. Eventually, he asked her to marry him. Through hard work and diligent saving, they were able to purchase the farm house and fifteen acres of land, which now belonged to Julie.

Much like her parent's journey, there were many heartaches and pains along the road to success. The search to find her brother, who had been adopted by a prominent family, had taken longer than writing the screenplay, but both had been worth it.

Jimmy touched Julie's hand and whispered, "I'm so glad you found me. We're finally home."

"Me, too. *Finally Home.* I thought it was the perfect title for a play."

POETRY
Any Sin or Virtue Goes

Saturday Writers 2017

Beatitudes
Cathleen Callahan

When I was small,
>with skinned, scabby knees,
>fly-away hair that escaped the bonds of every barrette and
>>braid,
>tiny white teeth wriggling free to make room for what was yet
>>to be,
>and chubby cheeks pink as bleeding hearts blooming beneath
>>the pear tree,

I would sit
>on the rough green spread of the daybed
>on the screened porch of ancient aunt Nancy and uncle Albert's
>>house
>with its narrow back stairway
>that wound to the third floor stuffed-with-yesteryears

next to my grandmother
>of strikingly bright blue eyes and beautiful hands,
>my back cushioned against the brown shake wall,
>my legs stretched out in front, toes pointed decidedly to
>>heaven,
>chin tilted up, eyes closed watching a pallet of colors swirl
>>inside my lids

and wait
>for a sweet warmth to wash from the top of my tingling head
>to the tips of my bare ballerina toes
>as my grandmother read—

>Blessed are...
>>Blessed are...
>>>Blessed are...

Latest Trade Show Notes
Prototypes
Larry Duerbeck

Two machines
The salesman pointed
In the first
Fourteen slots
Seven Virtues
Seen Vices
Each takes any payment
Any legal tender suffices
Your first, simple profits
Assured and reckoned
As for the second
Vending virtual forgiving
Salvation, damnation
That's where
Right there
Your future fortune's
Living

God the buyer—I'll take a flyer
How do You make 'em?
What do you call these two?
humans, said the Devil
That's the name they'll introduce
Production costs are few
Then wait: they'll reproduce!
Where should I haul these two?
—Commingled Mirth—
That little junkyard Earth?

Lost at Sea
Billie Holladay Skelley

Like the weary sailor, searching for the shore,
She knows his image will bring reassurance, comfort, and more.

Each night she grabs the remote, like the scepter of a queen,
Allowing her royal touch to bring life, to the dark and empty screen.

Her bidding produces a glow, that softly engulfs the room,
Bathing her face tenderly, and washing away the gloom.

Springing out of the darkness, at her regal command,
Her love comes to life, speaking phrases only she understands.

Rising toward her like a beacon, beckoning a lost ship,
His lips comfort with words, that cannot possibly be from a script.

Her brain knows this image may circle the planets and reach the
    sun,
But her heart is confident this prince's arrow is aimed at only one.

She treasures this nightly interlude that erases her daily life,
Worshiping a hero who can vanquish discord, conflict, and strife.

In the darkness of her room, they share a nightly embrace,
Always soothing her mind and bringing tears to her face.

While the light in his eyes faithfully brings peace to her soul,
Tragically, it never guides her, to where she truly wants to go.

This love soothes her daily burns, but never quenches her nightly
    fires,
Because she can never taste the lips, her heart so passionately
    desires.

Faithful to this radiant, celluloid image, she's afraid to admit or
    discover,
That she's trapped in a dark box, just like her televised lover.

Adrift in unfulfilled love and always left wanting more,
She has a welcoming harbor, but no access to the shore.

Secret Personae of the Mississippi as the River Styx
R.R.J. Sebacher

Over the centuries
Many of St. Louis's forsaken

Have thrown themselves away
At the riverfront

Sometimes disposal facilitated
By cops on this disciplinary beat

Do they realize when they rise
From the river of death

On the far boundary
They will be eternally in East St. Louis

A Gift of Spirit
Cathleen Callahan

I am not Catholic,
yet here I am,
on a tour of Ireland
with forty from St. Mary's in Illinois.

When I called to ask
if there was still a place,
Father Shawn enthused,
(as I found he tends to do),
Just one, surely meant for you.

He glows with spirit, this young priest,
whose dark eyes spark with delight,
who laughs from his toes,
harmonizes on key with our guide's glorious tenor,

And earnestly, with Sister Susan
of this patchwork green, Emerald Isle,
prays every day
for clear weather.

God enjoys him, too, I think,
for every day the rain stops
and the clouds unzip to the sun
whenever we step off the bus.

Except for today, our last,
at the cliffs of Moher, where the wind whips

and the rain pelts
and I dare not go
too close to the edge.

We clamor back onto the bus,
huddle near frozen in our seats
as Father explains that he had a talk with God
Who said we needed to have at least one day
of real Irish weather.

We can't help but laugh
and be grateful
for all the prayers for clarity
that had worked before.

Most of all I recall how,
clad in vestments arrayed with Celtic knots,
this man of radiant faith raised his arms to heaven
in preparation for mass at the rock of the Holy Well

and a beam of golden light
split the gray
and shone down
on his hands and face.

Any Sin or Virtue Goes

The Contract
Douglas N. Osgood

Pa used to say to me, "Tribulation is drawn to you like a tomcat to a fight."

He wasn't much wrong. I've seen more than most full-grown adults. Guess that's why I ain't afraid of it no more. When trouble finds me, and it surely will, we get right to the fightin'.

Like now.

I buried Pa under a cairn of rocks three weeks ago. He had been all the family left to me since smallpox took Ma and the others five winters back. As he died, Pa pressed his family ring into my hand and made me promise to fulfill the contract he signed last summer—at minimum four hundred beaver pelts delivered to a Mr. Jedediah Nash in Sutter's Fort.

So that's what I intended to do.

Flakes the size of popped maize whipped about in a swirling cyclone of snow and ice that stung my exposed skin. It was the kind of snow that comes in the early spring to the high passes of the Sierra Nevada Mountains—corpulent flakes heavy with the dampness clinging to the spring air. Visibility through the tumult was a yard or two at best.

Daylight disappeared and the inky blackness of night back-dropped the whiteout conditions. Temperatures plummeted. Cold became the greater enemy. My buffalo-hide cape and beaver cap kept my head and body warm enough, but did nothing to protect my face or feet. My animals suffered, too. All mountain bred and used to harsh conditions, even they would die if we didn't make it out of this storm soon.

Somewhere ahead of me was the forest and protection from the worst of it. The swirling wind pushed and pulled like a river's current, making it impossible to keep moving in a straight line. Was I still heading in the right direction?

A sharp crack cut through the howling wind. Dead leaves and twiggy branch ends slapped my face as a tree limb hurtled past in front of me. The safety of shelter must be close by. Leaning into the blizzard, I led my horse, Tornado, forward, along with the string of pack mules loaded down with that winter's work.

The snowdrifts piled higher, and with every step, I fell through to my hips. My legs wobbled as my strength waned. My eyebrows and lashes hardened with icicles while snow formed a moustache and beard on my otherwise smooth face. Stomping hard, I tried to get some feeling back in my feet.

The line of animals behind me stopped. The storm shrieked around us as I trudged my way back beside them. One of my pack mules was struggling on her front knees. I tugged at her lead.

"Come on, girl," I screamed over the fury. "Git up. You can do it."

With a loud bray that echoed ghost-like into the gale, she battled to her feet. The poor beast didn't have much left.

My tracks had already filled with falling and drifting snow, though I hadn't been gone five minutes. I followed the string back to Tornado, the mountain stallion Pa gave me years ago. He nuzzled against me as if to say everything would be all right. If I wasn't so cold, I might have believed him.

No longer aware of anything, I plodded blindly on. One foot rose above the thick, heavy snow, to again plunge hip-deep through the blanket of white. Another step forward. I couldn't stop.

How far did we go on like that? It felt like forever.

My legs gave out, and I collapsed into a cold comforter. Visions of Ma and her people beckoned me to join them in the Great Beyond. Surrender seemed so easy. I missed her. The divide between us narrowed. Grandpap, the great Shoshone chief Running Elk, stretched his hand to me.

So easy.

Pa's rasping voice filled my ears, crying out for me to complete my chore.

Surely Mr. Nash would understand. Death could not be predicted.

But Pa had promised. It was his honor, his word, on the line.

My will was all the strength remaining to me, and I drew on it to push myself to my feet. I had promised Pa. So now it was my honor, my word, too.

The wails of my ancestors drowned out the screams of the storm.

I trudged on.

Tornado stopped with a sudden hard jerk of his reins, waking me from my cold-induced trance. The mountain dropped off. Emptiness met my footfall, and I tottered on the lip of the chasm, my momentum hauling me over the edge. Tightening my grip on the lead with one hand, swinging my other arm in backward circles, fighting to regain my balance, I tried to signal Tornado to back up, to pull me from the brink.

My frozen lips couldn't pucker to whistle the command.

Gravity took over, and I tumbled face first toward the void.

A shrill whistle cut through the wind. Did I do that?

The reins pulled taunt. I lurched to a stop mid-fall. One slow step at a time, my stallion pulled me clear by the reins still wrapped about my fist.

Once I was back on solid ground, Tornado took over, turning us to the left.

Fifteen minutes later, we stumbled into a stand of pine that had been invisible in the swirling snow and darkness. Somehow, his mountain instincts found it. Inside the tree line, the wind died to nothing. We sheltered in the crater of a deadfall.

Soon, flames lapped hungrily at dry boughs broken from the fallen tree. Rolled in my buffalo-hide blanket, I lay between the fire and the dirt-encrusted root ball that reflected the heat back at me. White-hot needles stung the thawing flesh of my frozen face, fingers, and feet. Tears flowed over my cheeks. Warning from Pa of toes lost to gangrene filled my mind. I hoped they wouldn't need to be cut off, though I longed for the pain to stop.

Maybe it was the worry talking, sitting there, I got to thinking about how alone I was. I missed Pa. Ma, too. But I would see them in the Beyond.

My thoughts turned to the living—Pa's family—though we'd never met. My hand toyed absentmindedly with the heavy ring strung on a thong about my neck. The ring had no special meaning for me other than that Pa held it dear. It had been in his family for generations and was the only memento of his life with them.

Pa wrote to them about me many years ago. An ache grew in my belly, and I regretted not asking Pa about them. Would I be welcomed if I went to them?

An hour passed, and the fire warmed me enough to succumb to the exhaustion that over-powered my body.

The nightmares came again.

We were collecting our last cache of beaver pelts. I held our string of mules a hundred yards ahead, while Pa erased our sign. The high-pitched, demonic scream of a mountain lion broke the silence. Rifle ready, I raced back to Pa. He and the beast were locked together in survival's dance. Fear gripped my innards as I raised my Hawken. There was only time for one shot.

What if I missed?

I laid my cheek on the beaver tail carved into the stock. Sweat stung my eyes, and I blinked it away. Desperation guided my shot, and the shell took the catamount right below the ear, dropping her where she stood. Pa's Bowie, always honed to a razor's edge, protruded from her ribs. But each of her claws was their own Bowie. Pa's entrails spilled from between the fingers he used to hold them in.

My screams woke me.

The next morning, white wisps of cirrus drifted across the otherwise cerulean sky. The clean crispness that comes after a storm permeated the air. I rested that day and the next—we all needed it, the mules most of all.

Pa's people, the Fedicks of Baltimore, were much on my mind. Wealthy bankers, according to the only thing Pa said of them. I found myself gripping the ring. Would I be accepted by those who lived in such a different world? Could I accept them and their way of life? The wilderness was all I'd ever known.

The third day after the storm, I packed up and continued on for Sutter's Fort. A week later, I rode into town, dead tired, saddle sore, and hurting plenty. A place never looked so good. The town's doctor patched me up, and I found a room at Señora Alvarez's inn. A hot bath, warm meal, and soft bed sent me right to sleep.

The next morning, I walked to the bank to take care of my business with Mr. Jedediah Nash. Seated across his desk from me, he pulled a cheroot from between his lips, its sweet aroma filling the air already blue from its smoke. Through the large glass window behind him, I watched the flow of passersby on the busy street—businessmen in their top hats and coats, miners in dirty, patched coveralls, and women in colorful, lace-accented dresses. Lamp light gleamed off the freshly polished wood-paneled walls of his office. Rich red leather covered his desk, as well as the chairs we sat in. I had to lean forward to get my feet to touch the floor.

"Your father would be proud of you, Claire. Or do you prefer Running Doe?"

"Either is fine."

"When you told me about his death, I admit, the first thought through my mind was that I could get your pelts for far less than your father and I contracted for, but you surely dispelled that notion immediately.

"So, what are your plans now?" he asked me.

"I'm not sure."

"I could write you a letter of introduction to a wonderful women's college in Independence, Texas. The president is a personal friend."

My fingers found the ring and curled into a fist around it. Hugging it to my heart, I knew what I would do. "Thank you for your kind offer, Mr. Nash, but I'm going east. I'd like to find my family."

Saturday Writers 2017

Deadly Sin
Jeanne Felfe

Mary settled her generous girth into her boss's cushy leather chair and focused her binoculars on the brilliant blue sky outside the 40th-floor window. Two Peregrine Falcons snatched their breakfast in flight and swooped to the ledge overlooking the roof level of the C8 garage. Her hand dipped into the heaping bowl of snack mix she always kept close by—salted nuts, pretzels, chocolate chunks, sesame sticks, raisins,—heck, even chips, Fritos and the occasional Ding-Dong—well, just about anything she thought to throw in it before leaving the house each day.

Whenever her boss was away, she indulged herself with her tasty treats while engaging in her favorite pastime—watching the slate and blue-grey winged birds that the city had encouraged to roost in the tall buildings of downtown St. Louis.

Mary shifted her focus to the lightly colored concrete roof of C8. Few cars ever parked on the top floor, so she had come to recognize the regulars and their drivers. Her second favorite pastime was giving them names, at once describing both the car and its driver: Hippy Blue Prius belonged to the tiny woman with a single blonde ponytail who always dressed in flowing and flowery dresses; Staid Black Lincoln's driver always wore dark pin-striped suits and carried a dark leather briefcase; Hunky Red Jaguar—well, that one belonged to the man of her dreams—young, muscled, with a neatly trimmed beard and mustache, and a dark brown man-bun.

"Mysterious White 4-door. Prompt, as usual." This was a recent addition for her viewing. For five days it had arrived promptly at 9:25 a.m., and for the past four had left precisely twenty minutes later. It was the type of generic sedan usually seen crowding rental car lots. She couldn't place the make—it was just boringly white. Mary was intrigued because no one ever got out. Thinking no more of it, she continued watching the mated pair of falcons. She'd nicknamed them Blaze and Future for no reason other than she liked the names.

+++

On top of the C8 garage, he parked the white rental and waited. After four days of watching, it was time. He checked his watch and grumbled, "Late." If there was one thing he couldn't abide, it was tardiness.

The consuming hunger that had plagued him since Vietnam intensified until the red 4-door pierced the edge of the last turn, drawing his attention. The man opened his car door and strode toward the stairs, knowing she always walked the first ten flights before boarding the elevator to the ground.

+++

Glimpsing movement in her periphery, Mary diverted her attention from the birds back to the cars. "I don't believe it. Someone's finally getting out!" She focused as a tall man with a scruffy beard, wearing a red ball cap, white T-shirt, and jeans, got out of the white car and limped toward the stairs. A peculiar buzz of recognition disturbed her viewing, and she shivered as an unexpected chill skated down her spine. Seconds later, she noticed the buxom redhead she'd previously named Luscious Red Coupe also walking toward the stairs.

+++

Arriving first, he began his descent. Stopping on the first landing, he leaned against the concrete wall and bent to tie his shoe. The redhead approached as he straightened. He willed her to look at him—he wanted her to see. She glanced up for a split second and shifted to the open side of the stairwell.

"Good morning," he said, taking a small step toward her.

She didn't answer. Instead, she turned her upper body away from him, as if to create a wall between them, and hugged the railing.

With the silent fluid motion of a dance much practiced, he twirled as she passed, snapped her neck, and pushed, allowing her to fall to the concrete below. Entranced, he stared down at her lifeless form, as a pool of dark brown formed around her grotesquely twisted head, staining the strands of her long red locks. He inhaled a breath of appeasement as his gluttonous hunger for death was satiated.

+++

"Hey, there he is again!" Mary jumped to her feet, shouting as the man emerged from the stairwell, not two minutes after he'd entered. "Guess he forgot something," she said to the window and reached for another handful of snack mix, shoveling it into her mouth. She watched him limp back to his car, still unable to shake the eerie feeling that had attached itself to her moments earlier.

She refocused her spy glasses on the street below, waiting for Luscious Red Coupe's owner to appear at the exit. For reasons she couldn't explain, fear-tinged bile rose in her throat as the minutes ticked by. She was so busy watching the pedestrian exit she didn't register Mysterious White 4-door turning north on 9th Street.

+++

The white 4-door merged onto Highway 70 West. At the AVIS airport lot, he returned the keys to the counter seconds before a shuttle dropped off a full load of passengers.

"Was everything satisfactory, sir?" The clerk dismissed her tasks, barely acknowledging the scruffy man.

He grumbled, "Ya, sure," and left without another word.

He carried his bag into the men's room. In a private stall, he pulled a neatly packed suit from the bag and hung it on the inside of the door. He grimaced as he peeled off the beard, rubbing his cheeks to remove the last of the adhesive. After stripping off the ball cap, T-shirt, and jeans, he stuffed everything inside the now empty bag. He slipped on his three-piece designer suit and looped his handmade French silk tie around his neck, his transformation almost complete. Then he waited inside the stall.

Once the noise level in the lobby peaked, he left the bag behind the toilet on the restroom floor and paused to straighten his tie in the mirror. Slipping past the throng of people waiting for their cars, he boarded the idling airport shuttle.

After a short ride, he disembarked the shuttle and strolled into the airport lobby. Taking the escalator down to baggage claim, he approached the information desk.

"I'll be needing a cab, please," he said to the clerk, who looked up from her computer screen, brow creased with concentration.

Seeing him, her face shifted, and she fluttered her eyelashes in response, flirting coyly with the tall, devilishly handsome man standing before her. A perky grin lit up her face.

"Of course, sir." She giggled and then added, "Can I get you anything else?" Her tongue traced the curve of her full, red lips.

Responding with a playful smile of his own, he caught her gaze with his grey-eyed stare. He enjoyed watching the blush rise on her cheeks and felt the hunger rising within, rare so soon after a kill. *No,* he reminded himself. *Never anyone you've met. Well, maybe just this once.*

"Will there be anything else?" she asked with another lash flutter and a dimpled grin.

"Can I get your number?"

She giggled again.

With her number tucked securely in the inside pocket of his jacket, he strolled to the waiting cab. "BMW on Olive," he barked, his tone clipped and professional.

At the dealership, he handed the cabby a $50 bill for the $15 fare. "Keep the change," he said and waved at someone across the lot.

"Mr. Caron. Right on time. She's washed and ready to go."

He inspected his Beemer, then drove east, back toward the downtown skyline.

+++

"Bird watching again?"

Not hearing him come in, Mary jumped at the sound of her boss's voice behind her, spilling the last of her snack mix from the bowl.

"Mr. Caron." She rose and smoothed her skirt, glancing at the clock, even though she already knew. Of course—10:45—he was always prompt. "I'll clean this right up," she said, dropping to her knees and using her free hand to grab little bits of food from the floor.

"You look pale. Is something wrong?"

"There's an ambulance, and police everywhere." Mary pointed toward the window, offering her boss the binoculars with her other hand.

While getting to her feet, she added, "Earlier a woman went into the stairwell on the top and never came out." She leaned into the glass, staring at the street below before continuing, "Oh, by the way, Mr. Thomas called about the executive budget. I told him you were in a meeting."

"Thank you. Please dial him." He settled behind his desk and laid the binoculars by the phone without looking out the window.

Mary dialed the number. "Hi, Judy. It's Mary. Mr. Caron is back and can speak with Mr. Thomas now." She handed him the phone, grabbed the binoculars, and turned back to the window.

"They're bringing out a stretcher." She zoomed in and caught a glimpse of unmistakable red hair peeking out from under the sheet covering the lifeless form on the stretcher.

"It's Luscious Red Coupe!" Mary exclaimed, her hand flying to her mouth.

"John, I'll meet you in front of my building in 15 for lunch." Mr. Caron hung up the phone and walked to the window. "Mary, what's a Luscious Red Coupe?"

"Oh, it's a woman I've seen parking on the roof. She drives a red coupe, wears form-hugging dresses, and has long red hair, so I call her Luscious Red Coupe."

"You have names for the people who park on the roof? Mary, you need to get a life." Mr. Caron laughed as he grabbed his coat and headed for the door. "I'll be at the Media Club with John until two. We can talk more about this fixation you have with strangers when I get back."

"Good thing I called the police. They'll want to know what I saw."

Mr. Caron stopped with his hand on the doorknob and turned back toward Mary. "Just what...do you think you saw?" He fixed her gaze with his icy grey eyes.

She waved him on. "Oh, nothing that needs you. Go on. You don't want to keep Mr. Thomas waiting."

Once the door closed behind Mr. Caron, Mary again focused on the street below as the ambulance containing the body of Luscious Red Coupe wailed toward the morgue.

The commotion began to clear as the crowd, momentarily connected by tragedy, began to drift back to their separate lives and within minutes had disappeared as if sucked up by the city itself.

Mary observed Mr. Caron as he waved, greeting John Thomas on the walk. She watched as they moved toward the Media Club, recognizing his distinctive stride, the one flaw in an otherwise flawlessly handsome man. The limp, a leftover memento of time spent in Vietnam, was so slight that most people would never even notice. But Mary did. She noticed everything about him. As they disappeared around the corner, the feeling of familiarity once again raised the hair on her neck. She dropped the binoculars and ran screaming from the room, head-long into the police officer poised to knock.

Sky Burial
Tammy Lough

Shigatse, Tibet
May 2017

Zela Tsarong clutched the frayed handle of a woven basket as she zigzagged through a valley of oak, cypress, and maple trees. The medicine woman had placed five sprigs of Chinese juniper in the basket and ordered the eight-year-old to run straight home to where her sister, Deki, lay dying. On this day, the sweet scent of evergreen eluded Zela as she ran through a thicket, dodging unruly brush and shielding her eyes from the sun's lowering rays of red, orange, and yellow, as a pale moon peeked from clouds stretching across the western sky.

Feelings voiced about her sister's predicament would disrespect the family, so she vowed to silence her thoughts. Deki, and her husband of six years, Rimshi, broke the rules. Their governing country allowed each Tibetan family two children, three under special circumstances, and this was Deki's third pregnancy.

Zela rushed into the small hut she called home and stopped short. Her mother bent over Deki's cot and wiped the girl's brow with a cool, tattered cloth.

Turning to look at her youngest daughter, she shook her head and whispered, "Deki will not be with us when the sun sets."

Zela walked with trepidation toward her older sister, ignoring the distinct smell of iron from blood that dripped to form a crimson pool. She placed her trembling hands on Deki's upper body and felt her harsh, labored breathing. Her skin was reminiscent of the wild white lilies she and her sister liked to pick and place as ornamentation in their hair.

She had helped her mother prepare a tea of tansy and mugwort to expel the baby growing in Deki's womb. The aroma of menthol and cinnamon with a hint of rosemary filled the air, as all through the night she had touched the cup to Deki's cracked lips and urged her to finish the warm, aromatic tea.

Rimshi entered the hut, a trail of tears mixed with dirt ran down his sun-bronzed cheeks. His fists opened and closed several times before he knelt at Deki's side and brought her hands to his lips. After kissing each fingertip, he laid her tear-soaked hand back on the cot. His shoulders shook as he rocked his body to an unknown beat and controlled the volume of his grievous sobs. His voice cracked as he said, "Once the bleeding started, it flowed from her like a river." He bowed his head in prayer. Upon returning his gaze to Deki, he said between sobs, "Migmar, she is gone."

Her mother walked to the cot, and with a hand on Rimshi's shoulder for support, she brushed trembling fingers in a downward motion over Deki's face to forever close her beloved daughter's unseeing eyes. She bowed her head. "Om Mani Padme Hum." O Lotus Jewel, Amen.

The basket of juniper sprigs left Zela's hand and fell to the floor with a gentle thud. She glanced at the disarray at her feet. *Deki would no longer need them.* Her mother, so frightened the government would learn of her pregnancy, kept pushing Deki to drink more of the *abort* tea.

"Do not tell the medicine woman your sister died before we prepared the juniper," her mother said in a hushed voice. "I would like to keep the sprigs, as they may be useful another day."

Zela returned the stems to the basket before approaching her sister. She closed Deki's lax jaw and watched as her mouth returned to a slumped, flaccid state. She turned to her mother. "Deki did not have to die, Amma. You forced her to drink more and more of the abort tea." Her hands clenched into tight fists at her sides. "You forced me to keep her lips moist with tea. She died because of what we did."

Her mother remained calm as she prepared a solution to cleanse Deki's body. "Yes, you are right," she said. "She did not have to die. But, if found to be with child, they would have butchered her as they cut the babe away and sterilized her womb. She took her chances with the medicine woman's herbs and died at home, rather than among barbaric strangers."

Zela returned to her mother's side. "When will sky burial take place?"

"Your father must request permission from the National Civil Affairs Ministry. With approval, we shall have the ceremony."

"Permission? It makes me angry that Appa must receive permission to bury his *own* daughter."

Her mother poured two cups of tea and added a few drops of yak milk. She handed one to Zela and motioned for her to sit. "I agree, it is not right that we must receive authorization to bury our dead," she began. "But, it is the law, and we must obey. It was not always this way." Her mother took a sip of the warm tea. "Many feel the new laws were written to protect the government."

"I do not understand." Zela shook her head. "How is it protective?"

Her mother took a deep breath before answering. "So many of our people are arrested and beaten by officers when they chant for a free Tibet, the government fears the revealing of scarred internal organs during sky burial." She continued in a softened voice. "A government representative supervises the burials and controls the number of people observing the ceremony. Talk to Rimshi. We must notify your sister. Tell him to send word to Chensal. It will take days for the news to reach her in India."

Zela stood in respect for the man who entered the hut. "Appa," she said.

Her mother motioned for him to take her vacated seat. "Will you be traveling to Lhasa in the morning, Norgay?" she asked her husband.

"I shall. Rimshi will travel with me." He took his place at the table, his eyes avoiding his daughter's deathbed. "Now, I will eat."

#

Zela and her family halted when they reached the bottom step of Drepung Monastery. They listened in silence as twelve monks finished the monotone chant of the dead. She turned her head to watch as four men approached from the side of the temple. They carried Deki's corpse on a stretcher and stopped at the edge of the courtyard. The men lifted the body wrapped in white cloth and set it down atop the flagstones.

A knot wound in Zela's stomach as three men in long aprons exited the monastery and approached them. One handed her mother a silk scarf which she took and wrapped around Deki's neck. The men turned and walked away.

Zela touched the tail of the white silk between her fingers and looked at her mother for an explanation.

She laid the palm of her hand over the scarf and whispered, "To signify prayers and best wishes for Deki in her next life." She pointed to a high ridge above the monastery and said, "Let us follow to where the vultures cast their droppings. When the aroma of smoldering juniper rises in the air, they will arrive in great numbers. You will see."

The family fell into place as the group walked in silence along a well-trodden, dirt path. A fenced meadow confined two small temples and the charnel ground. The coroners knelt inside a large circle of stones surrounded by a cluster of colorful prayer flags. They unwrapped the white cloth surrounding the corpse.

Zela noticed how stiff and swollen her sister's naked body appeared. Her throat tightened, and she could not control the steady stream of tears flowing down her cheeks. She looked upward to see a bright blue sky with wispy clouds and felt the day should be dismal and thunderous for such a morbid occasion.

While the coroners sharpened their cleavers on the rocks, Zela directed her attention to the ceremony. They seemed so businesslike, she decided, as if they gathered to sign a banking contract. The overwhelming scent of searing juniper drew the vultures close to the ceremonial gathering.

Zela's mother gave her arm a gentle squeeze. "Your sister left her body as she made her way through Bardo, the intermediate state that proceeds rebirth," she said. "Her soul has already transferred to a celestial place, so now her body will be used to benefit other living things. Do you understand, Zela, that her remains are nothing more than a mere vessel?"

"Yes," she said and inched closer to her mother.

As the coroner made the first cut, the vultures crowded near. A group of men with long sticks waved them away. Zela watched as the coroner reached inside the body cavity and pulled out the internal organs.

He laid them to the side for later disposal, then raised his head and looked to the sky. "Shey, Shey," he called. Eat, Eat. The rush of enormous birds momentarily darkened the sky before covering Deki's body.

Zela grimaced when the huge birds tore away bits of flesh, the matted feathers turning rusty brown. The feeding frenzy seemed to go on forever. Six minutes had passed before Zela noticed a few of the satiated birds take to the air, leaving behind a bloody skeleton.

The coroners returned to the stripped bones with heavy mallets. They pounded them until only splinters remained. A monk placed an earthenware bowl on the ground and mixed the bone fragments with barley flour before throwing the dry substance to the awaiting crows and hawks. A few remaining vultures swooped to devour small bits of softened gristle.

Forty minutes after arriving at the burial site, Deki's earthly body became eternal dust.

*This fictional interpretation of events is dedicated to the people of Tibet, and to their continuing struggle to regain autonomy for their homeland.

Regal Forbearance
Wesley J. Ginther

One eye opened to confirm that I was still next to him on the couch. This was his domain, not mine. He tolerated my presence. He drew breath with measured patience. Body posture belied his alert attention.

His nostril twitched. Both eyes opened and focused on mine. His pupils, large and black, veiled any intent. I glanced away and cautiously inhaled.

He stretched his foreleg forward, sharp claws barred as a tease. As he slipped his paw across the top of my leg, the claws retreated leaving only the pad to touch me. A breath escaped his mouth, in a long sigh.

Our master approached with the morning newspaper underarm. "Max...get off the couch. You know you're not supposed to be up there." I jumped to the floor as he put his cup on the coffee table, leaned down and ruffled the hair of my head. "Good boy, Max," he praised as he settled where I had been.

The cat, still and next to him, closed his eyes in silent validation. Cats rule; dogs drool.

Saturday Writers 2017

The Fugitive
Douglas N. Osgood

Zebulon Price, U.S. Marshal, Dakota Territory, pulled the worn and dented field glasses from his eyes and let them settle to his chest by the leather thong hanging about his neck. The shadow of a cumulus cloud, mouse-grey topped with tall mounds of downy fuzz, slid over him, driven by the strong fall breeze that rattled the branches of the cottonwoods around him. He tugged the collar of his coat tighter. From somewhere, the whippoorwills' calls resonated across the prairie. With the palms of his hands, he rubbed his eyes. He glanced back at his only companion. Zeus, his massive speckled stallion, munched grass growing along the draw's bank. "You settled in just fine, but days in a cold camp's killing me." A yawn escaped his mouth, and he lifted his fist to meet it. "The worst part...," another yawn followed the first, "is two days without coffee." Zeb slapped his cheeks. "I hate the waiting."

He returned to his vigil.

A weathered shanty sat tucked into the notch between a pair of low hills. Shadows cast by the setting sun blanketed the building. In front of it, an old wagon lay turned on its side as if in preparation for Indian fighting. Dilapidated structures—a wood shed, privy, barn, chicken coop, and corral—were scattered about the property. What cladding remained to them had been bleached a blue-grey by the harsh Dakota elements. A few dozen cows grazed on the hillside pasture behind the outbuildings.

The place belonged to Bessie Godfrey, widow of one of the meanest rattlesnakes to ever live. Clive Godfrey had been involved in bare-knuckle prize fights in Boston, New York, Philadelphia, and all points in between. He mauled dozens of men, killing at least four. After his pugilistic days, he married Bessie—only sixteen at the time and twenty years his junior—and dragged her out to the wild frontier. The couple landed in Bijou Hills, three square miles of rolling landscape rising inexplicably from the otherwise flat and desolate prairie. Clive worked the farm some, when he wasn't sleeping off a drunk or beating his wife.

Until the day someone shot him.

Silhouetted against the setting sun, a lone rider crested the far hill and began working his way down towards the shanty.

A smile cut Zeb's face as he lifted the field glasses.

The notch swallowed the man, but he reappeared a few minutes later at the base and continued riding down the grade. By the time he pulled up outside the home of Bessie Godfrey, it was full dusk. Light spilled from inside the hovel as the front door swung open. The rider dismounted and looped the reins around the tongue of the old wagon. A woman came out to greet him, and he bent down to put his arms around her. She pushed the man away, holding him by his elbows at arm's-length, appraising him. The two hugged, and the rider pulled a rifle from his saddle before the pair slipped inside and the shanty's door closed behind them.

Zeb scrubbed his chin and waited.

An hour later, the marshal slid back into the draw and mounted Zeus. He rode upstream along the creek for a ways before turning back towards the farm. Out in the open, the wind was stronger, and he hoped approaching into the gusts would muffle any noise he made.

Leaving his horse ground-tied behind the barn, he eased to the rear of the shanty. He paused in the deep shadows created by a pair of lilac bushes growing a few feet from the kitchen window. Swirling waves in the glass, stained inside and out with years of accumulated grease and dirt, distorted and dulled the light from oil lamps inside.

The petite woman sat at a table. Fancy blue designs ringed the cup she held grasped between her two thin hands. Seated across from her, his back to Zeb, was the man she had greeted earlier.

Long, dark hair spilled from under the hat he still wore, to rest on shoulders no wider than a jug of 'shine.

The man matched the description of Dell, the only child of Bessie and Clive.

When the woman stood and turned to the fireplace behind her, the marshal slipped close enough to press his face to the glass for a better look. Only mother and son were visible in the front room— Dell was the first person Zeb had seen, other than Bessie, in the two days he had been watching. A revolver poked from Dell's waistband and an old flintlock hung over the fireplace. Leaning against the wall beside the front door was a Henry repeater. As the woman returned with a fry pan, the marshal slipped back into the deep shadows.

Somewhere a coyote barked. Another answered.

Crouching as he passed under the window, the marshal rushed to the front and rounded the corner. The startled horse snorted. Zeb paused, then hurried to take a position near the door. The sole window in the front stood on the far side of the entry. Soft lamplight glowed through it.

The horse snorted a second time, and Zeb pressed his back tight against the wall. He eased his Colt from its holster.

"Who's out there?" Bessie called through the door.

The marshal remained silent.

"I'll check it out, Ma."

A sliver of light escaped the hovel as the door creaked open. The distinct *snap, chink* of a rifle's lever action sliced through the silence and the barrel of a long gun poked through the narrow opening.

"Who's out there?"

Zeb said nothing.

Another creak warned him.

The marshal retreated deeper into the darkness, his weapon ready.

The door cracked farther.

The young man pushed it enough to slip through—dumping light into the night—and quickly pulled the door tight behind him. Dell hop-stepped sideways away from the entry. The soft thud from his boot—muffled by the thick grass—was no louder than the tap of a moth against a window.

Zeb cocked the hammer of his gun, the four clicks loud, even against the heavy breeze.

Dell tensed.

"Don't move." Zeb's voice was a rasp-filled whisper. "U.S. Marshal." He tapped the barrel between the man's shoulder blades for emphasis.

The young man froze.

"Warrant says dead or alive. I'd prefer alive. So would your ma. Why don't you set that Henry down real slow?"

The fugitive complied, laying the weapon at his feet. "You the one started that rumor 'bout my ma bein' bad off?"

"Been tracking you for months." Zeb kicked the rifle away. "You were always a jump ahead of me. Seemed the most likely way to find you was to let you come to me." Keeping his gun pressed into his captive's back, the marshal grabbed the revolver from Dell's holster and tucked it away in his own belt.

"On your knees. Give me your hands."

Zeb locked cuffs on his wrists and pulled him to his feet. "Now, wa—"

The door banged open. Bessie stood in the doorway, the stock of the old flintlock pressed to her shoulder.

"Dell, what's goin' on out there? Who you talkin' to?" Bessie's strong voice held a note of concern. She squinted into the darkness.

"Stay inside, ma'am."

Bessie swung her gun toward Zeb. "Who're you?"

"U.S. Marshal Zebulon Price, ma'am." Zeb swallowed hard. "Got a warrant to bring Dell in."

In spite of the weapon's weight, it never wavered in her grasp. "Leave my Dell alone. He's only seventeen. 'Sides, ain't done nothin'."

Stabbing his gun in the small of Dell's back, he jerked his prisoner between himself and the woman. "Mrs. Godfrey, he's wanted for holding up several banks. Killed a man, too."

"Sheriff told me he cleared Dell."

"Not talking about Clive. Shot a bank clerk in Pembina." He stepped back, hauling his prisoner with him. "Set your weapon down. Don't make this worse than it already is."

A glare holding more steel than a mile of rail was her only answer.

Zeb met her stare for several seconds, and no one spoke. The dim light cast its glow over part of her face, leaving part in shadow, but it was enough to allow Zeb to take stock of the woman. Wisps of her long hair—escapees from the bun perched on the back of her head—slapped at her neck. One cheek bone was less prominent, as if it had once been broken. A crook at the bridge of her nose told a similar story. Yet, underlying the evidence of a hard life were the curves of a desirable woman only just reaching her middle years.

"Ma, please," Dell begged, breaking the silence. "Put the gun down before the marshal..." Dell's voice broke. "Please, ma. I don't want him to shoot you." His whole body shook.

"Good advice, ma'am."

"Marshal, that child's the only one here don't know you ain't gonna shoot me." Her eyes narrowed. "No, you could no more hurt a woman than breathe underwater. You're the one with a real problem." She shifted her stance, and her gun's barrel drooped before she quickly corrected it. "Cain't bring yourself to shoot me, and my son's the only thing protectin' you. 'Cept, you gonna have to git him on a horse to git away. How you gonna do that?"

"I'll manage. Kill him if I have to. Is that what you want? At least this way you'll get to visit him in prison."

"Seems you're still the one with the dilemma. He's all I have left. Won't let you take him. You kill him, and I'll make sure you follow right behind."

"And he'll be just as dead, and you'll still be alone in this world."

The old flintlock wobbled again.

"We've been out here a while. Your arms are getting tired, ma'am. That's a heavy gun. In the hands of a strong man, practiced, it's accurate for fifty yards. The way you're shaking, I'll take my chances if it comes to shooting."

Doubt creased her face. "You promise my boy'll get a fair trial?"

"I do. Judge Thompson's as fair as they come."

"You take him off to prison, what'm I supposed to do?"

"Still got the farm."

"Don't own it. Clive lost it in a poker match—drunk. Thorrenson won it. Owns the saloon in town...and the whorehouse. I rent the cabin from him. Livestock's his, too. No way to earn cash money. Few years back there's a month we didn't have the rent." Her gaze shifted to Dell for a moment, a weary expression etched deep into her face. Her attention snapped back to the marshal. "Thorrenson suggested...I...I earn it..." Her voice faltered. She paused for a few seconds.

Zeb stood silent, weapon in one hand, the collar of her son's shirt bunched in the other, waiting for her to continue. Quiet sobs shook the youth in his grip.

She started again. "Suggested I earn it in the whore..." Her shudder shook the rifle in her hands. "Said...said I was still purdy enough to..." Bessie sniffled. "Made Clive mad when I refused. He took to beatin' me. Worst he ever give me." She paused again, but only for a moment. "Was then Dell kilt his pa and lit out. He been sendin' me money ever since."

Zeb's stomach clenched, and a bead of sweat rolled down his cheek—at least he told himself it was sweat. He paused long enough to get some iron in his voice. "I'm sorry for your troubles, ma'am. But the money he's been sending you was stolen from other people with troubles of their own. I've got a job to do. Don't want to kill him, but I *am* taking him in."

"Alright, Marshal." She let the flintlock sag in her grip. "I can visit my boy in prison?"

Zeb nodded.

Bessie glared at him. "I hate you, Marshal."

Smoke Gets In Your Veil
Sandra Cowan Dorton

I've always loved wearing hats. When I was a teenager, hats with veils were the style. A woman was not considered fully dressed if her outfit did not include a hat and gloves. Of course, I prided myself on being a woman of fashion.

Hats came in all colors with different lengths of veils. Some had a short veil that came just below the nose, but my favorite was the hat with the "full face" veil.

Since I had a part-time job, I bought several hats in different colors to match my outfits. I was always excited when spring rolled around so I could begin to wear my pretty spring clothes. My mother was an excellent seamstress who bought patterns in the current style, then made a dress to fit me perfectly. I wore white gloves, but my purse, shoes, and hat just HAD to match.

The type of hats I liked best had thin veils made out of mesh or lace with small holes. The veil would cover my face all the way down to under my chin. There was ample amount of material to reach up and around the back of my head where I would tie a pretty bow.

In those days, I was a smoker. Have you ever tried to smoke while wearing a full face veil? It was a feat in itself. I smoked Virginia Slims. Each pack of cigarettes conveniently came in a mix of different pastel colors. Again, a fashion statement! They were perfect.

If I was wearing a hat with a veil made of lace, all I needed to do was pick the color of cigarette that matched the color of my clothes. I would then carefully slip the thin cigarette into one of the holes in the lace, and I was ready to light up.

If the veil was made of mesh and I was wearing my usual pastel pink lipstick, I would ever so gently hold the tip of the cigarette as close to my lips as possible without actually touching the veil. I would then take a deep breath, light up, and get a puff without getting lipstick on the veil.

Picture it—what a visual—smoke pouring out of the head of a pink, blue, yellow, maybe lime green colored young lady with an outfit that matched her head!

I really thought I was one hot chick, and I would have been if one of those cigarettes had caught that thin material on fire.

Ahh—anything for fashion!

Showdown at the Lucky Mick Saloon
Douglas N. Osgood

In spite of its name, The Lucky Mick Saloon brought anything but good fortune to Sean Patrick O'Conner that day. Twenty years later, it haunts me like my first deathbed vigil, which in some ways it was.

It all started the day Margaret O'Conner and her thirteen-year-old daughter, Elizabeth, climbed off the stage in Santa Rosa, Arizona Territory. Just the two of them, no husband, no father. An unusual situation, but not rare. Life on the frontier was hard and things happened. Men died, went to prison, or drifted, leaving their women to care for the families alone. Folks naturally speculated about Margaret, even gossiped, but no one pried.

She purchased a large house on the edge of town and converted it to a boardinghouse, picking up odd jobs around to supplement. Elizabeth helped at the boardinghouse. The two kept to themselves. Neither spoke of Elizabeth's father. I should have realized who they were, who he was, but the small article I picked up for my local paper had been months prior. And from Kansas.

Santa Rosa grew around them. The O'Conner boardinghouse ended up in the center of town, situated between the barber and my newspaper office, across from the saloon. Now eighteen, Elizabeth had matured into the prettiest filly in the territory. She was tall and fair-skinned, with long raven hair. Every young man for fifty miles had it bad for Elizabeth O'Conner.

The day of the showdown, I sat tucked deep in the darkness of The Lucky Mick Saloon's back corner. From there I had a good view of the bar and the street outside. A half-dozen men sat, singly or in pairs, at tables around the room, most nursing a mug of McDaniel's fine homemade beer. Ian McDaniel, a tall red-head, joked and served frothy brews to three men who stood bunched together at one end of the bar. Their good-natured banter filled the room.

At the opposite end of the bar, a man sat alone, slumped over a bottle of cheap whiskey. No one I'd ever seen before. He tugged a sweat-stained hat low over his brow. Layers of grime and travel dust dulled his clothes, but the Peacemaker hanging from his hip gleamed.

"Fill that bottle for you, mister?" Ian asked as he stepped closer to the man.

There was no response from the stranger.

As Ian reached the man, he crinkled his nose. "Maybe a beer?"

This time a growl answered him.

The stranger piqued my curiosity. A less experienced observer might assume he was absorbed in his booze, unaware of his surroundings. I concluded this was exactly what he wanted folks to believe. He had positioned himself in front of a section of the bar-back mirror not obscured by bottles or advertising. Without moving his head, he lifted his eyes to the reflection, shifting his gaze left and right across its surface, scanning the room.

There was steel on the surface of his gaze, but something I couldn't place festered beneath.

He caught me studying him and stared into the mirror—at me.

And I knew then who he was, though it wasn't until later I made the other connection. I licked my lips and swallowed at the lump that formed in my throat.

The glint of sunlight from outside caught my attention. Glad for the excuse to break away from his intense scrutiny, I glanced out the front window. Kid Colt, his silver and turquoise conchos reflecting rays of the noon sun, exited the boardinghouse and crossed the dirt street. His wide-brimmed hat cast an obsidian shadow over his face, leaving his visage unreadable, but his rigid gait and stiff shoulders told part of a tale, for those who knew him.

His real name was Colton Reynolds. People took to calling him Kid Colt when he was fifteen. Killed a man with a revolver. It had been a fair fight. Kid didn't draw first, but he was fast, and the man was dead before he could fire his gun. A year later, Kid killed again. Bar fight ending in gun play. Self-defense. There had been two others. Both drifters. Both started it. Neither had a chance—Kid Colt was trouble.

And he had taken a shine to Elizabeth O'Conner.

Kid climbed the two steps to the boardwalk, the jingle of spurs faint behind the fierce thump of his boots on the wooden stairs. A moment later he stomped through the saloon's open double doors. The bright red handprint emblazoned on his left cheek told the rest of the story.

At the dance three weeks ago, Elizabeth made it clear to him she wasn't interested. Oh, she danced with him because she loved to dance and none of the other young men would look her way for fear of him. The embarrassment of her loud refusal afterward brought her relief from his advances that evening, though many of us wondered for how long.

Guess she just refused again.

Scattered chuckles from behind fists quieted when they drew a scowl from Kid. He brushed his fingers over the butt of the revolver holstered at his waist and scanned the room, daring men he surely knew would not draw. Not against him.

One laugh didn't stop. "Must've been quite the polecat to leave that," the stranger rasped.

The blaze in Kid's eyes deepened. "Mister, you oughta mind your own business."

"Only speakin' the truth. It's as plain as the no…uh…hand… on your face." The stranger roared then. A guffaw from so deep down, I couldn't believe such a man produced it.

Kid's fingers twitched.

Chairs clattered as men rose quickly and raced to line the far wall.

The stranger laughed on.

Kid Colt's expression changed to puzzlement. Then, as if the joke finally made sense, a huge smile creased his face. He sauntered up to the stranger and wrapped an arm around his shoulders like they were long lost friends. The two of them laughed together. Hard.

After the mirth quieted some, Kid leaned down and whispered into the stranger's ear.

A glower replaced the stranger's laughter.

Men caught starting to straighten overturned chairs, hurried back to their places along the wall.

With a casual grace, the stranger stood. Scarlet climbed his neck and stained his cheeks. Turning to Kid, he snarled, "You think so?"

"Sure and certain." Kid's cock-sure tone and crooked smile would have given pause to most men.

"I might have something to say about that."

Kid smirked. "Filthy old drifter like you? With her? Now that's funny."

The stranger stared at Kid.

Their silence thickened to a palpable fog.

"In the street," Kid Colt snapped. "If you ain't yellow." He spun on his heel and stormed out.

The stranger's eyes followed Kid, but he didn't move. I realized then what I had seen before. Sorrow. Soul-crushing sorrow. The kind men carry when they have hurt the ones they love. Or lost them. Or both.

The two minutes he stood there seemed two hours.

The newspaper man in me grinned inside. What a story! Two gunslingers in a shootout. In my town. An exclusive.

My feet fidgeted. Kid didn't recognize the stranger, I was sure. Should I warn him? Would he back down if he knew? I didn't think he could. And the stranger? Had he heard of Kid's reputation?

What should I do?

I opted to do nothing.

The stranger stepped forward.

McDaniel slipped from behind the bar and grabbed him by the arm. "Mister, that's Kid Colt. Mean as a momma grizzly and faster'n a frog's tongue. Best you stay right here 'til the sheriff arrives."

"It'll be okay, friend. Thanks for your concern." He shrugged McDaniel's hand off and kept walking.

At the doorway he stopped. As he turned around, I thought he changed his mind, but he beckoned me with his finger.

My hesitation seemed to annoy him. He glared until I hurried over. When I reached him, he cupped one hand around my ear and leaned in.

I can only imagine the shock that must have registered on my face as he whispered.

When he finished, he asked, "Understand?"

I nodded. The instructions were simple enough, and I would comply if the time came, but I didn't understand why.

With that, he strode out the door, chin held high.

Following him out, I stayed on the boardwalk. He descended onto the street. The other men joined me. Across the way more slipped out of the mercantile and barbershop to watch.

The man next to me stuck an elbow in my ribs. "What'd he say?"

"Asked me to pass on a message if he didn't make it."

"Against Kid Colt? Sure bet you'll be passing that message on. You know him?"

I shook my head. "Never met him, but I know who he is."

"Well?"

"Read about it in tomorrow's edition."

Tiny dust devils swirled between the two combatants, their tails leaving twisting snake-like trails in the street. Kid Colt and the stranger faced each other. Kid's curled lip twitched, and his right hand hung near his holster. He flexed his fingers.

Thirty feet away, a grim smile cut the stranger's face. His right hand poised less than an inch above his gun.

Bystanders stood tense and mute.

Kid's eyes shone as he broke the silence. "McDaniel, you say it." The words rattled out like a Gatling gun.

The barkeeper's eyes shot open. A bead of sweat popped from his forehead. "K...Kid, I...I, it...it wouldn't be right."

"Do it," Kid growled, "or I'll plug you first, then the old man."

The stranger spoke up, his voice calm and even. "It's okay, Barkeep. Go ahead."

The Irishman paused a moment before nodding his consent. He sucked in several deep breaths. With a nod, he said, "Dr—"

The boardinghouse door crashed open, and Elizabeth hurtled from it, legs churning as she raced into the street. "Daddy! No!"

Daddy? Oh. Of course.

In a blur of motion, Kid Colt's weapon cleared leather, and he palmed the hammer once.

Bang. Bang.

Kid's eyes formed wide circles to match the one on his lips, even as their light went out.

Stunned silence replaced the silence of anticipation. I never saw the stranger move. One moment he stood relaxed and waiting, a split second later, a tendril of smoke curled from the barrel of his six-shooter.

His slug took Kid just left of center. The force twisted the young man as he fired his own weapon. The errant shot turned the stranger's triumph into tragedy.

Kid Colt and Elizabeth crumpled together, at opposite ends of the street.

The stranger fell to his knees and pulled Elizabeth to him. His tears cut streaks through the caked grime on his cheeks. Blood oozed through the hand he pressed to the hole in her abdomen.

"Oh, Daddy," she moaned between sobs. "It hurts so bad."

"Doctor," he screamed. The stranger brushed hair from her face, his touch gentle and caring. "I'm so sorry." His sobs shook his entire body. "Daddy's sorry. I love you, Elizabeth."

"I love you, too, Daddy," she said between gasping breaths.

Doc White appeared. He knelt to touch her throat. A minute later he stood, shaking his head.

Tears continued to stream down the stranger's face, until he at last scrubbed them away with the back of his hand. He gently laid her in the dirt, mounted the nag he'd rode in on, and plodded down the dusty street out of town.

My headline the next day read:

RECENTLY RELEASED GUNMAN SEAN
PATRICK O'CONNER SLAYS KID COLT.
DAUGHTER HE CAME TO PROTECT DIES
IN CROSSFIRE.

The Ice Cream Lady
Tara Pedroley

Every year when summer rolls around, I become everyone's best friend. Wearing my white canvas visor with "Frosty Fun Treats" embroidered across the front, I sit inside a big white van with two huge coolers of ice cream bars and Popsicles. Four long, extremely hot days of the week, I cruise up and down each street, ringing my bell and listening to a high-pitched instrumental version of "Take Me Out to the Ball Game," waiting for the sweaty little kids on each block to run up with money in hand. Parents and older siblings of some of the neighborhood kids follow behind, faces flushed from the sun, sometimes carrying a baby or pet.

I look forward to this time of year, because I get to see some of the same faces from last year—only now their owners are a little taller. I smile inside when I realize that they remember me, too.

Tony, who lives on Echo Lane, was five when I started this route for Mister French. Today, when I see him approach my van, he is a tall, stocky boy wearing soccer cleats and a big smile.

"Heya, buddy!" I say, greeting him at my window. I realize just then, he is also missing his two front teeth.

"Hi, Sam!" he hands me a couple of crumpled dollar bills.

"You're getting tall, and you're missing a few teeth."

He nods, a strand of light brown hair falling in front of his face. "Yep, I just turned nine a month ago. Just before school let out."

"Wow, that's fantastic! How's your sister?" I ask.

"Tate is good. She is three, now."

"Three? Well, let's see…Nine and three. Both are good ages for some Frosty Fun Treats ice cream bars, eh?"

"Yeah." His smile grows even bigger as he points to the rainbow Popsicles on the ice cream sign on my van. "Two bomb pops."

"Comin' up." I reach into my cooler and grab the Popsicles for him. I turn around to find four or five more children forming a small line behind Tony.

"Here ya go, buddy. See ya later."

"Thank you, Sam!" He takes his Popsicles and starts up the street.

My next set of customers range from preschool age to middle school. A few are siblings. One teen boy with freckles and braces yells to his younger brother, "We are getting one treat, Mom said. That's it!"

Upon taking the requests of these young ice cream eaters, I notice a little girl waiting off to the side. Her long black hair is tangled, and a blue barrette holds a few strands out of her face. She's barefoot, with filthy elbows and knees. Her tank top is a few sizes too big, her shorts a few sizes too small.

As each child orders and hands me money, she stands and waits quietly. She doesn't request anything or ask how much the ice cream costs. Her face looks somewhat sad, licking her lips as she watches the other children remove the plastic and take huge bites of their selected treats. A boy about her age, who had ordered a bubble gum ice cream bar, holds it up after taking a huge bite and says, "Too bad you don't have money, Arleigh. This ice cream is awesome!"

She crosses her arms, managing a small smile, and mumbles, "Yeah, so what?"

After I serve the afternoon rush of overheated children, I notice the little girl is gone. It breaks my heart to see a child who has been outside playing in the hot sun for several hours unable to enjoy an ice cream treat.

This goes on for most of the summer. She shows up just before noon with a bunch of the neighborhood kids and waits off to the side as they stand in line and order their treats. She appears again later in the afternoon, once I finish both neighborhoods and begin the route again.

At one point, Keegan, an older boy, also a regular customer of mine, comes to my van to get a treat for his little brother Jack. Keegan's family has lived in their house since he was a baby. They know almost every child and family that has moved into the neighborhood.

I decide to ask about the sad little girl who never gets any ice cream when the rest of her friends do. And he's just the boy to ask.

"Hey there, Keegan! What are you boys in the mood for today?"

"Hi, Sam. Oh, nothing for me. But Jack wants an ice cream sandwich."

"You got it." I retrieve the last ice cream sandwich from the bottom of the cooler.

"Who's your friend over there?" I throw a nod in the direction of the little girl.

"Oh, her?"

I nod.

"That's Arleigh. Her dad lost his job earlier this year, so she and her family had to move in with their grandpa. She lives on Daly Street."

My heart falls. "Oh, that's too bad."

"Yeah. My mom told us that some of her friends are trying to get together a fundraiser to help them out. But for now, they can't afford anything."

I shake my head. "Not even a Frosty Treat from the Frosty Fun Treat van, eh?"

"Nope."

"Well, I will see what I can do to help our little friend Arleigh out, so she doesn't miss out on ice cream and can enjoy a little treat with her friends. What do you think?" I ask with a wink.

Keegan smiles. "I think that would be super cool of you, Sam."

He heads back up the street to the group of children who already have their treats and are eating them in his front yard.

Before Arleigh can step off the curb, I say, "Hey there, kiddo."

For the first time that summer, she makes eye contact with me. Her bright green eyes squint up at me, sweat beads resting on the end of her little nose. Her cheeks are lightly sunburned.

"Would you like a Frosty Treat, too?"

She shakes her head, a strand of long hair falls off her shoulder. "I don't have any money."

I give her a wink. "That's alright. This one's on me."

Her small pouty lips form into a smile—the first smile I've ever seen on her sweaty little face. "Okay!"

"Which one would you like, young lady?"

She points to a cherry bomb pop—the biggest, reddest Popsicle any child could ever hold. "Comin' up."

I hand her the Popsicle, and she jumps up and down. With her face lit up, she rips the plastic from the Popsicle and holds it to her tongue. As she slides it away from her mouth, she lets out a squeal.

"This is the best day of the summer! I finally get to try a Frosty Treat from the Frosty Fun Treat van!"

"You enjoy your bomb pop," I say with a smile.

"Thank you, Ice Cream Lady! I can't wait to show my friends!" She skips away, her long dark hair flying like a kite in the wind as she disappears up the street.

I didn't just make her day, I made her entire summer. To do something nice for a child is a wonderful thing, but to do something nice for a child like Arleigh is something beautiful. Because to me, she is beautiful, too.

Angel in the Night
Jeanne Felfe

The neon glow of the alarm clock taunted Annabelle as if laughing in her face—4 a.m.—again. Envious of her younger self, she wondered if she would ever again sleep without pain, the kind of deep, refreshing sleep that seemed to have abandoned her when her warranties, as she called them, ran out the day after her fortieth birthday. But truth be told, she'd had trouble sleeping since Samantha's death almost ten years before that.

As she usually did when sleep evaded her, she tossed back the covers and stepped into her house slippers. "May as well get the day rolling," she said aloud to the empty room as she tied her robe tight around her petite waist. She'd taken up talking to herself, and the hollow space in her heart echoed around her.

She flicked on the bedroom light and then the one in the hallway as she made her way to the kitchen, a habit she'd picked up after her beloved Maxwell passed, hating to be alone in a dark house. Pressing the start button on the coffee brewer, she pulled up a chair in front of the laptop her grandchildren had given her this past Christmas. She loved Skyping with them, but it was way too early for that. "Let's see what the rest of the world is doing at this dreary hour," she said as she opened it and swiped a finger over the screen to wake it up.

She did a quick check of email, knowing there wouldn't be anything important—there never was. Satisfied her private world was still spinning peacefully, she logged into Facebook.

"Hmmm…three new friend requests. Let's see who they are."

Her son's oldest boy, Sammy, had taught her well how to look at friend requests to verify they were indeed real people. "Grandma," he'd said. "You can't be too careful. There's a lot of trolls out there, and I don't want you getting hurt. If you're unsure of someone, either delete them or ask me to take a look." She hadn't been sure what a "troll" was, but she trusted her oldest grandson.

So, she clicked on each in turn and went down the checklist he'd written out for her. The first two were obviously lecherous men looking for a quick thrill, so she deleted them wondering what they'd want with an old woman like her. The third was different, and as she explored further, she was horrified by what she read. Something was seriously wrong with the young girl on her screen.

Annabelle glanced at the name on the account—John Brown. "What kind of a name is that?" she asked her computer screen. "And why does he have a video of this girl on here?"

Her finger hovered over the mouse button hesitating to open the video which had been posted just moments before, and her stomach lurched. She'd completely forgotten about the pot of coffee, having been drawn in to this peculiar drama. Worried about whether it was okay or whether her computer would self-destruct, she clicked on the "play video" anyway and held her breath.

The image of the young girl surrounded by darkness filled her screen. "Help me. My name is Millie Carthup, and I'm fourteen. I'm being held captive by this man. He got drunk tonight, and I took his phone. Please, whoever is watching. Please, help. I don't know where I—" A shrill scream interrupted the girl and the video went dark.

Annabelle checked her watch. It was still only 4:30, but she had to talk to Sammy, had to ask him if he thought this was real or a, what was the word he'd used...oh yes, poof. Or was it spook. She wasn't sure, but dialed his number.

"Huhlo," Sammy's sleep-drenched voice answered.

"Sammy, sweetie, it's Grandma. I'm sorry to wake you, but I need your help. Right now."

"Sure, Grandma," Sammy said through a yawn. "What's wrong?"

"Can you get on Facebook and look at the link I just sent you? I don't know whether to believe it or not."

"You woke me so I could look at a link? Can't it wait at least until daylight?"

"No!" Annabelle replied, more harshly than she'd intended. "I'm sorry, Sammy. I think a young girl may be in danger."

"Okay," he said through another yawn.

Annabelle tapped her foot under the table while waiting for her grandson. She hadn't realized she'd been holding her breath until he spoke.

"This is obviously a joke, Grandma. I mean, you think it's a joke, too...right?"

"She looks awfully real. What if she is and we do nothing."

"But we don't even know where she is. Look, I captured the video, so we'll have it in case it gets erased, and have taken a screen shot in case the account disappears. Hang on just a sec. I want to google something."

Annabelle sat in suspended animation until she heard, "Holy shit! Oh, sorry, Grandma. I googled that girl's name, and she was reported missing a month ago in Virginia. And her picture matches the girl in the video."

"I'm hanging up and calling the police. Hopefully, they can figure out where this guy is."

"Okay. Let me know what you find out."

She hung up and dialed 911. When the dispatcher answered, she said, "I know this is going to sound crazy, but I think I have a lead on a girl that went missing in Virginia a month ago. Her name is Millie Carthup."

"Ma'am, do you know this girl?"

"No, but I just saw her on Facebook. She made a video and said she was being held captive...and then screamed."

"Ma'am, that's probably a scam. You're kind hearted to try and help, but—"

"Son, do not patronize me. Can I send you a link to the page?"

"No, but if you look at the URL and read it off to me, I'll take a look."

Annabelle did as requested and waited. A few minutes later, the dispatcher came back on. "Ma'am, that URL is no longer valid. And no one in the area has been reported missing."

"Not missing here. From Virginia. Never mind. Where can my grandson send the video he made?"

"Your grandson made the video?"

"No, no, no…he made a copy of it."

Annabelle carefully noted the email address provided by the dispatcher. "I'm going to have Sammy Glischtock email it to you. Please, please, do something," she said before hanging up.

+ + +

Three days later, during the noon news, Annabelle watched through misty eyes as a reporter broke the story.

Millie Carthup Found Alive—Held Prisoner for a Month
Local Grandmother Hailed a Hero

Her hands shook as she dialed Sammy. "They found that girl. It was real."

"Wow, Grandma. You did good. Hey, I've been meaning to ask, why were you up at four in the morning?"

"Just getting old, I guess. The police said Facebook helped them locate the man. He was in the process of moving Millie to a new location, but wasn't fast enough, and they caught him. He was keeping her only four blocks from me."

"No way! How is she?"

"I wish I knew. I tried calling, but the police won't tell me anything."

"Well, it doesn't matter. Because of your kindness, that girl is home with her family."

+ + +

Two weeks later, Annabelle's phone rang shortly after she'd finished washing her supper dishes.

"Hello?"

"Is this Annabelle Glischtock?" an unfamiliar voice asked.

Remembering what her grandson had taught her about strangers on the phone, she asked, "May I ask who's calling?"

"Of course. This is Judy Carthup…Millie's mother?" the woman replied with a tremor in her voice.

"Oh, dear. How is your daughter?"

"Considering everything she's been through, she's doing as well as possible. She…she would like to meet you. Would it be alright with you if we came to see you in Tennessee?"

+ + +

Annabelle paced in the living room as Sammy lounged on the couch.

"Grandma, you're gonna wear a hole in the carpet if you keep that up."

"I'm just so nervous about meeting this little gi—" She was cut-off by the doorbell and raced to answer it, wiping her sweaty hands on her pants.

The young girl standing on her porch could have been her own daughter who had passed almost thirty years earlier. Same lithe, athletic frame, same straight, brown hair, same fawn-colored eyes. Annabelle held the door with one hand, while the other covered her mouth to stifle a gasp.

"Come in. Please."

The woman swept Annabelle into a hug. "I'm Judy Carthup. Thank you so much for listening to your instincts and calling the police. It's because of your kindness that my baby girl came home," she said between sobs.

Annabelle patted the woman on the back, then turned toward the girl. "You look so much like my sweet Samantha," she said while reaching her fingers toward the girl's hair. She pulled back before touching it.

Judy tilted her head. "Samantha?"

"Yes, my daughter. She passed away as a teen."

Seeing the looks of puzzlement on both of their faces, Annabelle shook her head. "What?"

"My middle name is Samantha," the girl whispered. "Something told me that night that I had to risk it all because an angel would be watching. When I searched for someone to add, your name was the first that came up."

+ + +

Annabelle rolled over in bed and stared at the sunshine streaming through her curtains. She looked at the clock and released a deep sigh of satisfaction at the 8:00 a.m. shining back at her.

POET LAUREATE'S CONTEST
Modern Sins and Mitzvahs

Saturday Writers 2017

When the Bough Breaks
Diane How

From the boughs of a cradle, much like you and me,
so dependent on others, so innocent and free.
He grinned with a smile that would capture your heart,
no clue that his world would soon fall apart.

Left alone once too often; forced to grow up too fast.
The pleasures that warmed him were soon part of his past.
The drugs and the booze became his whole life,
such a sense of abandon, such continuous strife

From street gangs to prison, he followed the path.
Consumed by his anger, his hatred, his wrath.
Now death by injection, the sentence he waits.
So hopeless and helpless behind steel gates

The cradle is empty, the smile worn away.
No family or friends to protect him today.
He was still just a child when he sealed his fate.
Can a difference be made or is it too late?

Is killing the answer for the decisions he made?
Is one life for another a meaningful trade?
Does the slaughter discourage repeat of the act?
Is revenge more important than facing the fact?

What lesson's excluded when just learning to crawl
that leads one man to stumble and one to stand tall?
Is it instilling belief in one's own self-worth?
Is it learning to love from the day of our birth?

What's missing from life that leads children astray?
When brown bottles and needles can lure them away?
Are they lacking the skills essential to cope?
Have they sunken so low there's no sense of hope?

To own our own actions, to build on mistakes
To take pride in achievements—is that what it takes?
How much is genetics and how much is fate?
Can a difference be made or is it too late?

Final Visit
Bradley D. Watson

Her hand was warm when I took it
    the hand that held mine crossing the street
    that held a spoon of warm oatmeal to make me feel better
    handed me money at the store
        and keys for the car

Her face was soft when she turned to me
    the first face seen every morning
    that smiled at my jokes and stories
    warmed my heart at the end of the school day
        and comforted me when hurt

Her eyes held mine with her gaze
    the eyes that watched me take my first steps
    that made sure I avoided the traps and snares of life
    showed compassion when I fell
        and brightened when I called her name

Her hand pulls back
    her face turns away
    her eyes are sad
        the light of recognition having dimmed

Saturday Writers 2017

Sailing by the Stars
Larry Duerbeck

Dedicated to
Edna St. Vincent Millay

My sails are set for midnight
They'll not see early light
Nor yet sunset
Catch nets all filled tight

My sails are set for midnight
My seas for every Star
Shakespeare, Milton
Millay
So close yet so very far
Away

My sails are set for midnight
Stars bid, they bid me bright
If a single running light of mine
Should ever find their Pack

See my little life ashine
At its eternal height
My sails are set for midnight
And not for coming back

Face
Bradley Bates

I look up to the moon of your face
and see eyes that span decades
beyond your own years. The smile
that hides nothing, it wants
to shine through alongside its
reflection. I just want you to know
the contours of your face bring
out a warmth not concealed by
the moon, only brightening the stars
as light falls all around me.

For Tiff

Go

Tara Pedroley

"Fly," she said, "Spread your wings, be
someone larger, be stronger, be wild…"
she gave me the pen, I signed the paper,
it was over, she'd set me free, mistakes were made,
tears were shed, the sand had run out, it
was time for me to go.
"You're not meant to stay here," and with
one more blink of long dark eyelashes, one
lonely tear
in our eyes, I was free

"Go," they said, "Be who you were meant to be
in the world. No more room to grow here."
my heart beat fast, my pulse raced. I was alone,
shoved away,
a rain began to fall, I had no umbrella. Clouds were
dark, restless above my head, I failed in that world,
familiar laughter had fallen away from me,
I heard nothing,
just silence and distance. I could no longer be a common
voice among them,
a sound opinion in the room, my family of eager lessons.
I'd been divorced, my absence grew around them.
A flower that only blossomed with guilt, a sunset of worry

The door was closed, the rain hit the windows. My cries of
loneliness were heard by only me.
Those faces, those hearts, those daily words and sayings had
disappeared,
so I build my wall, thinking that maybe one day,
doors reopen, yet with no wounds from the past,
lessons learned from new sunrises, from holding new hands.
One heart to be touched, it is not mine,
It's the mind of those who created the absence between us.
I climb the horse of my future,
I ride away.

Come On Over
M.L. Stiehl

I looked out the window and it was so very bright
After the snowstorm came through on us last night
There were trees all broken and scattered, limbs on the ground
The electric for some was out all around

I checked my electric. It was still on and my house all right
Yet all around outside, things were broken—it was a sight
Part of my neighbors were not so well off, I ask them and offered to
     help if I could
But they were taken care of, by others who would

The night was coming as cold as this day
So I checked some a few blocks away, they were okay.

The icicles were on the trees especially in the back
It broke a limb off and shattered my neighbors shed
As I checked further, a big limb in front had also broke
And fell on my roof like lead

I took pictures of the stuff outside of my place
And called the insurance man to come look for my case
Then I got a call from a neighbor up the street
Their electric was out, and they had no heat.

I said come on over, we'll find room
There was four of them, just three here
We all pitched in, ate, and made room to sleep,
without any more fear

So, goodnight. It's all right.

Saturday Writers 2017

PRESIDENT'S CONTESTS
From Sloth to Diligence

PRESIDENT'S CONTEST
Flash

From Sloth to Diligence

Don't String Me Along
Jim Ladendecker

Life has changed a lot, since the murder. Samuel doesn't smile anymore. No one knows, but me, and I won't tell. He didn't want to do it, I'm sure of that. He doesn't trust me anymore, but he knows to listen. I'm his business partner. You'd think that would make a difference, but he sees me as a stranger holding a bounty on his head. We were once tight as twins sharing everything, not anymore. Now, he hardly talks to me. It all started a year ago, when he met Sharon. Just saying her name makes me twinge.

* * *

It was mid-summer and we were doing a show in Hoboken, hot as hell. Sam was the main player. He set everything up; I played an integral part in the show, but Sam took care of all the details. I didn't mind being second banana; it worked well, until Sharon came along. That's when I felt manipulated. That probably sounds strange coming from me, but it's the way I felt.

* * *

She came backstage after the show, all perky and such with her pushup bra. Sam didn't have a chance, but I knew early on she was not right for him, not right for anyone. She knew what strings to pull to get him to do whatever she wanted. He couldn't see it, but I had experience. It went on for months. He no longer made his own decisions without consulting her. I tried to intervene, but he didn't listen.

* * *

Our shows got worse. Sam tried to go on his own without me, her idea, but it wasn't working. I was living my life in a box and I needed to do something. His life and our careers were flowing into the gutter. I knew it was up to me, I had no choice, but I needed Sam's help.

* * *

Early one day, when she wasn't around, Sam picked me up to practice our old act. I knew then how to get in his head and change our future. It was easier than I thought. Down deep he felt used by her, ready to retreat. My thoughts and plans became his. He knew too well she needed to go. It wouldn't be easy, and it needed to be fast. He followed her to a rundown hotel and plied her with booze until she collapsed. Sam was drunk as well, which is what I counted on. Her death was quick, and no weapons were used, just a soft plump pillow. His guilt made him submit to my every wish.

* * *

We still work together but it's not the same. He's the puppeteer, but I pull his strings. My mouth moves at his request, but now his words are from my thoughts.

"Who's the puppet now…Sammy Boy?"

Treasures and Stories
Sherry Cerrano

"Dan, we need to get outta here. The outer band of Harvey has started to come on shore."

"There's one last place I want to check."

"I don't know..." Curt said, looking at the palmettos bending to the wind. "We've pleaded and harassed. Everybody who's going to leave has gone. It's always like this. Some people won't evacuate."

Dan drove away from Shoreline Drive, heading west. He pulled the patrol car up to an old two-story brick home, an anomaly among the brightly painted pastel beach houses.

Before Curt could grab his partner, Dan disappeared into the house. Grudgingly, he followed. Inside, he found a maze of boxes and junk stacked higher than his head. A surfboard, rusty bicycle rim, and toaster impeded Curt's passage. The musty smell of paper and ink and unknown sources of dirty feet and fried bacon made him sneeze.

The path led to the kitchen. At the table sat a skinny man in his late sixties with a frizzy gray-and-brown ponytail, shaking his head no, holding tightly to his tea-stained mug.

Dan pleaded, "Pete, the storm surge will take your house. You gotta come with us."

"No. No, I'm riding it out. I appreciate you coming by. I'll be okay."

Curt interrupted, "Dan, you're wasting your time. Hey, old man, write your social security number on your arm so they can identify your body. Come on, Dan."

Dan scowled at his partner and slowly backed out of the room, imagining how the recovery team would find Pete, floating and bloated.

Curt planted himself behind the wheel.

Dan slipped into the car. "This one's going to haunt me."

* * *

Days later, Dan talked his way onto a rescue boat. He directed the team to Pete's neighborhood, now unrecognizable. In the distance, a brick structure eerily stood erect and alone, the flooding having washed away or collapsed the beach homes.

The boat motored to a window. Dan entered, crawling over the junk piles. He looked for a body, then climbed the stairs, ending his search in the attic. Among old furniture and the never ending piles sat a scruffy little dog and Pete, eating a peanut butter sandwich.

Seeing Dan, a smile spread across Pete's face. "Hey, man."

"You gotta come with me. How the hell did you survive?"

"House got good timbers. Mack, here, showed up, needed saving. We got industrious. Cleared the attic door and grabbed a few things.

Slacked jaw, mystified by Pete's view of life, Dan said, "Let's go," and led the man and dog to the boat.

Clutching his duffel bag, a tear rolling down his cheek, Pete watched his house fade into the distance and said, "I'll be back. So much ruined. The neighbor kids will miss it. We had fun trading my treasures and Vietnam stories for grocery runs."

Better Than 24-Karat
Larry Duerbeck

The boss called me in, but our business is none of yours. This may be. I told him what I thought. "That's one helluva picture."

"My fiancé. Back in my camera-toting days."

"May I?"

He nodded. I turned towards me a framed black-and-white outdoor shot of a dark-haired beauty, her burst-of-joy face to the viewfinder.

"We were flying a kite. Trying to. She just for sure got it aloft."

"A great portrait. You caught something."

"You're the writer here. Tell you what." He took the photo in his hands. "She still gets more than my kite aloft. Find me a word between exaltation and exultation. That's where I am with her. Meanwhile."

He set it back. "Anniversary's due. I'll buy her the traditional gold bauble. But you know. Words make better gifts than gold."

They're long gone now. A word between exaltation and exultation—they lived it.

Diligent though I was, I never found it.

Most Prized Possession
M. Rose Callahan

The handmaiden's scream pinged against my ears.

I froze. Stiff. Unable to move the one foot kicking back the hem of my gown, or the other foot flexed to support my weight on the pavestones in the garden. My arms stretched open for an embrace never to be felt. My father's greed coursed through my veins. Skin hardened and glistened in the sun. Onyx tresses matted into sheets of amber foil down my neck onto rigid shoulders. Loose hair fixed into thin wire wisps secured across brow and nose. My eyes, opened wide for eternity, only captured cold shades of yellow.

I hear King Midas sob, and I cannot shift my gaze to see him.

Saturday Writers 2017

Fresh Tracks
Judy Giblin

The man I'd picked up from the side of the road had a story to tell. It oozed from the valley at the bridge of his nose, between his eyes. But even though his eyes conveyed discontent, his body moved with purpose. Listening to his story made me reevaluate my own life. The ride I'd given him was worth much more than the gas I spent to drop him where he needed to be.

I also had let love go because of fear. Back then, I wanted to drop the sandbags from the basket, float up, and over—the world—to smell, see, taste, touch, and hear everything it had to offer. And I did. But the something that was missing might never have been revealed, had I not picked up the wanderer who wasn't really wandering at all.

It had taken him years to find her. I knew of her, had seen her in town on occasion. She was older than I, but her beauty shone through in her smile and her manner. And that poor fool had given her up.

As he climbed out of my truck, memories of laughter and take-me-to-the-bedroom looks from the smart woman I'd once called mine, flooded the roads that wound through my world, washing away old impressions and clearing the way for new ones.

I pointed and told him to follow the fresh tire tracks down the once muddy road beside us. And I watched him walk from his past—toward his future—while contemplating my own.

Saturday Writers 2017

Highballs, Hats, and Epitaphs
Judy Giblin

It was common knowledge that the dilapidated house in the woods behind my home was abandoned. But apparently no one had told the busy typewriter within it. I was not alone.

I'd moved to the country, attempting to flee my past. Though in some ways, the past never really leaves us. So, I tried walking—to exorcise my demons. Walking through the forest behind my little house was cathartic, not to mention good for me physically, which this abused body and mind could use more than an ushanka on a cold Russian night.

I remember the chilly fall day that I happened upon the abandoned cottage, which lay not so deep in the woods behind my hideaway. A sound caught my attention. It conflicted with the crunching of leaves beneath my feet, so I stopped walking, and I tuned into the noise. I heard clicking and clacking that stopped only on the occasional moment; the author was clearly gathering the next thought, the next plot point. I could relate to those pauses in thought. They were pauses I'd experienced—deciding which path to take, which path led to a more satisfying ending.

I continued my daily, yet evasive, dalliance with the author. Each time I walked by, the typing lessened. Until the day it stopped. Then I finally opened the door to the cottage and saw the typewriter—not clicking or clacking—but silently satisfied.

Should've Called in Dead
Sherry McMurphy

I zipped my tote bag, turned, and met Jack's eyes. We both smiled. "All ready," I said. "I can't believe our vacation is finally here."

"I know. Two weeks camping, hiking, and fly-fishing in Montana. It's a dream come true." He leaned down for a kiss and took my bag. Together we rushed outside to our Jeep.

Jack stored the last of the gear and lowered the cargo door. Immediately, I noticed it.

"Holy crap! Expiration date, June 30. That's today."

"What?" asked Jack, following my finger, which pointed to our South Dakota license plate.

"I'm sorry, honey. I totally forgot."

Jack checked his watch—7:30. "It's okay. The DMV opens in thirty-minutes. We'll get them renewed then head out." He opened my car door. "We can't travel on expired plates."

We pulled into the parking lot. Twelve people already stood in line. I shot Jack a worried look. "It can't take that long. Come on," he said.

Twenty-five minutes later, we stepped to the counter. The clerk's crabby face never made eye contact with us as she stated through clenched teeth, "Name and business."

"Carly Benson, and I need to renew my license plates."

"You got all your paperwork?" She continued to look down, organizing papers around her desk.

I read her name tag—Agnus. She looked to be in her late sixties. When I didn't verbally respond, she finally looked up and accepted the paperwork I held. Agnus read over the forms, slowly and methodically, before separating them to process.

Seriously? Does it really take this long? Not wanting to be rude, I tried my best to be patient, but I knew I wouldn't be able to handle much more of her painstakingly slow movements.

Jack leaned in to whisper in my ear, "What a sloth."

I grinned, working hard to suppress a giggle, and shook my head in agreement.

"Ma'am, is there a problem with our paperwork?" I asked. "We're leaving on vacation and need to get going." The wall clock stated 8:47. The sassy, gum-smacking coworker sitting next to "sloth" had already serviced five people while we waited. She grinned at us.

Switching my stance from one foot to the other, I looked around and gasped. I drove my elbow into Jack's rib, and swung my eyes toward Agnus when Jack looked at me. His eyebrows jutted up. "Sloth" sat fast asleep, eyes firmly shut, her head bobbing. She held our paperwork in one hand, a stapler in the other. "O.M.G." I mouthed.

Jack shook his head and casually nudged his hand against the pen container. It crashed over, spewing its contents on the counter and down below to "Sloth's" desk. She startled awake, refocused. We grinned.

The task finally completed, we rushed toward our Jeep. "That woman was awful. How can anyone move so slowly?" I asked. "She needs to give it up."

Jack laughed. "Better yet, she should've just called in dead today. She's practically there anyway."

PRESIDENT'S CONTEST
Poetry

From Sloth to Diligence

Saturday Writers 2017

Entertain Me
Judy Giblin

Entertain me;
Make me laugh
Or cry,
Or wonder why
I felt nothing.
But then, the nothing
Must be something
To make me wonder
About it at all.
And in my wonder
If I deduce,
Contemplate,
Or bristle—
I have been entertained.
Bravo!

The Dance of the Bird Feeder
Donna Mork Reed

Birds feed diligently
On seeds all winter long.
Cardinal red lands precariously
Gripping with talons sharp.
Shares a ledge with a chickadee
Spin your partner, promenade.
It's a bird brigade.
Red headed woodpecker
Trills his arrival.
Titmouse dashes in.
Watch the feeder suspended on string
Spin and spin and spin.
Purple finch saunters in
Blue jay hogs the feed.
On the ground, soft mourning doves
Feast on fallen seed.
Grand finale, in one accord
They launch into the sky
Leaving behind a sneaky cat
Who just now happened by.

At the Back of Tomorrow's Closet
Cathleen Callahan

I'm not sure I have a cure
for the mullygrubs,
or want one.
Lying around in a blue funk
may be just what I need,
a foyer to the rest of my life
dimly lit,
peer glass on the side reflecting a braless silhouette
in gray sweats
and pink turtleneck,
the woman within not yet sure
she wants to straighten up,
square her shoulders
and step into the oncoming future.

Maybe I just need to settle in
to weekend hair and naked eyelashes,
the audacity of unshaven legs
and funky flowered socks,
breathe around the aloneness
and bite my cuticles until I've bruised my thumbnails
into wavy hillocks.

Maybe I just need to sit here with my writer family,
notice the vascular artistry of spider veins tattooing my legs
and watch the last of the clinging dry leaves

of the neighbor's tree flutter last sighs
before new buds push through and unclasp their hold
on yesterdays gone.

Maybe I just need to be exactly where I am,
wrapped in mulleygrubs as in a prayer shawl
until baking a cake appeals
or I've wasted away enough to fit
into the secret size 12 red dress
waiting in a plastic sheath
at the back of tomorrow's closet.

California Burns 2007
R.R.J. Sebacher

This Halloween a dragon rides the Santa Ana winds
Spitting smoke and flaming embers, as sirens scream
One half million who did not flee
Huddled in churches and stadiums
Politicians and preachers to president and lord implore
No child of Satan, they cannot affect her
She is Nature's wrath for her laws ignored
Her work will release other elemental force
After she has scorched the earth
Her sister Water and Earth's mud golems
Will tumble and slide in her wake
Though they will slay her
Quench her fiery breath
Her revenge has just begun
They will rebuild on the same steep slopes
Amidst thick brush and pine
Child of Fire and Wind she will be reborn

Are You Sleeping, Muse?
Cathleen Callahan

Are you sleeping, Muse,
slumbering through ice-encrusted weeks
as this body grows cells to fill the spaces
created by the demise
of crippling debris?

Are you dreaming, Muse,
of a body renewed, frolicking through flower-strewn fields,
twirling like a child giggling as grasses and tender shoots
tickle her legs and cushion her toes,
wakening joy from winter's sleep?

Are you stretching, Muse,
as I sit beneath clear Western skies,
warmed by desert breezes?

Are you ascending,
unwrapping yourself from weighty blankets of silence,
peeling yourself from finished dreams,
surfacing,
sighing,
aroused by the coming caress
of tropical heat and volcanic fire?

The Shadow's Mistake
Tara Pedroley

I followed her, like a spy with many
Questions I needed answered
I waited for her to listen, I had
To try and hold her hand.
I saw her as a mystery, a dark shadow
That was only colored in my eyes.
I felt her sadness, smelled her anger
But I made a mistake.

I followed her too close, I couldn't let her go
Time fell away from me, I cared too much.
I framed her like a picture that no one
Wanted to look at,
But I saw it clearer
When I made a mistake.

I followed her through caves I barely fit
I tried to hold her hand, and tell her
The light is there for her to follow
I fought for her, doors were slammed
I bit down hard and cried because
I knew I made a mistake

I stopped following her, I saw the forest and got lost
It wasn't worth my heartache, it freed me first
I let it ache, turned to walk away telling myself
Not to make another mistake....

PRESIDENT'S CONTEST
Prose

From Sloth to Diligence

Misunderstood
Jeanne Felfe

The rap on the metal cubby frame forced the muscled young man to look up from his computer.

A tall man filled the thirty-six inch opening with little room to spare. "Marshall, are you done with that report yet? I needed it a half hour ago."

Marshall plucked one of his ear buds out and said, "Uh…that was due today?" He picked up a stack of papers and rifled through them.

The man heaved a sigh and ran a hand through thinning hair. "How am I supposed to run a business without the reports I need? This is the second time this week. When can you get it to me?"

Marshall glanced at his watch. "Uhm, an hour…maybe?" He bounced his left knee to silent music. As his gaze flitted around the small space, he nodded like one of those bobble-head dolls.

"One hour. No more. Bring it to my office when it's done."

Marshall touched the side of his head with two fingers in a mock salute and spun back to his computer.

An hour and fifteen minutes later, Marshall knocked on the door of Mr. Sampson's office. "I've got that report for you."

The man didn't look up, just said, "Never mind. I had Suzette do it."

Marshall strode into the room and dropped the pile of papers into the trash can next to Mr. Sampson's desk. "I sure wish you'd of told me not to bother."

"Excuse me? Next time, get it to me when I ask for it. Or maybe you'd like to go work somewhere else?"

Marshall held his hands in front of him, palms facing the senior man. "Whatever, man." He spun on his heel and walked out the door, heading straight for Suzette's cubicle.

"So, what gives?" he said, without announcing his presence.

Suzette held one finger up behind her, as if to indicate he should wait, and clicked with her mouse, before turning around. "What can I do for you, Marshall?"

"You did my report? You trying to show me up or something?"

A slight smirk crossed her face. "Well, if you'd gotten it to Ted on time he wouldn't have needed to ask me." She crossed one leg over the other and swung her perfectly clad foot.

"Oh, so it's Ted now? I think I'm getting the picture."

"Picture? What picture? I do my job. More than I can say for you. If you did yours, maybe you'd be getting the promotion instead of—"

"Wait. What? *You* got the promotion? But I've been here two years longer than you."

"Oh, crap." She held her hand over her mouth in mock surprise. "I shouldn't have said anything. They aren't announcing it until Friday."

"That shoulda been my promotion, and you know it." Marshall paced in the small space, like a caged leopard in a zoo.

"I know nothing of the sort. You don't get it, do you? You're lazy. You show up late, you leave early, you disappear for hours at a time, and no one knows where you are. What did you expect?"

"I get it now." He stopped directly in front of her. "You're sleeping with him."

Suzette jumped to her feet, shoving him out of her way. "Seriously? So you're lazy and a misogynist? The only way a woman can get ahead is to give head, is that what you're saying?"

A low chuckle rumbled from Marshall's chest and out into the hallway. "Well, I can't compete with that."

"You know, you don't report to me, yet, but when you do, I won't tolerate your sloth-like behavior. You keep doing what you're doing, and you're gone. You hear me? No way I'm letting some lazy slouch keep me from advancing in this company."

Marshall shook his head slowly. "You can't fire me, and you know it."

"Get out!" she hissed, pointing to her cubby opening.

* * *

Six months later, Suzette paced in her office, glancing at her watch. *Late again. That's it! Today's the day.* She moved toward her door but stopped when something that sounded like loud popcorn came from down the hall. That was followed by a scream and more pop, pop, pop.

She stepped through the door and was immediately grabbed and shoved back inside her office.

"What the—"

"Ssshhh." Marshall held a finger to his lips while he quietly closed and locked her door.

"Please, don't." She turned her head in the direction of more pop, pop, pop, and another scream, before looking back at him.

"Ssshhh," he repeated. He put his hand on the doorknob and turned to her. "Lock the door behind me. Get under your desk and don't come out until I tell you. And call 911—tell them we need SWAT and an ambulance."

He unlocked the door and eased it open, slowly sticking his head out and looking both ways. "Lock it," he said again, and then he was gone.

Suzette did as instructed, her hands shaking as she turned the lock. She kicked off her heels, ran to her mahogany desk, and grabbed her phone. Tucking her legs, she curled underneath and pulled her chair up close. Tears burned her eyes as she dialed. Her muscles trembled with each muffled pop and scream.

A few minutes later, the sounds stopped. She heard a knock on the door at the same time she heard the shrill wail of sirens.

"Suzette, you can come out now." Marshall's voice was loud and powerful. She'd never heard this kind of strength from him before.

She crawled out from under the desk and ran to the door. "What—" She stopped and gasped at the sight of his blood-covered shirt. "You were shot?!"

He looked at his shirt and shook his head. "Nah. It's not mine." He looked around her toward her in-office restroom. "You got towels in there?"

She nodded.

"Grab all the towels, rags, whatever you can. We've got wounded," he commanded before running back down the hall.

Suzette loaded her arms and raced in the direction he'd gone. She arrived in Mr. Sampson's office just as Marshall was standing, his shirt left in a pile on their boss's chest. He looked up and shook his head, then wasted no time running out of the office to the next person.

Suzette stared at Ted's lifeless body, swallowing the vomit rising in her throat.

"Suzette!" The sound of her name being yelled shook her from her haze, and she turned in that direction. She handed Marshall supplies and watched in terrified awe as he worked on Mr. Sampson's secretary, Linda. She noted the angry, raised scar across the back of his shoulder, but now wasn't the time to ask about it.

He pressed a towel to Linda's thigh, looked up at Suzette, and grabbed her hand, pulling her down. "Here, press down hard."

"Me?" she asked before dropping to her knees and doing as he instructed. Bright red soaked through the white towel almost instantly. She swallowed back her fear and kept the pressure on.

As Marshall reached the next person, a loud voice echoed through the halls. "Put your hands where I can see them." Marshall ignored the command and yelled back, "Gunman's dead. We need a medic in here, stat!"

* * *

After the last ambulance pulled away, Suzette stood in her blood-soaked dress, which had once been sunflower yellow, surveying the aftermath of the carnage. When Marshall reached her, she threw her arms around him and finally released the sob that had been lodged in her chest. "Ted's dead."

After a minute, she pulled away and stared at him. "Thank you. How—"

His single head shake stopped her from asking the rest of the question.

* * *

The office reopened a week later, a few days after Ted Sampson's funeral. Although the carpet had been replaced and the holes in the walls patched, there was still an eerie sense of something that might never be whole again. Mr. Sampson's office sat empty, leadership having decided to allow some time to elapse before announcing a replacement.

Suzette hovered outside Marshall's cubby trying to collect her thoughts. Finally, she tapped on the frame. "Marshall? Got a minute?"

"Sure." He gestured to his side chair and Suzette eased into it, tucking a designer-shoe clad foot behind one ankle.

"Thank you again for what you did. You could've been killed."

"Someone had to stop 'em." His left leg bounced as he waited for her to continue.

"It's scary that something like that could happen…here. Mr. Sampson fired that guy just last week. At my suggestion. I think he was coming for me next. You saved me and who knows who else."

She stopped and cleared her throat. "Do you like working here?"

He shrugged. "It's a job."

"Then, why do it?"

"'Cause I got a wife and two kids. My daughter has asthma, so we need the insurance."

"You know…my brother owns a company, and I think he could use someone like you."

"Someone like me? You mean a lazy slouch?" he said, a frown forming on his brow.

"No. I was…I was wrong about you. I mean someone…who can handle themselves in a crisis."

"Yeah, I don't want to be a security guard." Marshall turned his chair slightly away from her and looked over at his computer screen. "I got work to do."

"I'd be happy to talk to him about you. After what you did, I'm sure he'd hired you."

Marshall huffed, then asked, "Are you firing me?"

"No. God, no. I just wanted to do something for you to say thank you. If it wasn't for you, I might be dead right now. Look, my brother Ben…Ben's company works with at-risk teens in an Outward Bound type of program. Some of these kids come from violent and abusive backgrounds. He takes them out into the wilderness and teaches them skills to help them gain confidence."

"And you think I'd be good at this because I stopped a gunman?"

"Partly. But also I googled you, and I know what you used to do…used to be. Before."

"Yeah, before my partner and I were ambushed. Before I failed to protect him. Before he got killed. And you think I should be working with troubled teens. Lady, you don't know anything about me."

"I know you're not happy here. I know your family needs you. I'm offering you a chance to do something meaningful again. You weren't meant to sit in a cubicle and push paper." She reached out and handed him a card. "Just talk to him."

* * *

Suzette picked up her phone on the second ring. "Ben," she said, genuinely happy to hear from her younger brother.

"Hey, sis. I just wanted to call and thank you for sending Marshall my way. Man, this guy is a workhorse. He's here before anyone else and stays as long as anyone needs him. The teens love him, and he's good with them. We had this one kid have a major meltdown. We were all afraid of losing him, but Marshall stepped in and took charge. That kid became one of the leaders by the end of two weeks."

"That's awesome, Ben."

"If you find any more like him, send them my way. His work ethic is something you just can't teach."

"You got it, brother."

"Bye, sis."

Suzette hung up the phone and looked around the office she'd always wanted. She hadn't wanted to get it this way, but was grateful the lazy slouch she'd almost fired had been there to save her life.

Cold Case Diligence
Donna Mork Reed

"When you going to put away that case? It's cold as the tundra. Ain't nothing in there that hasn't already been beat to death." Officer Marco flopped into his seat, dislodging a precarious stack of paperwork on the abutting desk.

Sam leaned on his elbow and ran his hand through his hair. "I'll put it away when I can officially close it."

Marco shoved the loose pile aside, set his coffee front and center, and rolled his eyes. "You know what you are, Marco? A rabid dog with a bone."

"I've always heard diligence is a virtue." He shrugged and returned to the file.

One line in the Sarah Holloway file caught his eye. There was a brief mention of a café the missing girl liked to frequent, but no information listed as to whether there was an investigation beyond the initial questioning of the customers. Sam flipped through the file once more, but didn't find anything. That niggled at him. No stone left unturned, yet he could see several stones that were undisturbed. He put the file in his briefcase and finished his coffee, tossing the empty paper cup into the overflowing can by his desk. *Someone should really empty that*, he thought as he grabbed his jacket and headed out the door.

Pulling up in front of Maddie's Café, a local hangout for writers, artists, and college students, he scanned the scene, noting the exterior. A bike path meandered behind the building and into the forest. Pushing himself out of the car, he felt the extra twenty pounds he carried around that his doctor kept insisting he needed to lose. Doc might have a point after all.

He removed his shades inside the café, letting his eyes adjust to the dim interior. A middle-aged woman mopped the counter with a well-used rag, moving condiments around.

"Help ya?"

Sam approached, flashing his badge.

"Ma'am. Good afternoon. I was wondering if you could tell me anything about this girl." He held out a copy of the photo.

She paused in her endeavor and looked at it, then at Sam. He watched her face, half expecting her to chew gum while she spoke.

"She disappeared a while back. I didn't figure anyone was still looking for her."

"It's a cold case. Sort of my specialty. I'm just going over some of the details, seeing if I can find anything that might have been overlooked by previous investigators."

She shook her head and pursed her lips. "It's a shame. She was a sweet girl. Come in here about two, three times a week. Used to hike the trail behind here. Always very nice. Just a damn shame."

"Yes, ma'am, I agree with you on that note. Anything else you can tell me about her? Anyone she used to hang out with? Anyone you noticed around her the last day she was seen you didn't recognize?"

"Well, it was a while back. She had a boyfriend, but they had broken up. No one I saw with her. She was pretty much a loner, besides her boyfriend. I don't think I can help you. I really wish I could."

"You say she hiked this trail behind the building?"

"Yes. She enjoyed walking, and the trail back there is real nice. Goes into some real pretty wooded areas. Continues for several miles beyond the edge of town. I've only walked it a few times. I'm on my feet enough as it is, don't need the extra mileage on these dogs." She pointed at her tennis-shoe-ensconced feet.

"I see your point. I think I'll take a look at the trail. And if you think of anything else, give me a call, won't you? Or if you know of a regular that I could also talk to, I'd appreciate it." He handed her his business card. She took it, and after a quick look, placed it in her apron pocket.

He walked around the building, passing a bike rack on the side of the café. He followed the trail into the woods, finding the town quickly left behind and the rural feel of the trees settling over him like a blanket. He breathed in the fresh, crisp air, the first sign of autumn beginning to make itself known.

He kept his eyes on the trail and the surroundings, taking in the deep underbrush, the steep inclines. It really was a beautiful trail, but also was full of nooks and crannies and places a person could hide out and cause trouble. He almost wished he wasn't a cop and could just enjoy the sheer loveliness of the place, not seeing potential danger behind every rock.

A low rise sported a railing next to a drop-off that ended in a pond. He stopped and took in the view. Heavy brush around the pond, tall trees, thick leaf-litter covered the ground, and the clear water reflected a piece of sky that shone through the canopy. This was a beautiful trail. He could see why anyone would be drawn here if they had a love for nature.

He turned away and continued the walk. In another mile, the trail ran into a park that had picnic tables and a baseball field at one end with wooden bleachers for the local sports fans. Sam took it all in, then took a seat on a bench placed at an angle facing the park. Leaning his elbows on his knees, his brain would not stop going over the facts of the case. Last known location. Good student. Never late for work. Friendly girl. Favorite hangouts. Breakup with boyfriend. A prime suspect who was ruled out with an airtight alibi.

A mother sat watching her two young children playing on a dome climber. A man across a large grassy area was tossing a Frisbee to a border collie making amazing leaps into the air, catching the toy with ease and returning it to his master, tail wagging. A man near a swing set scanned the ground with a metal detector.

An idea struck Sam. He stood up and walked over to speak with the detectorist.

A week later, Sam strolled the path for the fifth time. Approaching the bridge, he noticed a young woman leaning against the banister, talking to herself. She stopped suddenly when she caught sight of him and gave him a quick nod.

"Good afternoon, ma'am. Great day for a walk."

"Yeah. This is my favorite spot," she said.

He joined her at the overlook and took in the view, the reflection as clear as the first day he had seen it.

"It's a very pretty spot," he conceded. He looked at her again, and something ticked inside his mind. He knew this woman. Or at least the face. "Sam. Sam McGregor," he said, sticking his hand out.

"Aurora. Nice to meet you," she took his hand in a nervous shake.

The name definitely clicked recognition in his mind. "Weren't you friends with Sarah Holloway."

The girl's eyes widened in shock. "I...uh...yeah. That was a few years ago." Her knuckles grew white as she gripped the rail. That was odd.

"Too bad about her disappearance." He decided not to tell her the nature of his job. She seemed scared, and that would only panic her more. "She seemed like a nice girl."

"As long as you didn't date her." Her eyes narrowed, and she stared into the woods across the pond. The nervousness dissipated, replaced by a tense rage.

"What do you mean? Did you date her?" he wondered how much she would share with him.

"No, I didn't, but Roger did. And she hurt him bad."

"Oh, yes, Roger was her boyfriend, wasn't he?"

"Was. She dumped him. Really broke his heart. It was a long time before I could get him to trust me. He thought I would crush his heart like she did, but I told him I wouldn't. I'd never be like that. I'd never be like her." She spat into the pond below, sending small ripples across the mirror face of the pond.

"Wow, that's a shame. Well, have a good day. It was nice to meet you, Aurora."

He walked away as nonchalant as he could muster, a new angle formulating in his mind. There were several unturned stones, indeed.

* * *

Each ping of the metal detector sent Sam's heart skipping. He tried to contain himself as the man, a local hobbyist named Stewart, dug up several old bottle caps, a license plate, and seventy-eight cents in spare change lost throughout the park. When the ding sounded on the far side of the pond, Sam felt it in his bones. This was the one.

Stewart kneeled and dug with his digging spade. After a minute, he called out, "Hey, Sam, I think you should look at this."

Sam pushed through the bushes, wiping a spider web off his face, then squatted. Stewart held a slim bracelet with a heart-shaped charm out of the dirt.

"I think it's still…uh….attached…" he stuttered, his tanned face paling visibly.

Sam poked in the hole, pushing dirt aside and found what could only be a bone inches beneath the bracelet.

"I think you're right. We need to call this in." He stuck his hand out. "Thank you, Stewart. I think you may have found our missing girl. We are one step closer to solving this case."

Stewart shook his hand. "Thanks. I'm glad I was able to help. But….wow….I've never found a body before."

Sam put a reassuring hand on his shoulder. "Good job. Sarah would thank you."

Stewart looked down, blushing under the compliment. The two men walked out of the woods, silent and introspective. Sam called for an investigative team and coroner.

"Do you know it's her?" Stewart asked, standing on the opposite edge of the path looking back into the woods they had just left.

"Well, it won't be confirmed until the coroner verifies, based on sex, age, and size of the skeleton, then checks the dental records. But I'd bet my next paycheck on it. That bracelet was described in the file."

Stewart shook his head. "Wow."

"Yes. Definitely a wow," Sam smiled at the bitter-sweet moment. In all disappearances, he always hoped for a person to appear in some distant city under a new name. A dead body always proved the worst in the human world.

* * *

One month later, Officer Marco stuck his hand out.

"Seems I owe you an apology. Congrats on closing the case."

Sam smiled. "Thanks, Marco. I just wanted justice for Sarah."

"I'm in awe," Marco said.

"Not necessary. I got a break. If I hadn't run into her so-called friend, I never would have followed up on that angle."

"But, I thought it was the boyfriend."

"Nope, he was cleared. Turned out, her jealous friend didn't like that Sarah broke up with Roger. And she took things into her own hands, in more ways than one. Tricked Sarah into following her into the woods, then buried her nearly in plain sight. She took some kind of maniacal pleasure in knowing Sarah's body was within sight of her walking hand in hand with Roger. As if that would affect Sarah after the fact. Even in death, Aurora wanted to flaunt the fact that she had Roger in her grasp."

"Stroke of genius, putting that detectorist to work on the case."

"Pure luck. It wasn't until I ran into Aurora I was able to redirect him to the part of the park I had a suspicion about. He wasted days searching areas not related to the crime scene. But once in the area near the pond, it was only hours when he got a hit from her bracelet."

"Well, your diligence paid off. I take back all those things I said about you before. Well, maybe not all I said about you," he guffawed. "Good job, man. Good job."

With that, Sam wrote "closed" on the folder and put it into the "To be filed" slot. Case closed.

The Coin Toss
Tammy Lough

Jack's pain escalates out of control, and he grabs the work-bench to keep from falling. Later, when his jaws ache, he won't remember how hard he had gnashed his teeth. Another wave passes through his body, and the pain bends him over 90-degrees as if he had reached to tie an unlaced shoe. The slightest movement feels akin to a knife sharpened to razor blade precision, slicing through his tissues.

Why? Is he a murderous psychopath receiving retribution for a hideous crime? What gruesome act did he execute to deserve such suffering? There exists no murderous monster attacking with sadistic weapons or the cutting of a surgeon's knife before anesthesia's merciful unconscious state. The monster lives within, stalking his every cell with what feels like a torch dipped in molten lava randomly tapping exposed nerves. The brain and spinal cord cancer are eating him alive.

He plummets to the floor with a teeth-jarring fall and glances upward. The tall, narrow curio cabinet he bumped is teetering and in danger of crashing on top of him. Will the tri-sided glass panels sever his arteries? Will he watch blood flow and puddle until the reaper takes his soul? Does he care?

The cabinet remains upright, and he rolls to his side. His left knee took the brunt of his fall and now resembles a super-sized, beefy, red tomato. For three years, severe pain has followed him like a dedicated sentry—never tardy or a no-show, and refusing to take a vacation day. Jack puts his best foot forward, never gives pain the power to declare victory from a man with cast-iron willpower. If the day comes when he no longer performs at his ultimate best, his creative woodwork projects unworthy of his name, he will pack his tools.

He lives alone, and his solitude would crack many, if not for a wide circle of family and friends. He relishes socializing and plays hard when given the opportunity, but also welcomes time alone to the rigor of preparing for an outing and attempting to exert energy from a near-empty tank. Falls come easy, falls hurt and happen too often, and sometimes glass-paneled curio cabinets topple over.

Today's pain is the worst this week, and he must obtain his fix. His company? His friend? His solace for mind, body, and soul? Food. He plans to binge and blanket his pain with the consolation of comfort food.

Come, keep me company glazed doughnuts, slices of pizza, baked potatoes loaded with butter, sour cream, and bacon. Visit tomorrow and sit by my side, apple Danish, fried chicken, pumpkin pie, and whipped topping. Ease my pain, give me a moment of euphoria, be my drug.

He cannot exercise away the thousands of calories after his comfort-binges, so the production of fat consumes his body more than the agony he attempts to console. He feeds his need with favorite treats, brings his taste buds companions of delight, and enjoys the pleasurable indulgences.

Not one task receives a checkmark on his to-do list. He cancels scheduled appointments and social plans. Most days, he pushes himself, hard. He has no choice. If he breaks and slows his life to a crawl, perhaps to a halt, will it rev up again? If he gives in and listens to the pain, will it become the master and he the slave? He is afraid not to fight, for if the fighting wanes, is that when death comes, or worse, assisted living? The fight is worth it today; he may not feel the same tomorrow.

He eagerly walks the aisles of the supermarket with ardent interest, holding the cart for support, as he chooses his evening's gratification. The high of unlocking the door to his home when he returns with bags of favorites has become a frequent, near giddy event. He pours himself a beverage, grabs the evenings binge food, and nestles into his recliner. The feast deadens his emotions, and he may doze from a sugar rush, but he doesn't care. The hour of contentment was his goal—his lustful escape.

The pain slathers his body. His cells fill with fat tissue and become obvious. So many people are heavy with physical and emotional pain that, for the most part, he goes unnoticed. Even though judgmental fools flash harsh looks, Jack continues to console himself with calories of enjoyment, albeit, for a short reprieve.

He kicks back with a cold beer to watch Monday Night Football and digs deep into the right pocket of his jeans. He pulls out a penny and drops it on the tray table next to a plate of chicken wings, a bag of corn chips, and a jar of bubbly-hot cheese dip. The opposing team's quarterback is an idiot, as are the referee's when a call favors the rival team. No one in Jack's apartment building escapes the wrath of his greater-than-90-decibel rage. The last swig of beer, and he reaches for the coin, tosses it, catches it, and slaps it atop his opposite hand. Just one time, one time he'd like the outcome to be in his favor. He concedes and stomps to the refrigerator for another cold one. The game ends. He feels heavy, but the presence of leftover wings and chips suffice until the empty containers match the emptiness of his soul. No matter the color of the various plastics holding his snacks, the treasures inside are what warm his heart, satisfy him unconditionally, and keep him alive on the days he contemplates the alternative.

He recalls the recent conversation with his doctor when, after pulling over a stool on wheels and rolling it near Jack's chair, he had leaned forward. He said he was unable to increase the pain medication dosage, and how sorry he was that arrogant lawmakers thought they could control drug addicts by punishing law-abiding citizens who required opiates to live a functional life. Jack had walked to the exit door, his hand devoid of a simple slip of paper, the prescription for a medication that gave him a fragment of independence, and a means to live with his pain until a promising treatment came along.

He returns the coin to his pocket and retreats to the bedroom where he lies down and rolls up with blankets. Pain apprehends his body, and he fears the forthcoming, dark images that invade nearly every waking moment. The pain closes him in, engulfs his body, and assumes control. He sees fresh blood and realizes his nails dug into the skin of his palm during the last bout of pain. A black cloud floats above his head, so near he can almost touch its sullen edges.

He places his feet on the floor and opens the nightstand drawer where he retrieves a key. With deliberate steps, he walks to insert it into a lock and allows the etched glass door of the gun cabinet to swing wide. He reaches for the cold metal of the loaded revolver his wife gifted him on their last Christmas together. He lays it atop the bed and digs the coin from his pocket.

He tosses it.

He catches it.

He slaps it atop his opposite hand.

This time, the outcome is in his favor.

The Lazy Traveler
Sherry McMurphy

The shrill whistle brought all seven survivors abruptly to attention. "Hey, can everyone gather around me?" asked Stone Weatherford. Three men and three of the four women trudged through the sand to stand in front of him. "As your pilot…" Loud cheers and clapping interrupted his words.

"Way to go, Captain," one passenger hollered.

Another cried out, "Thank you for saving our lives."

Stone grinned sheepishly. He wasn't used to praise.

The charter flight he'd commanded was en route to Playa Maya, Mexico, with three couples and one single woman for a week of fun in the sun. On the last leg of the flight, a sudden mechanical failure forced the plane down. Stone was able to glide the aircraft until its belly scraped the treetops before finally coming to rest in an area of grass on a remote, uninhabited island. Due to a sheer miracle, all travelers survived with only a few bumps and bruises.

"First, I want to thank the good Lord for saving us today. I have to admit, the closer we approached the ground, the more my stomach churned." *And my ass puckered pretty tight, too.* Stone laughed as cheers interrupted him again. "Okay, enough. Let's get serious. I already activated the rescue beacon on the aircraft and radioed 'mayday,' but I can't be certain anyone heard me. I received no response." The group nervously exchanged worried looks.

"How long will it take someone to find us," asked Mark, who traveled with his wife, Pam.

"Can't say, for sure, but we're only about forty minutes from Playa Maya. I'm hoping tonight, but could be a couple days." Groans rumbled all around.

"Okay don't get excited. We're going to be fine if we stay smart and follow basic survival skills. It's important we work together and prioritize our needs." Stone counted off on his fingers as he continued. "Water is number one, fire number two, shelter three. Storms are common out here and can be deadly. Number four is food. Do any of you have anything we can use in your bags?"

Joan and Steve rattled off several items as did Mark and Pam. Tim and Sarah offered bottles of water, blankets, and a travel size fishing rod. They'd planned to enjoy a camping and hiking excursion.

Responsibilities were divvied up and everyone jumped in to handle the tasks. However, passenger Ericka Emerson never spoke during the meeting. She'd sat on her Louis Vuitton luggage, unfocused, staring intently at the ocean.

Stone approached Ericka. "Ma'am, you doing okay? You're not hurt, are you?"

She rolled her eyes and stated, "No, Captain. I'm perfectly fine. Your atrocity of an aircraft has seriously inconvenienced me. I can assure you, my lawyer will be in contact once we are settled at the resort, which better be soon or I'll own your entire travel service." Ericka turned her back to him. He'd been dismissed.

Stone grinned, unaffected by her attitude. "Well, princess, have it your way. But you'll be pretty hungry and miserable tonight without food and shelter, if you don't get a move on it. You don't work, you don't benefit."

She angrily swung around and stood up in his face. "For your information, I already have shelter in the aircraft, and I have tons of nutritional bars in my bag. I don't need your benefits to stay comfortable."

His eyebrows jutted up as he cocked his head. "Oh? Is that right?"

"Yes, that's right. If there's nothing further, I believe I'll go relax on the beach. After all, I did take this vacation to work on my tan." Ericka brushed passed Stone, grazing his shoulder as she walked away, dragging her suitcase behind her.

Stone shook his head and mumbled "Dumbass" under his breath. *Not my problem.*

* * *

 High on a ridge, Stone stood watch, worrying his lip and scouring the horizon. He couldn't figure out why someone hadn't rescued them yet. The third night rolled in quickly.

Together, they'd developed an uncomplicated rhythm. Mornings, they fished, looked for fresh fruits, vegetables, and coconuts. Afternoons were spent collecting wood, boiling water to drink, and frolicking in the ocean to relax. Mark and Steve repaired the shelter following the nightly storms.

Tonight would be no different. Huge thunderheads brewed in the west, the skies darkened. *Why haven't we seen any fishing boats or a yacht? A tanker or military boat, for God sakes. It's not like the waters around here aren't trolling with drug lords.*

The day of the crash, Stone buried flares in the sand, ready to launch on a second's notice, and the men implemented a watch schedule over both the camp and the sea. So far, nothing. High society Ericka Emerson maintained her distance and contributed nothing. She spent her days privately lounging on the beach, her nights dipping into her stashed sauce, then sleeping it off. Hell, half the time the group had no idea where she was.

At the sound of loud voices, Stone turned his focus toward the campfire where six survivors huddled. He wasn't sure what they argued about the third of the day. *Dammit, come on. Somebody get us off this island.*

The first rumble of thunder echoed in the distance. As Stone approached camp, Tim and Steve exchanged heated words. "What's the problem here?" Stone asked, briefly interrupting their spat.

"I'll tell you what the problem is. Sarah here smart-mouthed my wife today," growled Steve, pointing his finger at Sarah's chest.

"I did not," Sarah shot back. "I told Joan she needed to stop being so prissy, worrying about her stupid nails, and stick her hand in the damn sand. We needed to collect a lot of clams to feed everyone tonight, since Steve couldn't manage to catch fish this morning."

Mark angrily piped in, "Steve didn't catch fish because he was too busy climbing palm trees, collecting coconuts you said we had to have, Sarah."

"Bullshit," raged Tim. "Sarah didn't want them. Ms. Hoity-Ericka-Toity wanted them. You're blaming Sarah because you're too afraid to admit you've been secretly catering to her every need, when she doesn't give a crap about anyone but herself. All because you have the hots for her."

"What?" screamed Steve. "I do not."

"Come on, Steve. Everyone notices you ogling her while she lies on the beach in her barely-there white bikini," said Pam in disgust. "Really, how gross. She's all of twenty-three and you're, what…sixty-five?"

"I'm forty-five…"

"All right, that's enough," yelled Stone, stepping in between them as they advanced on each other. "You're seriously going to argue about this crap? Come on. Our lives are in danger. We have to stick together," he demanded, eye-balling each one of them as if he were a father dealing with a pack of toddlers. "Apologize to each other and let the shit go. A wicked storm is brewing. I'm starving. Let's get some food in our stomachs and batten down the hatches before we lose the fire and end up drenched."

The word "sorry" echoed reluctantly around the fire. Tim left to assume guard duty. In the distance, the storm built intensity. They sat down to a meal of clams, mussels, coconut, and berries. The wind noticeably picked up, and they struggled to keep the fire from going out. The surf increased and strong waves crashed onto the beach, forcing water closer to camp.

"This storm is really going to be a doozy," stated Mark. "We better hurry up and fortify the shelter." As they began gathering up their belongings, a scream rang out. Startled, everyone froze.

"Helicopter! There's a helicopter," shouted Tim from the ridge.

"Did Tim say helicopter?" asked Mark.

Stone, already on his feet, raced toward the flares he'd staked in the sand. Two bright search lights flashed in the sky. He had to draw their attention to the island, to them. The others ran to the waterfront, screaming and waving their arms wildly. "Down here. We're down here."

Stone struggled in the intensifying wind to light the single wick after twisting the three flares together. He repeatedly struck matches only to have the flame blow out before igniting. "Come on!" he begged. Glancing up at the sky, he started to panic. The helicopters were turning away. "No! No, no, no…Come on, dammit," he bellowed.

Stone struck the last match, prayed it would take hold. The flame initially flickered, started to go out then fully burned. He touched it to the wick. It caught fire and Stone pushed backward to safety. In a flash, the flares shot out of the sand like a rocket, flew high in the sky, and burst into an explosive white light, similar to fireworks.

The castaways waited on pins and needles to see if the helicopters noticed the brilliance of their signal. Finally, they turned and the search lights grew closer.

Cheering, hugging, dancing, and laughing erupted amongst the survivors—two of the women burst into tears, while Stone fell to his knees and thanked his lucky stars. He bore a heavy burden on his shoulders these past few days. The relief was almost overwhelming. They'd made it. Tonight, they were going home.

The two helicopters landed on the beach. Stone waited patiently until it was safe to approach the aircraft, then ran and slid the side door open. "Oh, man, are you a sight for sore eyes," he shouted over the rising wind and rotor noise.

"Are you survivors of Flight 186?" asked the rescue pilot.

"Yes. We all made it through the wreck and have been out here for three days now," replied Stone. "We're so glad to see you."

"We're glad to finally find you all. Storm's moving in rapidly. Better get everyone loaded before we're grounded."

"Will do."

Stone helped three people jump in the chopper, while Steve helped the others board the second one. The rescue swimmer bolstered the door when Mark suddenly shouted, "Ericka. What about Ericka? We can't leave her behind?"

"Where was she tonight?" Stone asked.

"I don't know. I haven't seen her since around three o'clock. We have to go find her," he cried.

Stone looked to the pilot, struggling to control the joystick in a sudden wind gust. "We got time?" The other helicopter lifted beside them and flew away. A second strong gust struck their chopper, threatening to tip it over.

"No way," he shouted. "It's now or never. This is not a typical thunderstorm."

"Get to safety. I'll stay and find her," screamed Stone and reached for the door handle.

The rescue swimmer restrained Stone's arm as the helicopter lifted. "There's no time. We'll come back."

Swaying erratically in the wind, the pilot regained control, then headed west.

Stone looked at the others, silently sitting in horror, and mumbled under his breath, "God help you, Ericka."

* * *

Twenty-four hours later, Stone and the Rescue Guard returned to the scene of the wreckage to retrieve the black recorder box and Ericka. Everyone feared they were on a recovery mission, not a rescue mission, after the storm turned into Hurricane Juanita.

Stone was the first to discover Ericka's body floating face down in a pool of muddy water outside the twisted and bent metal of the plane. Maggots and worms had taken up residence on her face, crawling in and out of her eyes and mouth.

Stone fought back nausea, turning his eyes away before lying her down in the grass. He shut Ericka's eyes and placed his handkerchief over her face. Walking away, he left her remains in the care of the authorities and shook his head. Her stupidity, lazy and selfish ways caused her to die scared and alone. The thought had him feeling sympathetic and wishing things could have ended differently.

How Harry Got Religion
R.G. Weismiller

Harry stirred at a thunderous noise, but ignored it, falling back to sleep, snoring. Then, the clamor happened again—a loud unforgiving sound from the front door. With half-opened eyes, he groaned as his hands fumbled for the clock.

"Noon," he muttered. "Who could be here on a Sunday?" He rubbed his forehead and moaned. "Whoever you are, go away." His futile attempt to shout sounded more like a loud whisper. Rolling over, he placed a pillow over his head.

Another rapping, only louder and with more authority.

"Okay," he grunted. "You win—probably some Girl Scout selling cookies."

He rose, putting on a shirt he found on the floor, leaving it unbuttoned. He grabbed a pair of shorts and stumbled into them. Before he moved out of his bedroom, the banging occurred again.

"I'm coming," Harry bellowed, balancing himself against the walls as he staggered to the front door. Opening it, he stared at a group of neatly well-dressed people.

"Are all of you selling cookies?" Harry scanned the size of the crowd and buttoned his shirt. "I don't think I can afford to buy a box from each—"

"Mr. Robbins?" A small man, standing in front of the group, interrupted.

"That's me," the man in the doorway responded. "But call me Harry."

Harry belched without warning in front of the short man.

"Sorry about that," Harry chuckled. "That one was a surprise for me."

"Mr. Robbins," the small man said, waving his hand in front of his face, as if the motion would fan away the odor. "I'm Pastor Givens from the church next door. The people with me are my congregation."

"Nice to meet you, Rev," Harry said. "I'm just Harry. Mr. Robbins is my dad."

"Harry," the pastor said. "There have been several complaints about you from my congregation."

"Mr. Robbins." The woman, standing next to the pastor, glared at Harry. "Have you ever heard of sloth?"

"Isn't that an animal who hangs on trees?"

"I'm referring to one of the seven deadly sins."

"Is that a bad one, ma'am?"

"What my wife is referring to, Harry," the parson spoke before his wife could. "Is that our members have noticed the way your property looks."

"Why, thank you, Rev. I really can't take credit for that. It's just naturally beautiful."

"What my husband means," the woman said.

"Now, Gwendolyn," Givens said, patting his wife on the shoulder. "Harry, our members take pride in the Lord's house. Every home surrounding it is beautiful—"

"Except yours!" Gwendolyn put her hands on her hips. Murmurs of agreement came from the crowd.

"Rev, I thought you admired my humble abode," Harry said, slumping against the doorframe.

"Harry," Pastor Givens said. "To put it politely, it could use a fresh coat of paint."

Harry stuck his head from the doorway, straining his neck to look at the house. "You're probably right. But you see, I hurt my back on one of my many missions in Afghanistan—not sure which one." He grimaced, placing a hand on his lower back. "I was in the Navy Seals as a Weapons Specialist. That's a nice title, but what it really means is that it was my responsibility to carry the heaviest gear—whether it was weapons or communications or network equipment. I carried that burdensome gear, strapped to my back, up and down the mountains. Sometime I had to crawl up the mountains. Most of the time, our missions were at night, making it harder for our adversaries to see us. We had to be careful of the enemy's bullets raining down on us, as well as avalanches. Carrying that heavy equipment up and down the mountains with the enemy bearing down caused my injury."

"Wait," a man's voice called from the back. "You couldn't have helicopters fly you in?"

"Oh, no, sir," Harry said. "The Taliban sat vigilantly on the mountain tops, waiting for our Black Hawks, ready to bombard them with missile launchers." The homeowner moaned as he placed his other hand behind his back. "It's okay, I'll be better in a moment…You see, I can't lift heavy objects, especially over my head. A ladder is heavy—but don't worry, somehow, someway, I'll get the ladder up. Then I'll carry the paint can up and down the rungs."

The crowd fell silent for a moment, until a woman yelled. "Wait a minute, I saw you at the grocery store carrying two cases of beer last weekend."

Harry shook his head among the noise of the crowd. "That's my medication for my pain. I've been to every pain clinic in the country, and no prescription worked. Finally, all the doctors agreed—beer was the best pain reliever for me. It's the hops that do the trick. But, ma'am, I struggled just to carry it out to the car. Not only did my back hurt, but my arms and shoulders ached for days."

The eyes of the stunned crowd gazed at the man in agony. Finally, another woman spoke. "Mr. Robbins, put your mind to rest." She hit a man standing next to her. "Theodore, you get your no-good-for-nothing brother over to paint this man's house. Tell him it's for charity. He'd better do a great job, or he's gonna answer to me."

The woman looked at Harry. "What do you think about light gray with black shutters, just like mine down the street?" She pointed to a house.

"Ma'am," Harry said. "That would be wonderful. I knew by the way you were dressed, you're a woman of impeccable taste. Whenever I pass your house, I can't tear my eyes away from its beauty."

A few of those standing in front of the house nodded.

"What about your lawn?" Gwendolyn said.

"I like to think of it as the Garden of Eden," Harry replied.

"Garden," the pastor's wife exclaimed with her hands on her hips. "Why it's so tall, it would take a cow years to chew its way through it. A little mowing would be nice."

"Ma'am," Harry said. "I was on a mission with the Army Rangers—"

"Didn't you say you were with the Navy Seals," a male's voice blurted.

"You are so sharp, sir," Harry said. "I was in high demand among the Special Forces. So, one mission I was with the Seals and the next with the Rangers. On one occasion, the French Foreign Legion requested my services."

The crowd fell silent, all eyes on Harry. Finally, a woman broke the silence. "What happened?"

"We parachuted into the densest jungle of Kenya. Our Intel informed us there was a farm where terrorists had a small nuclear device just on the outskirts of where we had dropped. In order not to be seen, we crept through the crops to the barn where the weapon was stored. Somehow, the enemy knew we had arrived. The next thing we heard was the sound of engines being fired up. Tractors and combines started combing the fields, chopping down the crops, trying to find us. We couldn't stand—they would have spotted us. We crawled faster with the farm implements bearing down on us. To this day, whenever I cut the grass, that memory of those crops being sliced to the ground replays in my mind. The sound of the blades haunts me to this day—bringing me to the brink of insanity. I shudder with each step I take behind a mower. But, come hell or high water, I'll get the job done."

"Did you get the bomb?" a wide-eyed woman standing next to the parson's wife asked.

"Yes, we did," Harry said. "Not only did we dismantle it, but we captured all the terrorists."

"Mr. Robbins," the tallest man in the crowd spoke. "My boys will mow your lawn this summer. It will give them something to do besides play video games."

"You're too kind, sir," Harry said, stepping outside and closing the door so the congregation would not notice his PlayStation, Wii, and Xbox One consoles inside his living room.

Gwendolyn Givens turned to the crowd. "I can't believe you're all falling for this. This man isn't a hero. Almost every night he can be found at that tiki bar down the street. It is a den full of the lowest, immoral people who walk the face of this earth. Every night, sinners are being hauled off by the police from that lair."

Harry sensed the eyes of the crowd scrutinizing him. "Ma'am, you're right about that place being full of despicable people. I make it my job to route them out. Every time I walk through those doors, my life is in danger. But it's not about me. I do it for all of you and this great country. One less scumbag walking our streets helps us all to sleep more soundly at night. I fight motorcycle gangs, terrorists, and drug dealers—all for your safety, ma'am."

The crowd applauded.

The Parson's wife lips quivered. "You may have deceived this crowd, but you haven't fooled me. You're nothing more than a hedonistic playboy." She pointed a finger at Harry, shaking it. "Last Saturday we were having a funeral service for Mrs. Johnston while you had the gall to have scantily-clad women frolicking around your pool. Poor Mr. Johnston—he carries an oxygen tank, to begin with. His family said he began to breathe hard when he saw those Jezebels. It was only a block past your house where he passed out. They rushed him to the hospital—he's still in there recovering."

"I'm so glad to hear he's doing okay," Harry said, scratching his mid-section. "Alas, those unfortunate women suffer from a rare disease due to the lack of vitamin D…"

"Those poor girls," a woman gasped. "They can get rickets."

"That is so true," Harry said. "They need as much of that vitamin as they can get. The best way I could think of helping was to offer them my pool and let them soak up all that vitamin D from the sun. I think they are getting better. By the end of summer, they should have enough of the nutrient to last them through the winter."

The crowd nodded, smiling at the homeowner.

A young boy, standing between the Pastor and his wife, tugged at Gwendolyn's skirt. "Grandma, Grandpa said they were angels sent here from heaven."

Harry looked to the heavens and closed his eyes. "Son, they are indeed creatures sent from above."

"Gerald," Gwendolyn screamed, staring at her husband. Without saying a word, she stormed through the crowd, where a path easily formed for her like the parting of the Red Sea.

Less than a minute from his wife's exit, the red-faced parson spoke. "Harry, perhaps you could join us at one of our three Sunday morning services."

"Rev," Harry said. "If only I could. With all my escapades, I get these migraines every Saturday and Sunday morning—barely can move. The only thing that seems to help is my medication and sleep."

Harry turned to the crowd. "I just want to say, I'm so glad to meet you all. What you did for me today speaks volume about your kindness. You are the kind of people that give the human race a good name." He touched the clergyman's shoulder. "Rev, you should be proud of your congregation."

"I wish there was something I could do for you," the Parson said, shaking his head.

"Well, Rev." Harry brought his hand to his chin. "I am running low on my medication."

Top Salesman
Sandra Cowan Dorton

A salesman sits in his car, mumbling to himself.

It's too darn cold to be out here on these streets. I want to get away from here and head home, but with several more calls to make and my quota not met, I don't have a choice if I want to keep this job.

This morning, Melvin jumped all over me. He's such a control freak. Getting the promotion to supervisor has sure created a monster. Now he likes to strut around like a peacock in heat, but without all the beautiful colored feathers. He has feathers, all right, the kind I'd like to pluck. I've approached the Big Guy about Melvin before, but did it make a difference? Noooooo. When I told the Big Guy he had created a little Hitler by promoting that jackass, his response was, "Good." So, here I am out here collecting payments and trying to make a sale when I deserve to be home relaxing.

They expect way too much from a guy. I'm tired of going into that office every morning and having someone tell me about my appearance. What the heck, so I had a couple of spots on my tie. Big deal! Take yesterday, for example. Because I didn't have time to get to the cleaners, Melvin gets smart with me again. I told him the cat had pulled my pants down off the rocking chair where I'd hung them the night before. Is it my fault the stupid cat likes to sleep on my clothes? She loves me. I'm sorry I didn't notice those loose threads that Cat had pulled. And what is so funny about naming my cat "Cat"? That's what she is, isn't she? Makes sense to me. Jeezzzz. Stupid jerk! So, okay. I'll try to go by the cleaners and get my other suit cleaned, AND pressed. They sure expect a lot from a guy.

This morning it was the Big Guy's turn. Complaining about a couple of little cigarette burns on my shirt. They expect perfection. And even if they think so, I'm not perfect!

Now, where is Melvin? He's supposed to meet me here at the Piggy Barn to help me make some sales. I've been waiting here for a couple of hours. I'm tired of eating those bar-b-que pork sandwiches. I guess now he'll complain about the sauce spots on my tie. It's his fault for making me wait so long.

Oh, the heck with it! I'll just get going on my own. Can't depend on Melvin for a darn thing. He'll probably say I wasn't at the right place. Like he did last week. I still say he told me to meet him at the Get and Go Diner. Again, I waited all afternoon. By the time I left that place, I could have floated out the door with all the coffee I drank. And he wonders why I can't meet my quota. I spend all my time waiting for him. But does the Big Guy jump on Melvin? Of course not! Man, life just ain't fair!

I guess I'll drive through the alley and see if anybody's interested in buying something. Surely, someone will be hanging around out there.

Man, all these papers I have to carry around with me drives me crazy. It's a waste of my time moving them from the front seat to the back so I can get in to drive. No wonder they are always needing to order supplies in that office. If those secretaries weren't so lazy, they could come out to my car and get some of the forms that are all over my back floorboard. Or they could get some out of my trunk. I've told them that before, and all they did was shake their heads and walk away. What kind of response was that? No cooperation whatsoever.

Wait—there are two guys leaning over that fence. Surely one of them wants to buy something. I'll just roll down my window and try to get their attention.

"Hey, you guys. Wait, don't run. I want to talk to you a minute."

What the hell? Where are they going in such a hurry? It looks like they threw something over in the grass. Let me get out and see what it is. Why, it's a gun. Looks like a new one. Pretty nice.

Damn, what was that I just tripped over? For heaven's sake, looks like some guy taking a nap.

"Hey, fella, this here gun belong to you? Fella, I'm talking to you. Well, okay then, don't answer. Guess I'll just keep it. You sure look like you've had some of those bar-b-que pork sandwiches from the Piggy Barn, too."

See, other people get sauce on the front of their tie, not just me.

"Well, if you're not going to answer, I'll go back and wait for Melvin, and show him this here gun I found. Maybe I can sell it to someone."

Saturday Writers 2017

CONTRIBUTORS

Contributors to This Anthology

Sarah Angleton

Sarah Angleton is the author of the essay collection "Launching Sheep," as well as a couple of forthcoming historical novels and at least one pretty good short story. She lives with her family in St. Charles County, Missouri. You can follow Sarah on Twitter @SarahAngleton, or find her blogging most weeks as the Practical Historian at www.Sarah-Angleton.com.

Bradley Bates

"I graduated with my BA English/BA Interdisciplinary Studies (Dec. 1994) from the University of Missouri-Columbia, my MA English emphasis Creative Writing (May 2001) from Northern Arizona University and my MFA in Writing (June 2007) from Pacific University.
I have published in small presses both online and in paper stock as well."

Phyllis Borgardt

"Writing is my passion since joining Saturday Writers. Before that I was an Occupational Therapist with a degree from Washington University and a Master's Degree from California School of Psychology. A widow with three children and four grandchildren, my family has always been supportive of my writing, painting, and educational pursuits.

I've completed two books: 'Moments from My Wild Childhood' and 'The Doctor and the Pole Dancer.' I'm presently writing a sequel to the latter."

Cathleen Callahan

A mathematician who discovered a poet/writer within when a numinous dream awakened inner realms long ago…the thread [I] follow…[that] goes among things that change (William Stafford) is this writer. A high school drop-out (ah, a story) with several college degrees and careers in teaching, counseling, and poetry therapy, I'm now a retired visual arts teacher (yet another story) who has never let go of the thread of joy for life through all its wonders and tragedies.

M. Rose Callahan

Rose's love for fiction started at the age of four when she snuck out of bed at night to listen as her mother told her older sisters bedtime stories. She was found hiding in a darkened hallway, was properly spanked and put back to bed. But she kept going back to listen. Today, she still searches for those hallways, looking for stories of her own to tell.

Sherry Cerrano

"Writing has been an integral part of Sherry's life, never off her mind nor far from her responsibilities. For thirty-seven years she taught high school English in the Quincy Public Schools, making a living that incorporated her lifelong love of literature and writing.

Now retired, she is finally experimenting with her own creative writing. Sherry's goal is to finish a novel that is fun to read, a work which is still in progress."

Sandra Cowan Dorton

Sandra Cowan Dorton is a retired Office Administrator. She enjoys traveling, writing and genealogical research. She is in the process of writing a memoir and a book regarding the discovery of her African American heritage. After discovering that her maternal grandparents traveled north during the Great Migration and passed for white, she attended college for the first time at the age of fifty, earning her Certificate of Specialization in African American Studies.

Larry Duerbeck

"I have been involved with show dogs since circa 1975. There are other aspects to my life, but not many, and they are of limited interest. Even, I must say, to me."

Jeanne Felfe

Jeanne is the author of The Art of Healing - A Novel—published in June 2016. Her first essay—*Yes, It's Personal*—was published in 2014. She's had many short stories published in various anthologies since. In May of 2017, her personal essay, Amidst the Weeds, won first place in the Fiftiness.com "Renewal" competition. Jeanne is currently working on her second novel. She resides in St. Charles with her fiancé and two dogs who believe they are tiny humans.

Sue Fritz

"I am a retired elementary teacher. I taught for 23 years. Upon retiring, I chose to follow my second passion in life, writing. I have taken several online writing courses. I have also attended several conferences in order to hone my writing skills. I am a member of Saturday Writers, as well as the Society of Children's Books Writers and Illustrators. I have been married for 24 years and have two children, both boys."

Judy Giblin

Judy Giblin writes for children and adults. For many years she has volunteered in elementary level classrooms and libraries, encouraging children to love reading and writing. She has degrees in marketing, management, and psychology, and retains a substitute teaching certificate. Recently, she finished her first novel. Judy enjoys reading, writing, watching thunderstorms, exercising, and driving the 1973 Mustang she's had since high school.

Wesley J. Ginther

Wesley J. Ginther is a retired newspaper-advertising executive of The Santa Barbara-News Press, Santa Barbara, California. He retired in 2004 as National Advertising Director and moved in 2010 to Cottleville, Missouri, with his wife, Mary Beth, a financial analyst with Monsanto. He is freelance journalist, graphic artist, landscape artist, accomplished photographer and avid golfer. He writes short stories and essays.

Heather N. Hartmann

Heather N. Hartmann resides in St. Peters, Missouri, with her husband, one son, and four crazy animals. She is working on self-control I the area of multiple manuscript writing while editing her current work in progress. Heather has been published in the St. Charles Suburban Journal and SW Anthologies. Seeing her work in print fulfilled one part of a lifelong dream. She is determined to fulfill part two of her dream, a published novel.

Diane How

Life is simple. Live, laugh, love. Make someone, think, smile, want more. Don't make it harder than it needs to be. Diane writes from her heart with these thoughts in mind.

Nicki Jacobsmeyer

"I started entertaining my imagination by writing stories in elementary school. A few years ago I realized writing was my true passion and haven't stopped since. I write historical fiction and non-fiction, children stories, short stories and poetry. My work includes "Surviving the Iditarod" (Capstone, 2017), "Images of America: Chesterfield" (Arcadia Publishing, 2016), and several anthologies. I live in Troy, Missouri with my husband and two boys."

Jim Ladendecker

"I retired from Boeing in 2011 and after a year of adjusting to retirement life, I started to write a few things down in a blog.
Initially, my stories were from personal life experiences, with a splash of humor containing interesting anecdotes and opinions.
A year ago, I started writing some fiction stories. To my surprise this opened up a whole new avenue to me, and reinforced my interest in writing."

Tammy Lough

"I have two amazing sons and three cherished grandchildren. My memberships include Saturday Writers, Missouri Writers

Guild, Romance Writers of America, and Pen to Paper Writing Group. I also head Round Table Writers, a writing/critique group under the auspices of Saturday Writers. I am honored to write a monthly column for the Saturday Writers newsletter titled *On The Back Page With Tammy.* I have a BSN in Nursing and spent my career as an intensive care nurse-manager."

John Marcum

"I am a Missouri native and graduated from St. Louis University in 1965 with a Bachelor's degree in Arts and Science where I excelled in English composition. After graduating I worked in sales and as a factory Rep. to the steel industry.

In 1985 I began fine art painting as a hobby. I joined a local artist's group and did some newsletter writing for them. I have since written two full novels and several short stories, all unpublished."

Sherry McMurphy

"All my life I have had a strong passion for reading. When I began mentally changing 'features' in the stories to match my preferences, I considered writing my own stories. I was published eight times in the Suburban Journal as an Opinion Shaper columnist and have written two books participating in NaNoWriMo. In addition, I am published in the Saturday Writers 2015 and 2017 Anthology."

Douglas N. Osgood

Doug Osgood's grandfather was raised on a reservation, was taught to shoot by a wild west show's trick shot artist, and eschewed that life to marry the love of his life. He taught his love of westerns, especially Zane Grey, to his grandson, who now translates that love into fiction he hopes his grandfather would have enjoyed reading. Osgood, a long-time resident of Missouri, has traveled the country seeking stories to write.

Tara Pedroley

Tara Pedroley discovered the joy of writing in grade school. An award winning poet, she also loves children, holding a degree in Early Childhood Education. She authors several blogs, including one with advice on relationships and dating. Though she spends a lot of her time writing, she also enjoys various other interests, including dance, art, photography, and creating fun projects for friends and family.

Donna Mork Reed

Donna Mork Reed grew up in the Ozarks and resides in St. Charles with Dave, her husband, and Newfie dog, Barnabas. She authored an inspirational true story published in "Joys of Christmas 2015," a Guidepost Publication, and is published on Tin Lunchbox Review and Ibis Head Review. She holds an M.L.S., a B.S. in biology, and works as a librarian. She won awards for her photography at the 2015 and 2016 Douglas County Fair.

R.R.J. Sebacher

R.R.J. Sebacher is an evil old bear—poet—midwife to the world's collective unconscious. His short term goal is to write poetry layered like an onion, which makes his reader weep I joy or grief. His ultimate desire is to focus the light of poetry so fiercely that it burns through the paper and sets the mind on fire. He would also like to remember where he left his car keys and his last girlfriend.

Billie Holladay Skelley

Billie Holladay Skelley received her bachelor's and master's degrees from the University of Wisconsin-Madison. Now retired from the nursing profession, she enjoys focusing on her writing, and she is a member of the Missouri Writers' Guild, Joplin Writers' Guild, Ozarks Writers League, and the Society of Children's Book Writers and Illustrators. Her poems, articles, and essays have appeared in various journals, magazines, and anthologies in print and online. She also has written books for children.

M.L. Stiehl

M.L. Stiehl spent her childhood on a large farm in the country. Her school years were spent at a one-room school house, where she had plenty of extra time. To fill it, she began writing stories about her life on the farm, and about the things in her imagination. In those days, her stories only entertained her fellow students and teachers. Now, she hopes to entertain a much larger audience with her tales.

Bradley D. Watson

Brad has always lived in his imagination—reading comics, building models, and writing/playing music. With his daughter's help, he rediscovered his love of the world of fantasy and set about writing novels. His short stories have found their way into several Saturday Writers anthologies.

R.G. Weismiller

R.G. is fulfilling a lifelong dream to write. He feels fortunate to have a support from his wife and encouragement from a group of talented writers. He is working on his first novel. He may be reached at rgwstl@hotmail.com.

Susan Gore Zahra

Susan Gore Zahra has been writing since hand-printing the single-page "Neighborhood News" when the Globe-Democrat went on strike in 1959 (total distribution: 3 copies). Her most recent work appeared in Saturday Writers Writing Sense-ably: Anthology #10.

"The comingling of good and evil, sin and virtue, in families, communities, and individuals fascinates me. This year's theme of seven deadly sins/holy virtues gives me the opportunity to explore the interaction of the two in each story."

Saturday Writers 2017

JUDGES

2017 Judges

We would like to thank all of the judges who volunteered their time and expertise to read, compare, and rate the entries for each contest, showing us once again that those in the writing industry are among the most generous, knowledgeable, and helpful people in the world.

Prose Judges:

Renee' La Viness is a writer, editor, speaker, instructor, and event organizer in the publishing industry. In more than four years with 4RV Publishing, she spent two as the Children's Corner Imprint Editor and was recently promoted to Special Projects Editor. She enjoys helping authors polish their stories. Renee' has written for magazines, newspapers, anthologies, and other projects. She lives in Oklahoma with her husband, a nervous Corgi, and five ornery chickens. www.reneelaviness.com.

Laura Matheson has written and told stories for as long as she can remember, and when she's not teaching technical writing, watching her two boys at the hockey rink, or busy herding rogue space dragons and random little green army men, she can be found writing (and drinking far too much coffee). Originally from the Canadian west coast, she now lives in rural Saskatchewan with her boys, husband, and two crazy English Springer Spaniels. Twitter @mustwritenow.

Joe Baumann's writing has appeared in Zone 3, Hawai'i Review, Eleven Eleven, and others. He is the author of Ivory Children, published in 2013 by Red Bird Chapbooks. A PhD in English from the University of Louisiana-Lafayette, Joe teaches composition, creative writing, and literature at St. Charles Community College. Nominated for three Pushcart Prizes, he was recently nominated for inclusion in Best American Short Stories 2016. Joe runs The Gateway Review Literary Journal—https://gatewayreview.wordpress.com.

Donna Essner is the Publisher/Editor for Amphora Publishing Group, and Acquisitions Editor for Walrus Publishing. Her writing experience dates back to high school. She has a MA in English with a focus on creative writing, and was the Assistant Editor of The University Press at Southeast Missouri State University. Now she focuses on providing editing services for other writers as well as continuing to pursue writing and publication of her stories and novels. http://www.amphoraepublishing.com/.

Steve Wiegenstein is the author of Slant of Light, This Old World, and The Language of Trees, all published by Blank Slate Press of St. Louis. The novels follow the trials and triumphs of a utopian community in 19th century Missouri as its residents cope with the coming of the modern age. He is a native of southeast Missouri who now lives in Columbia. Website—www.stevewiegenstein.com. Blog— http://stevewiegenstein.wordpress.com.

Alex Balogh is author of the poetry collection *& Yet*. He has been writing poems and songs for more than four decades and currently teaches creative writing at Lindenwood University. His debut novel *Accidental Destination*, set in 1970s' countercultural Oregon, was recently published by Cool Way Press.

Emily Hall is co-owner of the Independent bookstore, Main Street Books—serving St. Charles, MO since 1993. She graduated from Truman State University in 2011 with a BA in English, and has been an avid reader her entire life. When not at Main Street Books (which, frankly, is most of the time), she can be found reading YA and romance novels, chattering to her parakeets, and trying to write a book of her own. www.mainstreetbooks.net.

Poetry Judges:

Christina Gant is Assistant Professor of English at St. Charles Community College, teaching courses on composition and literature, Introduction to Creative/Poetry Writing, and honors seminars. Her publishing credits include: thirty+ poems in a variety of magazines and journals, fifty+ articles and essays, and a co-authored textbook on world mythology. She earned her BA Certificate in Creative Writing at Washington University in St. Louis and her MA at UMSL. She hosts The Coffeehouse, SCC's open-mic event.

Linda Barnes is a Certified Applied Poetry & Journal Facilitator. Past-president of the International Federation for Biblio/Poetry Therapy, she is a retired counselor who began writing in childhood and remains passionate about the written word.
Early in her career, Barnes was a contributor to Tristine Rainer's classic book, The New Diary, and sponsored a Denver appearance by Anais Nin, with whom she corresponded for several years. She is on the faculty for the online Therapeutic Writing Institute.

Jane Ellen Ibur is the author of *Both Wings Flappin', Still Not Flyin'* and *The Little Mrs./Misses*—PenUltimate Press. She has garnered recognition as an Arts Educator with 35+ years of experience teaching writing in public schools, jails, museums, residential schools, social service agencies, with veterans, homeless men, the young and old. Lead Faculty and a founder for the Community Arts Training (CAT) Institute. She co-hosted and co-produced Literature for the Halibut on community radio.

Sins and Virtues

Made in the USA
Columbia, SC
30 April 2018